"WHAT THEY'RE HIDING IS SO DANGEROUS THAT THEY CAN'T EVEN LET THEIR OWN SECURITY KNOW IT'S HERE!"

The animal who had been stirring opens eyes the color of brass.

"Just look at them—these aren't dogs. I doubt they're even terrestrial."

At the sound of my voice, it raises its head. Close as I am, I can see that the pupils are neither round like a human's nor slit like a cat's, but somehow pyramidal—a triangle with depth, set inside a circle of sparkling metal.

"Tammany! Vance!" I whisper urgently. "This is them."

Other AvoNova Books by
Jane Lindskold

BROTHER TO DRAGONS, COMPANION TO OWLS

MARKS OF OUR BROTHERS

JANE LINDSKOLD

AVON BOOKS • NEW YORK

MARKS OF OUR BROTHERS is an original publication of Avon Books. This work has never before appeared in book form. This work is a novel. Any similarity to actual persons or events is purely coincidental.

AVON BOOKS
A division of
The Hearst Corporation
1350 Avenue of the Americas
New York, New York 10019

Cover art by Matt Stawicki
Published by arrangement with the author
Library of Congress Catalog Card Number: 94-96560
ISBN: 0-380-77847-5

First AvoNova Printing: June 1995

AVONOVA TRADEMARK REG. U.S. PAT. OFF. AND IN OTHER COUNTRIES, MARCA REGISTRADA, HECHO EN U.S.A.

Printed in the U.S.A.

RA 10 9 8 7 6 5 4 3 2 1

To Roger—
After everything, Whitman's
"When I Heard at the Close of the Day"
still says best how I feel. Gramercy.

Feet that leave no mark
Eyes that see in the dark
Ears that can hear the winds in their lairs
And sharp, white teeth

These are the marks of our brothers
Save for Tabaqui and the Hyena, whom we hate.

—spun from Rudyard Kipling

ONE

My martial arts instructor says that I'm a hopeless cause.

"Do you really want to learn this or is this some kinda joke?" she growls.

I don't answer except by hopelessly screwing up another attempt at a breakfall, but I really do want to learn. There are six people that I have to kill and I figure that some idea of how to defend myself might come in handy.

Five, I remind myself as I leave the dojo, stiff in body and fatigued from the instructor's impatience.

Five. I killed the first last night and he died painfully, slowly, but with no chance to warn the others.

I smile and straighten despite my sore muscles.

Five left.

At home, a tear sheet hangs limply from my fax phone. The green ink tells me that the message was coded "Urgent" and I smile a little as I rip it free.

"Karen: Rhys is dead—apparently a freak accident. Thought that you should know before Monday. Tammany."

My smile broadens. If Tammany has dismissed Rhys's death as an accident, the rest should, too.

Tammany, stingy Tammany. (Who else would fax such a message?) Soon there will be four, but you won't be around to wonder if this is coincidence.

A cup of coffee later, I go and shower off the sweat from class. It seems to me that my first murder should have changed me, but the body I scrub off is the same lean, average thing, topped with the same straight brown hair, seeing the world through the same brown eyes. "The Invisible Woman" Mr. Allain called me and in a way he was right, because no one ever looks twice at Karen Saber.

As I'm toweling off, my phone pages me—doesn't it always? I step into the bedroom and give the word for voice only.

"Hello? Karen?" The voice is male, baritone, and familiar.

"Hi, Toshi."

"Have you heard about Rhys?"

"Tammany sent me a fax—something about a fatal accident."

"Oh."

I hear him considering.

"She tell you how?"

"No, she was keeping the message short."

Toshi laughs dryly, "That's our Tammany. Rhys was poisoned by oleander smoke. Apparently some of the wood he had bought for that fancy illegal wood-burning fireplace in his house had oleander mixed in. The fumes are deadly."

"Oh," I manage to sound shocked, glad for the relative anonymity of the audio-only connection.

"Can you come in about an hour early on Monday, Karen?" Toshi asks, suddenly crisp, all business.

"Uh, sure," I pause, "Why?"

"We'll need to prepare some sort of formal statement for our clients. I thought that you and I would be the best at framing it and leave the others to review and initial."

Angrily, I run a mental translation. He thinks he has something to gain and figures that I'm his best sidekick. The anger roiling inside me doesn't touch my voice as I agree. We chat for a few more minutes and then he signs off.

Shaking, though I'm no longer wet, I curse him. You'll be Three, Toshi, or maybe Four. Your ambition makes you dangerous, but makes you safe, too.

Digging out jeans and an old shirt, I collect my laundry. No matter what else I'm doing, somehow I've still got to find time for chores.

When I arrive at work the next morning, I'm the promised hour early, but Toshi is there before me. He waves me into his office.

''Read what I have here, Karen,'' he says, swiveling his chair about so that I can read the computer screen over his shoulder.

As I read, I can see Toshi studying me from his reflection on the screen. He's mostly Japanese, but some Danish blood has given him a pair of the bluest eyes I have ever seen, eyes that seem all the more blue against the yellow ivory of his skin.

''What do you think?'' he says, almost as soon as my eyes stop scanning the print.

''Don't you think that 'heartfelt grief' is a bit overdone? Wouldn't 'sincere sorrow' do just as well and be more—proper?''

Toshi nods sharply, ''Yes, more professional. We must not seem to feel too strongly about this. Can you polish it off and have copies ready for when the others come in?''

My turn to nod, though something burns in me at his request. Toshi periodically forgets that I am no longer clerical staff, that I am a Director, and that I hold the post at his instigation. I stifle my reaction, tamping it down with a reminder that I need Toshi to need me, to trust me. Right up until I kill him.

Sending the file to where I can access it from my office, I bid Toshi good morning.

I love my office mostly because it is mine, and because of that I've done my best to make it as beautiful a place as I can. The one narrow window was little more than an eyesore looking out into the cinder block grey of an alleyway until I convinced Mr. Allain to have a holo window put in; now it glows with light shining through a tangle of stained glass clematis in the rich jewel-tone purples of wine when the light hits it just right. My computer station is a donut of oak-and mahogany-toned plastics that grow over and embrace the monitors and other machinery the way a tree grows over a fence rail. The carpet is the color of moss and the walls fade from green into blue in an imperceptibly slow cycle.

Smooth. Peaceful. My refuge. A place where I have done some of my best work, a place I may need to abandon soon. The thought still hurts, but some things are more important than creature comforts.

I remind myself of that as I log onto the network and scan my messages. Toshi has about twice as many messages posted as anyone else. He's become a fiend for administration since Mr. Allain died and that's impressive since he started as a Knife rather than a Hand.

Me, I'm a Hand all the way and have been since I was just a clerk with a bunch of penitentiary degrees and a sixth sense for how languages work. I must not let myself forget how deadly the others can be and as I remember I am frightened.

Hastily, I shove my doubts to one side. I don't dare let anything confuse the hot, dull core of anger that I have stoked ever since I learned . . .

I reach inside and find it there, hot and pulsing at the memory. Good.

Comforted, I polish the death announcement before returning to my messages. Most are routine, but one cipher has resisted the computer decoding. It's a really devious thing consisting of an old standby: words cut from a newspaper and glued to a sheet of plain paper. This one has some neat twists, though—the message itself makes no sense, and the words themselves are cut from at least four different newspapers.

I recognize the typefaces of the *Wall Street Journal*, *Washington Post*, and *New York Times* immediately. The last one takes a cross-check through my files, and even then all I can do is narrow the candidates down somewhat. It's definitely a small-town or low-circulation paper. I'm sure of that, though more on instinct than anything quantifiable.

Temporarily blocked, I summon up the "Holmes"—the check sheet of data our labs pulled from the actual material (I just get a copy at this point). Again, a block. Apparently to stop precisely this type of analysis, the message was photocopied before being sent—so, no glue clues or paper clips, and certainly no fingerprints or blood stains.

Sighing, I have my printer cough out hard copy. The page is headed by a date two days earlier. The message begins further down:

> cabbage disproves questionably that the common diaper is unintelligent. Bangkok tartan Opal released for bad of seaweed. Auntie agreement disorganized.

Yeah. Right. I stare and wonder if this can possibly be important. Even as doubt niggles at me, part of my mind is wondering why the "writer" bothered with four different newspapers. Surely the *Washington Post* alone would have contained all of these words. Unless . . .

I don't even let my mind finish shaping the thought, shrinking from startling my intuition. Instead, I hurriedly type the message into my machine, picking a different format for each newspaper. *Washington Post* gets bold; *Wall Street Journal* gets italics; *New York Times* gets underlining; and the unknown paper gets standard. The message now looks like this:

> **cabbage** *disproves questionably* that the *common* <u>diaper</u> is *unintelligent.* **Bangkok** <u>tartan</u> **Opal** *re-*

leased for *bad* of seaweed. Auntie *agreement disorganized.*

Shit.

I put a save on the file and cut out for coffee. Arriving in the break room, I pour something that looks like black sludge into my mug, shudder, and set up a new pot. While it's dripping, Tammany comes to the door.

Tall, slim, with dark, satiny skin, Tammany was born within a stone's throw of the River Niger. Her close-cropped hair emphasizes her broad, high cheekbones. She destroys any resemblance to a professional model by dressing in clothes that even the Salvation Army would refuse.

"Karen," she says, crossing to the coffee and replacing the pot with her mug, somehow managing not to spill a drop.

"Tammany," I reply, taking the pot from her.

"Vance has checked Rhys's packet and he says that there'll be a wake of sorts, but Rhys wanted to be cremated."

"What time?" I say, covering my discomfort with a quick sip of coffee.

"This afternoon. Four. In the Atrium."

I wave my mug at her.

"I'll be there."

Back in my safe haven, I stare at the words on my screen. I'd never thought about the funerals when I started this, about maintaining my cool while the friends—well, at least the associates—of the people I'd killed discussed them, mourned them.

I'd only thought of Mr. Allain.

Now I wonder what else I might have forgotten.

Scared, I hit the button that will unfreeze the words on my screen. They glow turquoise against fog grey.

"Cabbage disproves questionably . . . common diaper . . . Bangkok tartan . . ." What craziness was this?

I stare, concentrate, let my mind associate. Anything is

better than thinking about killing Tammany. Patiently, I reorganize the sentences, anagram the words, try reading every second word, every third. Nada.

As I lose myself in the game, the intuition that had prompted me earlier to recast the words within different formats brushes like an icy wind against the contours of my brain. Trusting it, I align the words in columns according to their typeface:

Post	WSJ	NY Times	unknown
cabbage	disproves	diaper	that
Bangkok	questionably	tartan	the
opal	common	seaweed	is
	unintelligent	Auntie	for
	released		of
	bad		
	agreement		
	disorganized		

No meaning there, but I feel that there is something. Right off, I realize that the nameless paper contributed only the commonest of words—an article, a "to be" verb, a couple of prepositions, a indefinite pronoun. For the first time in hours, I smile.

Chortling madly, I select the list from the *Wall Street Journal*; one of the first rules of cryptography is to work with the largest body of material possible.

A whine from the intercom at my elbow makes me jump, banging my knee against the tabletop.

Rubbing the sore spot, I touch the answer tab.

"Director Saber."

"Karen." The voice is silky, male, with a whisper of a Southern accent. "Are you aware that it is nearly four? We are expected at poor Rhys's wake."

I hear the reprimand despite Vance's courtly tones and try to sound sincere.

"Dear Lord, Vance! I didn't notice. I've been working on a message that was forwarded up to me."

A pause, then, "I saw your light as I was closing down," he says without acknowledging my explanation, "Would you care for a ride?"

I sigh, resigned. "Thank you, sir. I'll meet you in the outer foyer as soon as I shut off my stuff."

"Very good. I'll bring my car around."

I look back to turquoise on fog, then tap keys and let ebony eclipse the screen.

TWO

ALLOWING VANCE TO DRIVE ME TO THE WAKE IS AN INdulgence since the Atrium is only a quarter mile across the Corp's private park. Vance, however, would have driven anyway and I need to soothe the waters I've roiled by nearly missing the wake.

The low-slung shape of his red Gemster hums outside of the building, a glittering, impossibly large oval-cut ruby. Ever courtly, Vance leaves the driver's side to hold the door for me.

Silver-haired and nearly as slender as Tammany, Vance is in his seventies but moves with only slight hesitation. His features are fine and his usual expression is so prissy that he comes across as effeminate.

The Gemster rises on a cushion of air and wafts us to where the Atrium glows from within like an enormous sea green diamond. Constructed along the lines of the famous Victorian Crystal Palace, the more modestly named Atrium is a repository for several hundred varieties of rare plants, including one of the continent's largest collections of orchids.

When I first came to the Corp, Mr. Allain told me that the Atrium had been constructed and maintained as a tax loss, but had begun to pay for itself some years ago when several varieties of orchid believed to be extinct in their native habitats were found to be part of the collection.

Now the rare plants provide the seed stock used to clone and synthesize numerous medically beneficial compounds. The countries that had once considered their botanical wealth expendable now clamored for their "national treasures" to be returned.

Mr. Allain had loved the irony.

Vance reluctantly turns the Gemster over to a very pleased minor security op doubling as a parking attendant for the evening and stiffly offers me his arm. With a gracious nod, I accept his escort and together we sail up the carpeted walk and into the main reception area.

Since this section of the Atrium is often used to entertain clients, it is less oppressively planted than other areas. An artificial stream twists itself under artful bridges and plashing cascades. The air is heavy with humid greenness and buzzes with a dozen muted conversations.

Vance stops where Tammany leans against a palm tree, in conversation with a stocky, dark-bearded man. Only when he smiles and raises his glass in greeting do I recognize him.

"Anton!"

He puts his glass down on a passing tray and embraces me, brushing my cheek with his lips.

"Kari, I hope you're well."

I accept a glass of wine from the server Vance waves over, considering my words.

"As well as can be expected."

Anton's eyes spark green.

"Yes, shocking thing to have happen, but at least we can be certain that Rhys died happy."

Vance coughs lightly, clearly finding Anton's banter in very bad taste.

"We should circulate," he suggests. "Has anyone seen Qiang?"

"Not yet," Tammany replies, "but she'll be here."

Taking Vance's hint, we separate and circulate among the curious, the polite, the proper, all of whom have come to pay Rhys their final respects. There do not seem to be any mourners, but this does not surprise me. If Rhys came to the Corp as I did, he might have been cautious about mingling his private life with his work.

After nodding to a brace of Brinx executives, I cross to greet a balding former pop idol with whom Rhys had once toured. He is stoned enough to be genuinely upset that Rhys is dead and begins babbling a confused tribute that seems half confession. Gently steering him to a discreet alcove, I stay until a glass of wine seems to have steadied his mood.

The alcove puts me in the perfect position to observe the Chirrs' arrival. Like humans, the Chirr are bipedal and bilaterally symmetrical, but there any external similarity ends. Unlike humans, who evolved from omnivorous, probably arboreal primates, the Chirr evolved from herbivorous tunneling creatures more like Terran rodents than anything else. A highly social race, they rarely travel alone, and even when speaking individually usually refer to themselves in the plural.

"Coordinator Wheep!" I call to the leader.

With two short hops, rather like a gerbil, Wheep orients on my voice. She stands less than a meter and a half high—average for her race—and is stocky like a prairie dog. Her lightly furred tail extends from beneath the many-pocketed vest/robe that she wears over her dense golden fur. Her long whiskers curl forward in friendly greeting.

"Directors Saber," she replies, the words coming from a translator, underscored by the whistle that marks the languages of her race. "We are pleased to see you, although the occasion must be sorrowful for your Corp."

"We mourn," I whistle in her own language, "but we are pleased to see y'all nonetheless. May I know your other names?"

Wheep makes introductions. Two of her party I have met before. The third, a piebald individual with the title of "Discoverer"—something like Scientist/Adventurer—is a stranger.

"Shi Freesh is just arrived to us some days ago,"

Wheep explains. "He has come to announce study results on a planet in a system found some time ago and under inspection since."

"Would that be Xi-7?" comes a deep voice from over my left shoulder.

I turn and find that Anton has come over to join us.

"Yes," Shi Freesh says, "We returned from our survey a short time ago."

"And your report?" Anton asks.

Freesh's eyes are so dark that they seem to lack a pupil. Calmly he stares up across the meter plus that separates his head from Anton's.

"Our report is confidential," he says, "as you know."

Anton chuckles and gives a short bow.

"Excuse me," he says, "I see that Qiang has arrived."

I look across the foyer and wave to the Chinese woman in the jade silk pantsuit who has just entered, but I remain until the Chirr become involved in a conversation with a representative of a Terran mining company. Then I excuse myself and drift over to where Anton and Qiang have just finished accepting the condolences of a botanical company representative.

"That was a bit careless, Anton," I chide, deciding that he looks good in his new beard.

"What?" He collects himself. "With the Chirr, you mean? Perhaps it seemed so, but I am very interested in knowing what that report will say."

"Why? What report?" Qiang asks.

She is short and almost as plump as a Chirr. Her shiny black hair and ivory skin are unremarkable in one of her heritage, yet she has a steadiness about her, a presence, that makes her compelling.

"Later," Anton promises, "Not something to be lightly chatted up, especially with people getting ready to come over and say good night."

"Later then," I agree and Qiang nods.

When the last guest has left the wake, Vance dryly offers me a ride back to my office so that I can finish my project. I refuse, laughing at his implied joke, wishing that there were not times that I so liked my fellow Directors.

My fingernails bite into my palms as I remember suspicion flowering into certainty, how I had realized that Mr. Allain's Corp had turned against him. Even then I had felt the bitter irony that the group he called his corp—his body—had turned its own Hands and Knives against their wielder. The Body assaulting its own Head; there was the taint of the primal sin in the crime. In that moment, I had vowed to avenge him.

Yet, yet, the others are somehow part of me because we're all part of the Corp, Mr. Allain's Corp. Killing them will be like killing me. And a bit like killing him, too.

These thoughts trouble me throughout my train ride home and keeps me sitting in my darkened living room for a long while before I finally stumble off to my bed.

I awake the next morning feeling as if Chirr have been burrowing through my mind. Groaning, I sit up and tousle my hair with both hands. Given how I am feeling, it seems almost unfair that the day outside is bright and clear, that the air has the sharp snap of a perfect autumn.

When I roll out of bed, I hear the shower start and the first gurgle of the coffee maker. Muttering blessings to automation, I stagger for the shower.

Warm water brings me around, and by the time I've finished my coffee and an English muffin I find myself actually anticipating getting to work. The puzzle that Rhys's wake had forced me to leave the previous afternoon had been the backdrop to all of my dreams. Somehow, I feel certain that I will break it today.

Humming, I shoulder into my quilted denim jacket and head out. Unlike Vance, who will never walk when he can drive, I usually leave my skimmer in its cradle and walk down to the public rail system. I live far enough away from the City center that getting a seat is not a problem. I settle back and skim the local paper's headlines on the seatback monitor.

MR. AMERICA PROTESTS PADDING CLAIMS
JETS OVER FLARES IN DOUBLE OVERTIME
XI-7 SURVEY RESULTS PROMISED AND PROMISING

Xi-7? Yes, Anton had mentioned it last night. Reaching up, I run my season ticket through the credit slot and obediently the monitor shows the complete story. It is fairly short:

> UAN delegates who arrived on Terra last week announced yesterday that they would soon be reporting the results of their extended survey of the planet currently designated Xi-7. Xi-7 is one of the most promising discoveries in recent years, possessing both an atmosphere compatible to UAN lifeforms and a rich and varied ecosystem. However, in accordance with the treaty entered into by UAN members, any planetary system must be proven to be without native, sentient life before colonization can begin.
>
> The UAN delegation's report will let the allied races know whether we can expect the bounty of this new world to be opened to general use or whether a more complex situation exists.

It continues, but I am fascinated more by what this piece does not say than what it does. I had been twelve when the Chirr had "discovered" Terra. I remember the excitement of learning that there were other intelligences "out there." Had thirty years or so been enough that a new piece of real estate was more exciting than the possibility of a new race?

Vaguely troubled, I let the paper go back to running headlines and watch the landscape flowing by in a green blur outside the train's window.

Stopping only to get a cup of coffee, I go directly to my office. E-mail mercifully does not bring me any new jobs that I cannot deal with quickly. Blowing softly on the mug in my left hand, I mutter responses. Then, putting aside the throat mike, I reach for the keyboard.

Mr. Allain often teased me about my reliance on such

an out-moded crutch and I would plead in return that I needed to be able to feel the words form in response to my touch, not just see them conjured by some insubstantial djinn.

Sliding open the drawer to my right, I pull out a pretty box embossed with a tiger lily. It holds heavy paper and a fountain pen, both as untouched as the day Mr. Allain handed them to me. Only the top sheet of the creamy bond paper is marked: "To Karen Saber, who likes the feel of letters as she shapes them. Remember, the pen *is* mightier than the sword." It is signed Benjamin Allain.

Touching his signature before shutting the drawer, I turn to the puzzle. The list of words from the *Wall Street Journal* awaits me, still patiently highlighted within a lemony nimbus: disproves, questionably, common, unintelligent, released, bad, agreement, disorganized.

I run the words in a loop through my mind, letting my unconscious seek patterns. Every cryptographer acknowledges the role of intuition, of luck. Champollion with hieroglyphics, Ventris with Linear B—never mind the egos involved, they had paid their tithe to luck. Ciphers and cryptographs aren't "real" languages like those, but that doesn't matter; real or created, there must be a pattern or no one can make sense.

My coffee is gone but for a cold puddle I dribble down my throat. I'm considering another cup when a possible similarity strikes me.

"Dis-proves," "un-intelligent," "dis-organized"—so contrary. "Questionably," "bad," "common" all fit with this tone, but "released" and "agreement" do not.

But all—my hand strikes the wrong keys in my eagerness—but all, contrary in tone or not, are easily reversed—"common" becomes "uncommon," "bad" becomes "good." And if the words in the unknown typeface are meant to be read as they are, I have half of the message deciphered.

My momentary elation fades. Even if I *am* right, and I feel certain that I am, what can I make of the remaining words? The three from the *Washington Post*—cabbage, Bangkok, opal—or the four from the *New York Times*—diaper, tartan, seaweed, Auntie.

My stomach growls; glancing at my watch, I see that noon is rapidly approaching. Stubbornly, I refuse to go and soothe my appetite, alternately staring angrily at the words and spinning about in my chair to better glower at the walls.

They are no help, but the volumes that reside in the low cases which line the walls give rise to a peculiar line of speculation. I lift a heavy volume and leaf through until I come to *The Valley of Fear*. Sir Arthur Conan Doyle's tale of treachery, pursuit, and revenge tempts me with its familiar texture, but I stop at the beginning and join Holmes in puzzling through the peculiar message sent by Porlock.

My job is nothing like his and yet there is something that gnaws at me. Holmes's answer lay in words in an almanac, a standard book for his day. Mine must be in these newspapers—why else would the sender have used the different typefaces? Holmes had column and number to guide him. I have just an odd assortment of words. By themselves, they mean nothing, but perhaps they are guides.

Computers, God love 'em. Holmes never had such servants. I log into the *New York Times* and with a grin select the edition for the date that is lettered onto the top of the sheet of paper.

Tap-tap-tap-tap-tap-tap: "diaper" glows on the screen for a brief second before the search command goes galloping through what would be a good pound or more of heavy, dirty newsprint. It freezes thrice at the word "diaper"—the first two times I discard it, but at the third I pause.

"Next the handler takes out a fresh diaper. Animal though she is, Tiko appreciates adornment and . . ."

There seems to be no clue in this sentence, but perhaps

as in *The Valley of Fear* the code indicates proximity rather than anything in context.

On a scratch screen split from my search I type "fresh diaper. Animal."

Next I set the search for "tartan." Here I find the word only once, in an article on the upcoming season's fashions.

"Gilberte claims that Scottish kilts will be the next big thing in men's wear. Industry sources report that tartan orders from France alone have tripled."

Smiling at the thought of Vance or Toshi in a kilt—though Anton would look rather good—I tap: "that tartan orders" onto my scratch screen.

"Seaweed" offers more of a problem, since there is a long article on seaweed farming. However, most of the sentences use the word "kelp" rather than "seaweed," and I finally choose two sentences that seem promising.

The search for "Auntie" goes quickly. After discarding a bit of dialogue from an advertisement, I find it in an excerpt from a forthcoming novel about eighteenth-century Boston. Lining up my selections and their surrounding words I have:

fresh diaper. Animal
that tartan orders
the seaweed tastes
a seaweed. UAN
Jim's Auntie selected

Both the proper name and the articles and pronouns lead me to discard the preceding words, even though "fresh" could be a candidate. The remaining words seem hardly more promising, but I put them in their places and move on to the three from the *Washington Post*.

I've just finished finding "cabbage" in an article on winter vegetables and am searching for "Bangkok" when the intercom signals.

"Director Saber," I reply.

"Qiang speaking," she says without preamble. "Karen, when will you have an answer to the piece you have been working on? When I spoke with our clients on another matter they mentioned that they are anxious."

"Why don't you ask me *if* I'll have an answer," I growl, sending the search after "opal."

There is a breathy laugh.

"Because you will. You have been working steadily—it is only when you do not have any idea how to solve a puzzle that you roam the halls with coffee mug." She laughs again. "What shall I say?"

I glance at the clock. Two o'clock.

"Say tomorrow—I'm onto something, but I'm not sure if it's the right track. I'll know by then and I'd rather have the time."

"If you know sooner," she says, "let me know."

She clicks off, but I hardly notice. My three new fragments await my inspection.

in government tests cabbage was shown
has been selected by DuPoy. Bangkok is
Australian sources of information. Opal mines

Immediately, I flag the preceding words. DuPoy is a UAN Minister for Interspecies Relations. The common verb "is" hardly competes. Without hesitation I select "tests," "DuPoy," and "information" and plug them into the gaps in my message. The final result shows me that I am on the right track.

Tests prove unquestionably that the uncommon animal is intelligent. DuPoy orders information suppressed for good of tastes (UAN). Selected disagreement organized.

Yes! There is something here. I drop "tastes" in favor of "UAN." Fiddling about with synonyms, I fuss particularly with the awkward "uncommon." DuPoy's name in the message is an inspiration and I substitute "alien" for "uncommon."

A chill hits me as I realize the significance of what I have found.

"Qiang!" I yell, hitting the intercom tab, "I have something, but don't tell the client yet. I want a Directors' meeting soonest. I'm not putting what I have on the E."

"You have something?" I can almost hear her nod. "The others are about the facility—I believe we can meet in a half hour."

"Great, I'll be there."

Only after I sign off do I realize that I'm shaking. Could DuPoy do this? And what will it mean for me?

Pushing questions away, I busy myself sealing files, erasing my scratch notes, and securing my data. When I'd learned how Mr. Allain died I'd thought I'd uncovered the cruelest plot I could imagine. Now I am forced to admit that perhaps there might be worse.

THREE

QIANG LOCATES THE OTHER DIRECTORS INSIDE THE promised half hour. Deliberately, I wait to be the last to enter the secured conference room. Although I am older than any of the other Directors but Qiang and Vance, I am the most junior in position. Even in Mr. Allain's lifetime I was never more than a prized specialist. If I was offered the opening left by his death—well—I suspect that I know why.

When I come in, all but Toshi are already in their seats at the crescent-shaped table. Toshi is standing near the wall by the further of the moon's horns, obviously just finished with a routine bug sweep. When I come in and flip the toggle that automatically activates the security screen while locking the door, he takes his seat. Rhys's chair has been pushed back against the wall, but his space remains conspicuously empty.

Licking my lips nervously, I set my datapad on the table in front of my seat, but remain standing.

"As I'm certain that all of you know," I begin, "since yesterday morning I have been working on a cipher that came in from . . ."

I pause, realizing that I don't know.

"From one of our clients in the interstellar shipping industry, StarUs," Tammany supplies. "The story they gave is that the message was found in the public rest area of one of their research buildings."

"Hmm," Toshi says, "Who found it?"

Tammany checks her datapad, "A member of their cop force who went in to take a leak. Apparently, she was tempted to dismiss it as a joke, but had second thoughts. Her superiors passed it on to us when they couldn't make sense of it."

"Wise," Vance says dryly.

"Yes," I say, redirecting attention back to me. "I won't trouble you with the details, but essentially what we were given was not one, but four cryptograms. Each style of newsprint had to be decrypted in a different fashion. When I finished, the message was—wait, I'll put it on the screen."

I click my datapad into the table monitor and the words are suddenly black against the pale cream of the wall across from the table:

> **Tests prove unquestionably that the alien animal is intelligent. DuPoy orders information suppressed for good of UAN. Selected disagreement organized.**

"Shit!" Anton exclaims, hitting the table so hard that coffee splashes from his cup. "The bastard! What does he think he's doing?"

"Protecting the UAN and Terra," Vance replies. "Obviously. Though I must admit that this is an odd way to go about it."

"If anyone learns—especially any of the Chirr or suankh," Tammany says, "we may see the UAN shattered. If anyone learns—Karen, you were right to keep this as quiet as possible. We don't even dare let StarUs know we've solved it."

Toshi grimaces, "That's not part of our usual procedure. This may be volatile, but our client will only pay us for a job completed. Beyond that, what can we do?"

"Toshi! We are contemplating interspecies, interstellar

conflict,'' Qiang says, her almond eyes wide with shock. ''This is the issue and you worry about payment?''

''That's why we're in business,'' Toshi counters, ''or have you forgotten, too?''

His words hang pregnant with a threat that I am not intended to comprehend. I see Vance glance at Tammany.

I decide to interrupt before they remember too vividly what I would prefer them to believe forgotten. Anton, however, speaks before I do.

''Actually,'' he says slowly, stroking his beard, ''we may be able to find a client. Karen's information connects in some interesting ways to what I have been working on. I was not going to report until things were more certain, but perhaps now is best.''

He pauses, enjoying the suspense he is creating. I sink into my chair and dim my display.

''Speak,'' Qiang demands, less patient than I with Anton's theatrics.

''Two weeks ago,'' Anton says with the faintest of smiles, ''we were approached by representatives of StarUs, who requested that we undertake an investigation of a possible information leak within their company.''

''I remember,'' Toshi nods. ''Their stock had been fluctuating wildly and they suspected that someone was leaking insider information about some of their R and D work.''

''That's right,'' Anton continues. ''I was given the job and after some research decided that my best bet was to become an insider myself.''

''We set you up as a product liaison,'' Tammany says, ''with a B.S. in physics and an M.B.A.''

Anton runs his hand over his new beard again before flipping on his datapad. I fidget slightly.

''I'm not as far off topic as it may seem, Kari,'' he says. ''My time at StarUs confirmed what my external research had led me to suspect. Nothing they were doing would contribute to the stock fluctuations that I was seeing, but there was an acute interest among the staff about new developments in interstellar travel.''

''Not so strange,'' Qiang says. ''They are the foremost manufacturer of interstellar vessels on Terra.''

''No,'' Anton objects, ''not the usual interest—the personal plans, dreams, speculations. There was a sense of expectation, of big things about to happen. In the lower echelons, the rumors were diverse, but the higher up I listened, the more centered they became on expectations of a new market opening.''

''You think they have Xi-7 in mind,'' Vance says.

''And when the report came in that there might be a sentient race on Xi-7,'' Tammany continues, ''those operations were doubtlessly threatened.''

The conference room falls silent while the assembled Directors weigh the information. Toshi speaks first.

''Then StarUs cannot be who you have in mind to pay our fee,'' he says. ''Who do you mean?''

Anton laughs, ''Why, whoever drafted this portentous message of Karen's.''

''An interesting idea,'' Vance says dryly, ''but, if you recall, the Corp's charter mandates against our taking a job against a current client.''

''But we wouldn't be,'' I say, speaking up at last. ''This message was brought to us by StarUs. I suspect that it was written by someone within the company. It does mention 'disagreement'—couldn't we interpret that as 'resistance'?''

''Perhaps,'' Vance agrees reluctantly, ''but if the writers are resorting to complex codes, they are hardly likely to be the people with the money to pay our fees.''

''If I said I had reason to believe otherwise,'' Anton counters slowly, ''would that make a difference?''

''It might,'' Vance says, locking his pale gaze with Anton's green.

''Oh! Stop your male posturing!'' Qiang sputters. ''Anton, speak what you know if you believe it important. Otherwise, I move that we turn this fine job of decoding over to those who commissioned it and move onto new business.''

''Qiang's motion seconded,'' Tammany says, leaning back in her chair. ''Do we need to go through the rest of this nonsense or will you give us the dirt, Anton?''

He shakes his head, suddenly grim.

''No, no need, but I remind you, none of this must go beyond the six in this room.''

''So noted,'' Toshi says. ''Go on.''

Anton draws a deep breath. ''Aliens were brought to Terra from Xi-7. After extensive examination by a mixed-species scientific team, the team concluded that their initial judgment that the aliens might be sentient was erroneous and that they were merely highly versatile non-sentients.

''My information, however, has led me to believe that a member or members of the Survey team somehow tampered with the results. In other words, the aliens are sentient, but the report the UAN will receive is otherwise, and the planet will be opened to exploitation and colonization.''

I steal glances at my fellow Directors; each is trained to hide reactions, but still shock, horror, disbelief flicker through their facades.

''They cannot do that!'' Qiang exclaims.

''Can't they?'' Vance counters with a humorless chuckle. ''Can't they now?''

''This would mean that far more than DuPoy are involved,'' Tammany says. ''The Survey team was mixed-race—he must have alien allies.''

''My thoughts exactly,'' Qiang agrees.

''Do you vote to at least hold Karen's code?'' Anton asks. ''We can say that Kari hasn't broken it yet.''

Nods around the table, although Toshi's is last and slowest.

''If I can find where the Xians are being held,'' Anton continues, ''I'm going to pull them out—with or without the Corp's support. All I ask is that you consider whether you'll assist me."

"Outrageous!" Toshi sputters.

Tammany nods, "Yes, but a reasonable reaction to this information. If the UAN is willing to misrepresent these creatures, then their lives are not safe."

The room erupts into fierce debate. After a time, Qiang moves that we adjourn and consider our options. Vance seconds and the vote passes.

Stepping out of the building later that night, I stop on the pathway and look up at the sky. Milky nighttime clouds veil those stars the urban lights haven't already washed out. Could that be the same sky that once arched over my happiness?

"It's over there," says a deep voice and a broad-fingered hand gently turns my head. "Up there, to the right."

I let Anton turn my head, smelling the sharp scent of his cologne mixed with a faint tinge of sweat. I feel a tremble deep within the marrow of my arm bone as I suppress the urge to drive my elbow deep into his solar plexus.

He had not mixed the poison, nor had he helped it find the vein, but he had stood by while it did its work. And for less reason than some. As I weigh his passion for justice in the conference room against what I know of his guilt, this time I do shiver.

"Cold, Kari?" he asks, letting his arm slide down around my waist.

"No," I reply, twisting away with a grace that I think would please my martial arts instructor. "I was just somewhat—overwhelmed."

"By the distance? Or the crime?" he asks.

"Yes," I answer, walking briskly down the path toward the rail station.

Anton stands for a moment, then hurries after.

"A bit late for the rail, isn't it, Kari? Let me give you a lift."

"I've taken the rails home far later than this," I answer without slowing.

"No, Kari," he says, breaking into a trot to catch up with me, "Let me give you a ride. I need to talk to you."

"Talk, then."

"Kari!"

"It's a short drive to my place, Anton."

"Maybe you'd invite me in for tea, then." He darts past and blocks the path with hands outspread. "Please."

I sigh, "You win and I may even see my way to tea—but don't press for more."

"Never! Thank you, Kari." He grabs my hand and presses his lips to it.

A few minutes later, we're humming along. Anton's vehicle isn't nearly as flashy as Vance's Gemster, but it's just as plush in an understated way.

"I've gotten Vance to agree that we should at least try to release the Xians if they are being held against their will," he says without preamble. "It's not so much that he's an idealist, but I get the feeling that he's scared of what might happen if the UAN treaty is broken."

"Isn't it already?" I reply hesitantly, "if DuPoy has the Chirr and the su-ankh agreeing on this cover-up?"

"No," Anton shakes his head, "A couple of corrupt politicians doesn't violate the integrity of the system. And I suspect that there are Chirr scientists who don't back this approach. Your friend Shi Freesh, for example."

"Freesh? The Discoverer? I never met him before Rhys's wake."

"Whatever. I think he's less than happy over something and I'll bet that it's this." Anton lets his hummer idle in front of my door. "I checked him out. His specialization is biology, but he's been dropped from the delegation making the UAN presentation. I find that rather interesting."

"Are you coming in for tea?"

Anton pauses, his hands tightening around the wheel for the briefest moment.

"No, I'll see you tomorrow."

He waits until I am inside before speeding off. As I undress for bed, I am struck by how little he really had told me, just that he thought that Vance would go along with his operations. I could have guessed that for myself.

There had been the bit about Freesh, but he'd been guessing there—hardly worth spiriting me away. I'm relaxing into the warmth of my bed when another thought jars me awake.

Could Anton like me? Romantically? I stare into the octopus shadow of the ceiling fan gently whirling over my bed.

Oh, God, no. Not this. Not when I've sworn to kill him.

Sleep is again a long time coming, but when it does I tumble, almost welcoming nightmare's embrace.

FOUR

LIFE, I DECIDE AS I SIP MY MORNING COFFEE ON THE long patio that wraps my backyard, has become too damn complex, too damn fast. There's no way I'll manage to kill Tammany if I go into the Complex today; I'm just not good enough at this. After yesterday's immersion in code breaking, no one can bitch if I work from home—hell, most of the other Directors are field ops as things stand.

Resolution made, I "E" in my plans, get my messages, and switch off the phone. Let 'em use fax.

Second cup of coffee in hand and cinnamon donut ringing my index finger, I take my messages back out into the autumn sunshine. Most are simple things I can dispose of with a one- or two-word reply; one stops me.

"V & I going X. A."

The encrypting is so simple, I find myself sputtering at Anton: "Vance and I are going for the Xians. Anton." But my initial indignation is washed under by something stronger. They've decided.

I try to recall whether they had to vote before taking an action like that. It seems to me that they did not, but in the old days Mr. Allain would have had the ultimate veto. Now he wasn't around to ask, but I couldn't help but think he'd approve of Anton's course of action.

Would he approve of mine? He must. After all, I'm doing it for him.

Later, a loud buzzing stalls me from a series of tests into the synergistic effects of various household cleansers. My hands still in gloves, I reach for the phone and then yell for the monitor to answer for me.

"Phone service blocked per your command. There is an incoming call coded 'Urgent,' " the voder replies.

"Damn! I'll take it." Glancing at my lab coat I amend, "Audio only."

"Kari?" Anton's voice comes, echoing a bit strangely. "Where are you?"

"Home," I laugh. "You did reach me here."

"Yeah." He pauses. "Listen, I've decided we need you for this."

"This?" I understand, "That?"

"Yes, I was going to ask you when you came in, but you didn't. Tammany's coming and Vance, but I really want you along too."

"Me?" I repeat, knowing, as he must, that field operations aren't usually my thing.

"Yes," he sighs, "A feeling. Can you come?"

"Sure," I agree, knowing my curiosity would never forgive me otherwise. "What should I wear?"

"Something simple, I've got the trims. An hour then."

"An hour," I repeat.

When I get off the train closer to forty minutes later, dressed in blue jeans, sneakers, and a white tee shirt with a Michaelmas daisy embroidered on the pocket, the station is nearly deserted. With a soft hum, a service van parked on the edge of the lot comes alive and Anton leans out the side window.

"Karen! We're saving you the walk. Get in."

The door facing me opens and Vance, dressed in navy coveralls with a cap over his silvery hair, reaches to help me in. Tammany, dressed in a tidy mint green pantsuit, gives me a sleepy wave from the other front seat.

"Coffee?" she asks, handing me a plastic cup.

"Thanks," I say, sipping gratefully. "Where are we going? And why do you need me?"

"Where? About an hour away—to the west, a complex owned by Lantic Labs, a subdivision of StarUs," Anton replies. "Why do we need you? Well, apart from the brightness of your company . . ."

I cough theatrically. Vance chuckles.

"I'm not certain what the Xians will speak—if they speak any of our languages—but if they do, you're the best linguist in the Corp, so we brought you along."

"I wish you'd let me know. I could have brought some equipment that would have helped."

Anton concentrates so intently on driving that Tammany answers.

"We're breaking in, Karen; we're carrying weapons and what's between our ears."

"You'll have your datapad, Tammany," Vance objects softly.

"Weapons," Tammany replies, fingering her computer pad. "This'll let me shut down their security and rape their records. If that doesn't make it a weapon, I don't know what is."

I huddle down in my seat and concentrate on my coffee. Next to me, Vance checks the works on a small gun with the meticulous care of long practice. I shudder desperately. Why after Rhys, after my plans, should the dull-finished deadly thing scare me so?

Check done, Vance slides the pistol into its holster and swings it to me. I balk, disbelieving his intent.

"I'm a Hand," I protest, even as my fingers accept it.

"We ran your last couple of firing range tests," Anton says, "and selected this for you. Accuracy isn't really important and it doesn't have much recoil."

"Why do I need it? I thought that I was coming along as a translator."

"So, you still need to be ready to defend yourself," Vance scoffs. "Don't worry. The load isn't deadly—it's something Qiang cobbled up for us a while back. She calls it 'Oblivion.' In most cases it knocks the target cold. When the vic comes around, memory for the last several hours is wiped clean."

"Most cases?" I ask, feeling more assured.

"In about 25 percent," Tammany clarifies, "the subject has a reaction—usually fatal. Don't land more than two darts if you can help yourself. Overdose ups the bad reaction chance big time."

"Oh," I strap the holster over my tee shirt, and Vance hands me a set of coveralls similar to his own.

"We three are going in as Maintenance," he explains. "These should fit, but you may need to get rid of your jeans. The middle fasteners are dummies so you can get to your gun. Your shoes are behind the seat there."

I shake the coveralls out over my knees; they do look like they'll be too close-cut to put on over my jeans. Vance seems so indifferent to my presence that I guess I'm supposed to change right here.

Blushing, I kick off my sneakers and peel off my jeans. Vance doesn't even turn his head, but I see Anton glancing up in the rearview mirror.

"Eyes front, Anton." Tammany pokes him. "Isn't that our turn coming up?"

Anton grunts and turns onto a road marked by a sign reading "Lantic Labs: Private." The road surface contains a liberal mixture of a blue gravel that coats the van with a gritty dust. A simple but sturdy barred gate blocks our way, a storklike guard-pad off to the right.

"Your turn, Tammany," Anton says, "Got the code?"

For answer, she fingers a few icons on her datapad, scans the information that blurs onto her screen, and nods once.

"Got it. Press 825493."

Pulling up next to the guard-pad, Anton lowers his window and, coughing slightly at the dust, reaches out with a gloved hand and enters the numbers. My heart is racing wildly, but Tammany seems only mildly interested, and Vance is apparently dozing.

When the gate jangles open, Anton smiles slightly and raises his window.

''Nice, Tam, keep scanning. Kari, you might want to get those shoes on.''

As I scrabble for the crepę-soled work boots, I listen carefully to the instructions Anton fires out.

''We're going around to a side building where—I believe—the Xians are being held. Tammany has made IDs for us that should cover us if we're stopped. The floor plan is simple enough, but I don't know where in the building the Xians are quartered. You three will go in; I'll back the van into the loading bay and make sure that things are clear on that end.''

''Sounds good,'' Vance says, ''but I notice that you are not going in.''

Anton glances back, ''But I'm sending Karen with you. I'm counting on her to keep you out of trouble.''

The Lantic Labs industrial park is not as decorative as the Corp's. Most of the buildings are lumped in a central group awkwardly connected by breezeways and gerbil tubes. Artistic landscaping cannot make them anything but Bauhaus horrors.

The sweet gums, showy scarlet, orange, and yellow, are certainly pretty though. I remember collecting their prickly seed pods when I was small, swinging them like miniature medieval maces or tossing them as caltrops under the feet of imaginary pursuers.

Anton drives us past the main complex along a curving, downsloping road. A smaller building of the same boxy construction as the rest is nestled into an island of asphalt off the road.

''That's it,'' Anton says somewhat unnecessarily. ''According to my research there should be no one much about at this hour. There's some important reception that most of the big shots will be attending and the work day is over for the rest. There will be at least one on-site security officer.''

"Only one?" Tammany asks as the van halts by a side door. "With what they're hiding?"

"Could be more," Anton replies. "You'll know what to do if there are."

"Yes," Vance says, and his matter-of-fact tone makes my skin chill.

"Wait here," Tammany orders as she gets out. "If I can't get the door open, there's no sense for you to be seen."

I want to protest—anything rather than seeming scared—but since Vance only grunts, I lean back and watch. Tammany walks up to the door, her datapad swinging from a long-fingered hand. At the door, she bends over a keypad, her body carefully masking whatever she is doing. In under a minute the door opens.

Without looking back, she walks in. The door closes.

"Come along, Karen," Vance says, picking up a tool kit.

I don't see anything for me to carry, so I jump down after.

The keypad bears a light film of white dust on certain numbers. Pulling a work glove on over his hand, Vance presses down on them simultaneously. The door opens; as I follow him inside, I notice that every trace of dust is gone.

Clever.

A woman with iron grey hair, wearing a dark green uniform, sleeps behind an orange plastic desk, her head resting on her folded arms. Tammany stands next to her, watching the scenes flickering by on a monitor set flush with the desk top.

"Hey," she says softly, "this thing scans room by room, and the halls. I've got a feeling that one picture is a dummy—that one."

She points to a view that to my eyes is little different than the others—pale cream walls hung with various tools, long lab tables stacked with a bewildering array of equipment.

"The light in that one is different from the others on the same corridor—see?"

The views flicker by again and Vance grunts. I nervously glance past Tammany, expecting another guard any minute.

"You see," Tammany says, "they're showing a fake scene and that can mean only one thing."

I catch on.

"That what they're hiding is so dangerous to them that they can't even let their own security know exactly what they are guarding!"

"Seems about right to me," Tammany agrees. "This scan assumes that the viewers know what room they're seeing so there aren't any room numbers. We'll still need a closer search, but at least we know that there is something to find."

She turns away and starts down the corridor.

"I haven't seen any other security," she says in low-voiced afterthought, "but we know that their cameras lie."

I get the tail position and follow, resisting the impulse to glance back over my shoulder every few steps. Tammany is calm, consulting the datapad she holds in one hand, the other carefully left empty for her hidden weapon. I gather from what she softly mutters to Vance as they stop at each door that she has a life detector, similar to those that rescue teams use. With it, she gives each room a tentative "all clear" before Vance opens the door.

They are quite efficient, and I find myself admiring them the way I had before, but that admiration brings with it a new form of jitters. A broom closet, two offices, a cross-corridor, and three labs later, I am a tangle of nerves.

We are checking the rooms down a corridor that angles toward the loading bay when Tammany signals that her detector registers something. Glancing back over my shoulder, I realize that I am praying that we'll find lab animals—mice, rats, illegal kittens—like we have twice before. All I want now is out of this place.

Vance slides the door open and steps quickly in. Tammany is his shadow, and I third. We have done this enough times that our movements are like some strange dance. The room is dimly lit. At Tammany's silent signal, I find the dial that raises the lights.

"Just some dogs," Vance grunts, already turning to leave. "I wonder if Anton's scouting was off."

Stepping back so that he can precede me into the corridor, I try not to look at what Lantic's scientists have done to these animals. Four metal barred cages hold sleek black dogs about the size of Labrador retrievers, but much thinner. IV drips taped to their necks seep some bright fluid into their systems. To keep them from dislodging the IV's or assaulting their handlers, their paws are strapped down to the cage's floor. Three seem comatose, their slat-ribbed sides raggedly rising and falling; a fourth stirs weakly.

Even knowing that Lantic is probably searching for a cure for some debilitating illness or making sure that some wonderful product is safe doesn't keep me from turning away.

"Get the light, Karen," Vance reminds me as he opens the door.

Reaching for the dial, I look back, wanting to leave the animals with at least as much light as they had had before we came in. The one who had been stirring opens eyes the color of brass and with difficulty raises its head to get a look at me.

"Tammany! Vance! Come back," I whisper urgently. "This is them!"

The two step back and Vance lets the door shut.

"What? Karen, we don't have time for pity," Vance says.

Raising the lights, I go over to the cages.

"Just look at them—these aren't dogs. I doubt that they're even terrestrial."

Crouching next to the cage with the most active one, fear making breathing difficult, I gently stroke the bars to get its attention. At the soft ringing sound, the "dog" raises its head.

Again eyes the color of highly polished brass open. Close as I am, I can see that the pupils are neither round like a human's nor slit like a cat's nor even rectangular like a goat's, but somehow pyramidal—a triangle with depth, set inside a circle of sparkling metal.

"Shit," Vance hisses, "You've got something here. But how do we know they're not simply Xian life-forms brought in for study?"

My certainty makes me brilliant.

"Tammany, this room wasn't on the security vid when you scanned before. Was it?"

She shakes her head, her clever fingers already examining the cage. Then she looks at Vance.

"Vance, these have built-in wheels and limited lift. We can move them quickly and we'd better. Someone may be looking for us about now."

Vance squats next to another cage and finds the release. The "dog" doesn't stir, not even when the cage thumps onto its wheels.

"I hope we're right," he's saying as the door from the corridor opens, framing two security guards with leveled weapons.

"Ping-pong," Vance says in the tone of someone calling a pool shot.

Obviously, Tammany knows what he means, because she rolls deeper into the room and continues readying cages. I simply freeze, watching as Vance pulls his gun and tacks two Oblivion darts into each guard, alternating one, then the other, and back again.

"Get those men out of the door," Tammany calls. "We're ready to move. Karen, take these two. I'll get the others."

Vance bends and lifts the guards out of the way with an ease that his slender form belies. Tammany lashes her two cages train-car fashion and pulls them into the corridor. I imitate, breaking into a trot as soon as I'm out. Vance closes the door and follows.

As we near the loading bay, we hear shouting—one of the voices is clearly Anton's.

"Blindman's Bluff," Tammany calls, tossing her pullrope to me and fumbling for her datapad.

"Tag!" Vance answers.

My head reels, but I can see the reasoning behind their words—after all, battle language is a code of sorts. I throw myself into pulling the cages forward. Vance runs ahead. I hear the hollow report of his weapon and what sounds like a glad cry from Anton.

Tammany heaves an access panel from a wall. Whatever she does with the circuits there makes the lights flicker and the security cameras flash and wobble on their mounts.

Behind me, I can hear wheezing breaths and the impotent scrabble of strapped paws against the flooring of the cages. Reluctant to speak and screw up communications for my embattled teammates, I subvocalize.

"Easy, now, easy. Everything will be fine."

My desk-bound muscles, more tortured than toned by the training I've been taking, are aching as I pull my little train to the bend in the corridor.

Tammany has vanished and I am left to interpret the noise—or lack of—as best I can. A breeze, slightly cooler than the air around me, touches my face, leading me to believe that Anton had opened the loading bay. A faint sound of ragged breathing, shaded with a tremolo whistle, from ahead of me adds a person or persons to the picture.

Vance? Anton? Or other?

My mind refuses to believe that either of the Corp ops could be so out of shape as to wheeze and the noise is too regular to be a pained gasp. Extracting my pistol from under my coveralls, I flatten myself to the floor so that I will be as small a target as possible when I look around the bend.

A voice makes me jump.

"Give it up," it commands—male and authoritarian—"Backup is on its way. You are surrounded."

"Don't believe it," Tammany's voice says, the timbre flattened as if she is outdoors and calling in. "Your communications system is disabled; this immediate area has been jammed."

Tammany must have gone out another door and slipped to join the fellows. Uncertain whether I should feel flattered or angry at her abandoning me and the aliens, I peek around the corridor.

A man crouches in the shadow behind a packing case, intent on the end of the corridor. In the uncertain light, I cannot tell whether his uniform is blue like my teammates' or the green of the front-desk security guard's.

Suppressing a wild urge to giggle, I aim the gun. Whoever it is, if Oblivion does its job, he won't remember. And if it's Vance or Anton, I guess I can see the shot as practice.

My first dart buries itself in the man's right buttock; my second lands in the middle of one thigh as he jumps to his feet with a shout more of surprise than of pain.

I drop my weapon to keep from hammering dart after dart into him, and before he crumples in a heap to the floor, a sequence of orderly shots tells me that someone—hopefully on my side—has taken advantage of my diversion.

The building falls absolutely silent except for the complaints of the tortured security cameras and the incongruous twitter of a bird from outside. Anton's voice breaks the silence.

"Karen?" He doesn't bother to ask if I'm okay, "Let's get those creatures out of here. Someone's going to notice this mess."

Angry, I start hauling again. When I clear the corner, Vance is moving three figures in Lantic's green security uniforms out of my way. The van has been backed into the loading bay, the doors opened, and a ramp dropped.

A pattern like a half-melted snowflake on one of the windows shows where something went off very hard, or maybe merely very close.

The cages are too cumbersome and the corner too sharp for me to manipulate the load alone. Finally furious, I snap.

"Anton! Stop making like James Bond and get over here. Tammany and Vance can watch for trouble. We need to move!"

His green eyes widen and his omnipresent smile vanishes into his beard, but he leaps from the back of the van and lopes over to assist.

"You pull," I say, tired of draft-horse duty. "I'll go behind and steer."

He takes the line that I shove into his hands and quickly we have the first pair of cages clear and moving. Vance arrives in time to take the next pair. By the time we get them down to the van, Anton has his set on and is moving to help us.

"Drive," Vance orders economically.

Twice reprimanded, Anton is glowering as he moves to the driver's seat. He starts us moving before we have the doors shut or ourselves seated, but the Xian animals are aboard. Vance adjusts to the motion and finishes locking things down.

I topple flat on my ass, biting down against yelping at the sharp burst that jars its way up from my tailbone.

When, with a trace of his courtly social manner, Vance helps me to my seat, I realize that he considers us safely away—or maybe he's simply better at putting his fate into others' hands than I am. Whatever, I sit chewing my lip and wishing there was a dignified way to rub a bruised backside. Finally, Tammany lets her headset fall around her neck.

"No sign of physical pursuit or of any reports going out," she says. "Where next? Qiang?"

"Yes," Anton replies, "She'll be the best to tell us if we've guessed right."

He looks worried for a moment. ''And maybe she can tell us if those creatures look as sick as I think they do.''

I turn to get a clearer view of the cages. Only one of the ''dogs'' is at all alert—I think it is the same one as before. The other three have subsided into unconsciousness, their slumped posture and pinned feet giving them the look of melted sphinxes.

The brass eyes study me carefully, then squint—painfully I think—shut.

''I think they're bad off, Anton,'' I answer his tacit question. ''I think they're very bad.''

As if to confirm my statement, the brass eyes flutter as if trying to open once more then fail.

I accept Anton's offer to drop me off on the way to the Corp Complex. Once again clad in jeans and tee shirt, the events of the morning seeming cast off with the clothes, I catch the rail home, resolving to have at least a quiet afternoon.

Safely inside my house, I scan the phonefax, decide that I can ignore all my messages, and on impulse take a hot shower. With my hair still dripping down my back, I fix a sandwich and a bowl of vegetable soup. Only when I'm at my kitchen table, realizing that I don't remember a word of the magazine article I've been reading, do I face my internal uproar.

What I'm feeling isn't just a reaction to being part of a field strike, nor is it resentment that my part—despite my being a Hand and not a Knife—was accepted so matter-of-factly. Honestly, I'm irrationally pleased that the experienced field ops took my role, including plugging that one guard and breaking the stalemate, as a matter of routine.

My own pleasure in their acceptance is what makes me quiver with suppressed disgust.

That I should care! That I should care about their opinions and acceptance after what they have done!

A section from Yeats' *Autobiography*, wherein he reflected how in his search for spiritual guidance he had abandoned those who did not prove to be "the lonely mind," rises from memory. I am so disgusted with my own lack of resolve that if at that moment I could quit myself I would and consider the parting well chosen.

But I had learned long ago that the one person I can't escape is myself. The knowledge had cost me my husband and two children, far too costly a lesson to ever forget.

No, that lesson is behind me. Before me is only memory, oath, and resolution.

Standing, I reach up to where a spice rack is built into the side of a kitchen cabinet, so cunningly crafted that it is all but invisible. Anyone noticing the extra inch or so of depth and pulling along the edge would quickly dismiss the supposition as fancy. Long ago, I had secured the space by drilling a hole through the door and into the frame and then pegging it shut with a length of doweling. Later, I had finished the peg so that it was a perfect match for the surrounding surface.

The cubbyhole might not fool a determined member of the Corp, but otherwise it was perfectly undetectable.

Drawing the peg free, I grasp the door edge and pull open the door. Inside rests a fabric bag with my jewelry, a roll of currency, some credit slips that can't be traced to me, a duplicate set of my ID documents, and another set made out to Kathy Spring. I ignore all of these and pull from the back of the highest of the four shelves a triangular tube, cut so that it fits into the angle of the back shelf like a piece of molding.

This I take down and, after shutting the compartment behind me, carry to the table.

My hands tremble slightly as I unroll the brittle papers inside.

The first document is several pages long—line after line of criminal charges and convictions: disturbing the peace, drunk and disorderly, resisting arrest, shoplifting, breaking parole. As the dates go by, the crimes become more serious: possession of illegal substances, burglary, embezzlement.

The name at the top of the arrest report isn't mine—not anymore—but the charges are mine, perhaps more real to me now than they were then.

Then the only thing that was real was drinking and, later, some designer drugs that helped with the hangovers and the furry mouth; drugs that helped when I had to pretend to cope with my job, with my kids, with Will.

Will.

I put the police blotter down and move to the next page—a divorce decree between William Raymond West and the person I once was. My—her—signature is shaky, but not because of any emotion. I'd had to be sober to be permitted to go through the court proceedings. They'd been rather rough because we had minor children and Will was determined that I'd never be permitted to see them again.

He'd probably been wise.

I'd gone downhill from there until finally I committed the crime that even the overtaxed judiciary system couldn't ignore. Prison had room for me—long-time room, not a week or a couple of months like other times—and once inside to stay I'd started sobering up.

It wasn't that I couldn't get the stuff. Hell, even I had the connections and sex will buy a lot. No, it wasn't that I couldn't get the stuff. Later, I began to suspect that drying out was the last type of hell I could put myself through.

Turning over those pages, I come to a flimsy of the diploma for an M.A. in foreign languages; under it is the second, this one for alien anthropology—a rather ironic degree for a person who would never see a Chirr or a suankh except on vid. I'd felt the irony then, too. Probably reaching out to stars I'd never visit was another way of beating on myself.

I'd been working on a third M.A., this one in the classical languages, when Mr. Benjamin Allain decided to change my life.

To pay my tuition (the prison system didn't give lifers education for nothing), I'd been doing a variety of translation jobs. The majority were pretty routine, but sometimes there would be a piece that would hint at events between the stars, events that spun the bridges of the UAN.

Even as I had buried myself in developing fluency in Latin and Linear B, I'd found time to improve my command of the commerce patois that the Chirr and su-ankh had developed before encountering Terrans. I pretended to care for nothing later than the high point of the Roman Empire because admitting otherwise awakened a pain more intense than I'd felt even when drying out, even when Will took my kids away.

Then the first present came. It wasn't much, just a slender volume with color plates of the treasures of Schliemann's Troy. The note inserted between the frontispiece and the title page said simply, "Thank you for your work. You have an extraordinary gift. Mr. Allain."

That note, its pale blue stationery yellowing around the edges now, tries to curl into itself as I pull it from beneath the diplomas. The paper is somewhat tattered from the many times that I had read it in the shelter of my bunk in the quad I shared with two murderers and a woman who had found that a woman can rape a man if she is creative enough.

I'd looked at the book nearly every day until it was stolen by a guard who was one Christmas present short. But the note had fluttered to the floor and had become my talisman, a charm reminding me that someone believed that I was special.

Mr. Allain sent me other gifts: books, scented notepaper, a lavender sachet. All were always gifts meant for a woman, reflecting a strange, Victorian ideal of what a female is. His notes, increasingly personal, were never less than formal and were always signed "Mr. Allain." Nearly two years passed after that first note before I discovered his first name on an order form and I hugged that knowledge to me like a secret.

To say I was happy in prison would be a lie, but I did find a strange form of contentment. My alcoholism was quiescent and my early disdain for the vices of my sister prisoners left me fairly free from temptation. Because of the nature of my crime, I was never approached to become a trusty, but because of my lack of inclination to cause trouble I was also left alone.

My quad had been cramped into a sextet when Mr. Allain made his pitch to the judicial authorities. I never learned the details, but in six months I was free. In a year, I was dead—or the person I had been was dead to all but a few people—and Karen Saber was born.

The last page in my pile is a copy of Mr. Allain's death certificate. Under "Cause of Death" is printed "Massive systems collapse due to chronic condition."

I knew better even then. I knew that he had been murdered and I determined to avenge him, no matter how impossible killing the Directors of the Corp that he had built and that had buried him would be.

Rolling up my memories, I ease them back into their tube. Then I bury my head in my hands.

Damn. Life is getting awfully complicated.

Heading for the fridge, I break out the chocolate ice cream. There are times that I regret—or at least my hips regret—that I gave up drinking.

The rest of the day is spent between methodically calling up every news report on Xi-7 and winterizing my rose garden. The news isn't promising, especially when I compare the reports to those that came out when the Chirr and su-ankh made contact with us. There is nothing—after the first few columns—of the curiosity and delight I had remembered.

One does not need to be an expert on semantics to see that some group had a vested interest in making Xi-7 seem nothing more than a chance for the UAN races to expand their territory.

Thoughtfully, I heap mulch to protect the bud unions from frost, my mind hovering above fields never cut by human hands, on a far away green planet.

FIVE

When I go into the office the next day, no mention is made of the Xian animals, though both Anton and Tammany stop in my office to chat. Taking my cue from them, I hold my questions. This does not stop me from doing some quiet snooping.

Qiang is nowhere to be found and so I assume that she is working with the creatures. Putting my curiosity aside, I settle to work. The hours pass in an easy flow that bounces from task to task without any more interruption than a stream finds in a well-worn course.

The buzz of my intercom is hardly an interruption to my thoughts.

"Yes?"

"Director Saber, there are some—people—here to see you."

"Send them down, thank you," I answer, and hardly have time to swing my chair to face the door before there is a soft rapping for admittance.

"Come," I say, and as the door opens I am on my feet, understanding instantly the hesitation in the receptionist's voice.

Terra has had commerce with aliens for some thirty years, but for the average person to meet a Chirr or a su-ankh is as unlikely as it would have been for the average

Londoner to meet Pocahontas. Yet through my doorway comes one of each.

Chirr I have done work with—for—in the past. As different as the Chirr and Terrans are, we are close cousins when we compare each other to the su-ankh.

The su-ankh who stands before my desk is tall—taller even than Vance. It resembles a bipedal salamander, as much as it resembles anything terrestrial. Its torso bears four arms: two heavily muscular ones nearly where a human's are, a second comparatively frail set growing gangly and multijointed from below the first. This su-ankh is covered with silver-green scales so fine that they shimmer.

Even stranger than the four arms are the large round eyes that bulge like half-spheres from the flat, wide-mouthed head. A su-ankh's eyes are almost always monocolor, without apparent pupil, and whether they are black or gold or green or blue, the legend is that to look fully into the eyes of one of the su-ankh is to look into the very soul of the cosmos.

With two such visitors, I don't have time for wonder nor time to remember the strange treaty that our three races all share.

Instead, I bow.

"Coordinator Wheep," I greet the Chirr, "Welcome. I regret, but I do not know your companion."

"Such regret," the su-ankh says in a deep voice that reverberates from within its chest, "is mannerly, if not reasonable. I have not entered your personal orbit before this time, although I am not unknown on Terra. My name is difficult for Terrans to pronounce, but I would be pleased if you would call me Chiron."

I don't know whether I am more astonished by the su-ankh's fluency in pan-lingi or his identity. Chiron is—as best as Terrans have been able to judge—an important member of his people, although whether that importance is official or merely because he is a xenophile is a matter of constant debate.

Whatever the reason, I must restrain myself from bowing again at his introduction.

"Please," I say, "make yourselves comfortable if you can. I can have appropriate furniture brought for you if what is here is not suitable."

"Thank you, Directors Saber," Wheep replies, "I can manage."

"And I," Chiron adds, leaning back on his long tail into what I take as a resting posture.

"Can I have refreshments sent?" I offer. "Coffee, tea, or fruit juices?"

"We," Wheep says, settling herself onto a padded footstool in what looks like an uncomfortable crouch, "would drink apple juice."

"And I am fiercely fond of orange soda, if it can be had," Chiron says. "The carbonation is fascinating."

After I get on the intercom and order refreshments, we exchange formal chitchat until the server is gone from my office.

"If we may press to the business that has brought us to you," Wheep says, "we believe you would be interested."

"Please," I reply, striving to maintain my poise, "I am at your disposal."

The Chirr dips her furry nose in deference to the su-ankh and Chiron continues.

"The matter is absurdly simple and dreadfully difficult," he says, pausing for so long that I wonder if he has drifted off into one of the trances for which the su-ankh are notorious. Then he lets out his breath in a long hissing stream.

"A group of my people, a group of the Chirr, and a group of Terrans have been in deepest negotiation regarding some future trade and development possibilities," he says. "We have, at last, come to a consensus, but find ourselves in an awkward position."

"We are, you see, Directors Saber," Wheep interjects, her synthesized words tumbling in rapid contrast to Chiron's deliberate speech, "not 'government' bodies, as we understand you Terrans to have them. We are independent groups."

Mentally I translate this: these commercial negotiators are representing themselves as independent of their planetary governments, thus avoiding making their actions policy. However, I know enough about Chirr, at least, to know that Wheep cannot be completely independent.

About the su-ankh I am less certain, but Chiron is different from the majority of his race—at least of those who have ventured into space. Some do serve in administrative and exploratory positions within the UAN, but most prefer the company of their own kind.

All I reply is, "Yes, please continue."

"We have settled the terms in the trade tongue, but before we ratify the document we wish to have it translated into our own languages," Wheep touches her mechanical translator for effect, "to make certain that we understand each other."

"Since we are unofficial bodies," Chiron says, "we do not wish to involve government translators. Machines are inadequate for the subtlety of this project. Our inquiries came up with you as one of the most fluent linguists readily available in the private sector. As Coordinator Wheep was already acquainted with you, you were our logical choice."

He stops and, as if by mutual consent, they both sip their drinks. I mouth cooling coffee and consider my reply.

"I am only Terran," I finally say, "with Terran limitations."

The two aliens nod quickly.

Somewhat miffed, I continue, "May I see the document?"

Coordinator Wheep reaches into one of her voluminous pockets and produces a folded square of paper.

"We have it on computer as well," she says, "but this is as quick."

And harder for me to copy without being obvious, I qualify.

Stepping around my desk, I accept the sheet of heavy paper, unfolding it as I retreat to my chair.

"It is quite brief," Chiron says, "and, I believe, fairly clear."

I grunt, forgetting my manners as my brain assimilates the remarkable document in my hands. Simply, it shares among three groups the rights to an unspecified piece of land. The rights are neatly—in fact, quite fairly—divided. What chills me is that I suspect I know what the nameless property is.

"I see that your Terran partner is StarUs," I say, looking up.

"Yes," Wheep nods, "but they have said that they will themselves be looking for partners; they are primarily a shipping concern. They will be interested in a more versatile organization, perhaps one involved with creative problem solving, to help them."

"A creative group," Chiron adds, "such as your own Corp."

I hold his universe-swallowing gaze, testing his offer, wondering how the others will react when I tell them that we have been offered a chance to join the first ones who will exploit the wealth of Xi-7.

After the aliens depart, I sneak home, hoping that the absorbing activities of the other Directors will keep them from noticing that I have had two alien visitors—at least until morning.

I had accepted the translation job, promising to do it myself. Their payment, of course, would not go to me directly, but to the Corp. Specialists, whether Hand or Knife, draw salaries and success bonuses. Mr. Allain had felt that this kept internal competition down. Perhaps he was right.

Perhaps.

Shrugging, I put the translation from my mind and head down to my basement lab, telling my home computer to ignore/refuse all calls and visitors. I certainly don't want to be interrupted during what I'm about. My research must be jinxed, because I'm not even down the basement stairs when a loud noise startles me.

"What?" I mutter to myself, "Or who?"

A rhythmic thumping by the patio door brings things into focus. Stripping off my gloves, I run up to find Vance already inside, pocketing an electronic skeleton key. Anton, pushing a plastic crate in front of him, is coming through the door.

"Thank you so much for knocking," I growl.

"We did," Vance replies unperturbed, turning to help Anton with the crate, "and called from the van and rang your front door as well, but when you took your time coming we could not stand out in the street."

"Not with this, at least," Anton adds.

"This?" I ask, my annoyance fading into confusion.

"This," Vance says, putting his hand on the crate, "the last surviving member of the Xian creatures we liberated."

Words jam in my throat, but finally I manage, "Here? In that crate?"

"Oh, Kari, it was bad," Anton says, slumping into a chair, "The Xian is unconscious now, the only way we could get it out. It wouldn't leave the others."

He trails off and I realize that he is still stunned. Vance looks calmer, but the lines around his eyes are set in an expression of apprehension. With certainty, I realize that what has shaken Anton and what has shaken Vance are two completely different things.

Irrationally, I am scared.

"Why did you bring it here?"

"Why?" Anton stops. "Because our labs have been sabotaged. Qiang may be dead, and we need you to find a way for us to prove that this 'dog' is indeed an alien sentient and not a beast, or we may have made a very costly mistake."

"I wish that Rhys was still alive," Vance says. "I'd

send him to go out and sweep some retribution, but we're shorthanded as it is with Ben's death."

My head pounds until a faint scratching noise focuses my attention on the crate. Sinking to my knees, I peer inside. Strange brass eyes meet my gaze. I want to believe that this is the same one who was so fearless back at the Lantic Labs complex.

"Easy, boy," I croon, "easy."

The Xian settles back on its haunches, but regards me suspiciously. I look up at the two men—even Vance's expression holds some hope mingled with the uncertainty.

"Did you bring its chow?" I ask. "And I notice it isn't hooked up to an IV anymore. Will it need something that it was getting from that?"

"Qiang didn't think that the IV was helping at all," Vance says. "Toshi is seeing what he can resurrect from the ruins of the lab. For now, we're to treat it like a Terran creature."

"Except that I'm supposed to try and talk with it."

"Yeah." Anton shrugs, then gets to his feet. "We had better clear out—we've been here too long."

When they are gone, I kneel before the cage. Again, I stare into those disturbing eyes.

"Bet you want out of there," I say, reaching for the leash that Vance has left on the counter.

The Xian doesn't move, but suddenly I feel ridiculous. If this is indeed a visiting alien, a delegate of some sort, putting it on a leash would be an incredible insult. Of course, if it's an animal, if I don't leash it I could be letting myself in for a tremendous amount of trouble. And the people at Lantic Labs did have the creatures strapped down, which would seem to indicate that they are dangerous.

That, more than any other factor, is what decides me. I don't want to do what Lantic Labs does. Dropping the leash on the counter, I squat in front of the cage.

"Okay," I say slowly, "I'm guessing that you must

understand at least one UAN language or they would have had difficulty deciding—hell! Let me start over."

I plop onto the floor.

"I'm going to let you out. Stay calm. I won't hurt you. I promise. Okay?"

I repeat the message in Chirr whistles, su-ankh hisses, and in as many Terran languages as I can. Then, keeping my motions slow and steady, memories of telling my son how to approach a neighbor's dog trembling from where I've kept them buried, I press open the door latch and slide back to give it room.

Hesitantly, the Xian rises to its feet and, lowering its head to avoid bumping the cage's roof, steps out. I expect its claws to click against the tile floor, but its footsteps are marked only by the faintest whisper of leather. It walks toward me, step after tentative step, until we are nose to nose. The black nostrils widen and it whuffles slightly as it sniffs me.

I return the favor. Its odor isn't like a dog's. It doesn't smell like any animal I've ever been near. Beneath the sharp scent of medical alcohol and the sweeter scent of the adhesive that clings to its fur from where the restraints had been fastened, there is a spicy smell—something, but not quite, like apple pie.

"Not bad," I say, "I could get to like you."

The Xian seems indifferent to my approval. Its curiosity regarding me apparently satisfied, it now begins to inspect the kitchen. Everything is sniffed carefully before being approached, then studied. Only rarely does it touch anything. Even when it seems most absorbed, those silky ears track sounds, seemingly independently of the creature's actions.

I settle cross-legged on the floor where I can see through the kitchen and into my small dining room, watching the methodical inspection continue. Nothing the creature does seems to indicate any intelligence more sophisticated than that of a Terran dog or cat. Although clearly curious, the Xian creature makes no effort to manipulate its environment. Nor does it attempt to communicate with me. It simply inspects everything in these two rooms.

My home computer breaks into the comparative quiet.

"Incoming message coded 'Urgent.' Do you wish to accept it or shall a message be taken?"

The Xian stiffens, but rather than fleeing, it slinks down, pressing belly and tail flat to the oriental rug in my dining room.

Watching the creature so that I'll be ready for any panic, I answer, "I'll take the call."

The next voice is Toshi's, "Karen, Qiang is dead—she died about an hour ago from a combination of burns and chemical fumes from the fire in her lab."

"Oh, God!" I manage, remembering that Qiang had been the strongest advocate—after Anton—of Anton's plan to help to uncover the Xi-7 fraud, remembering, too, that I had wanted to kill her.

"Oh, God," I repeat weakly.

"I realize that this is a shock, Karen," Toshi continues, "and that you aren't feeling well, but we need to have a Directors' meeting. Can those of us who remain come to your house?"

Translation: You're not sick, but for the record that's why we're meeting at your house. We can't exactly leave the alien creature alone.

"Uh, sure," I answer. "Are you certain that this is a good idea?"

Translation: Will it be safe?

"Yes, Karen, I can bring the necessary gear along. Will two hours be enough time?"

"If you don't mind a mess and will settle for coffee and grocery store cookies."

Toshi's laughter is deep and rusty, as if he hasn't laughed in too long.

"Karen, I promised you I'd take care of all the details. Just change out of your robe and fluffy slippers and dose up on cold tabs and look for us in a couple of hours."

When he signs off, I tell the computer to refuse all calls except those from the Corp. Then I uncross my legs and bury my head in the shelter of my knees.

Toshi. Vance. Anton. Tammany. All here. All of them, here within a mere two hours. I had never dared hope for such luck. With Qiang and Rhys dead, these four are the end of my problem.

Can I manage anything effective in so little time? My house doesn't have a shielded conference room. Toshi's cryptic wording, even over the private line, tells me that he fears a leak within our own system. No wonder. Given his own conspiracies, he will see them anytime that something goes wrong.

This time he may have cause, which means that whatever Security he will bring will stay outside of whatever room we will be in. Can I exploit this? The house is mine; the choice of meeting room, within reason, will be mine. But with guards outside it is unlikely that I could pass the others' deaths off as accidents without careful planning. Not unless I also kill myself and I realize that I am not yet ready to die.

My frenzied musing is interrupted by the lightest brush of something cold against my arm. Raising my head, I see that the Xian creature has crept disconcertingly close.

"I'd nearly forgotten about you," I say, breath catching in my throat at the Xian's nearness.

The creature studies me silently. Despite its doglike appearance, it has yet to bark or whine or yip . . . or anything. Suddenly, I realize how completely silent it has been. How does it talk? Does it even understand that I am talking or does it just dismiss my words as aimless noise?

No. There is something in the way those brass eyes study me. I cannot believe that there is not understanding of some sort there. More important, someone else believed it too.

Even as I contemplate the thought, the creature steps delicately onto my leg and then across me into the rest of the house. Its touch dispels the wild fantasies that I have been brooding on. Even if I could come up with a plan within the next ninety minutes—a plan that would take out four assassins—I could not hope to deal with Security. Nor could I hope to deal with the Xian problem with a shattered Corp as my only resource.

Laughing like an idiot at myself, I get to my feet. Damn! I always preferred Monte Cristo to Hamlet.

Leaving the alien creature sniffing around my house, I brush my hair and, almost as an afterthought, change out of the kickarounds I had been wearing and into a neat skirt. As I'm stepping into my flats, I notice that the Xian has come to the door of my bedroom and is watching me with the most lively interest that it has shown about anything thus far.

The creature shies back for a moment when I drop my tee shirt onto the bed, but only for a moment. Nose wrinkling, it steps cautiously over the lintel and carefully inspects the discarded clothing. Inspired, I shake the shirt out so that the creature can see the shape.

"See," I say, "arms go through here, head through here, torso through here."

The Xian tilts its furry head. I laugh and pull the tee shirt on over my blouse.

"Like that," I reach and pick up my jeans. "These are pants: two legs and a waist."

Again a tilt of the head and this time a perking of the large ears away from the smooth skull.

"All right."

Sitting on the edge of the bed, I step out of my flats and pull the jeans on over my stockings, lifting my skirt so that the Xian can see how the zipper and buttons at the waist work.

Letting the skirt drop, I find that the Xian is studying the pairs of shoes scattered on the floor.

"All right," I say, plopping down on the floor beside it, "Shoes. They protect feet. See?"

I put one shoe on and let the Xian inspect. It tilts its

head at me, apparently confused. Chuckling, I turn my unshod right foot up against my left thigh.

"These are really soft on the bottom." My finger drags against my stocking. "Oh, this stuff isn't me—it's more fabric."

The Xian's eyes are wide, the dark triangles within the brass seeming somehow deeper. Clumsily, it lifts a paw and touches the sole of my foot. The gesture is awkward rather than tentative and I wonder if it is trying to imitate me.

"That's it," I encourage, chilled and delighted all at once. "Can you feel the difference between that and the skin of my hand?"

Moving slowly, I put my hand down next to my foot and again the paw extends to touch my palm. Its skin feels rough and dry, so much like a dog's paw that I am amazed that something evolved elsewhere could be so like.

Emboldened, I touch the rest of the Xian's foot. There are four toes, the center two stronger and thicker. I press as I would on a cat's paw, but the claws I can feel sheathed within do not extend.

"You do have claws, don't you?" I ask. "Are they vestigial?"

If I expected it to suddenly extend the claws, I am disappointed. Since it hasn't bitten me yet, I mime stroking it along the flanks and shoulders. The brass eyes follow my gesture and its breathing comes slightly faster, but it neither moves nor flinches. I let my fingers lower into fur that is deceptively deep and faintly oily. What I can feel of the skeletal structure beneath the muscles seems oddly designed, yet there are bones of some sort and a spine. Aware that its breathing has picked up, I take my hands away.

"You're pretty," I say soothingly, "and very soft."

It looks at me and, placing its front paws on my thigh, stretches its neck to bury its nose in my hair. Its motion brings it nearly into my lap and I am conscious of a myriad of tiny details that bring its alien nature home to me. Later, I will try and sort them out.

For now, I am content to suppress a tremor at skin that scales like a star beneath fur that is constructed of hairs more rhomboid than round. For now, I feel the soft warmth of alien breath against my scalp and wonder if it is studying me as I am studying it.

Certainly this seems to be the case, for when it has sniffed my hair—jerking its head back once with a damp sneeze—it moves to inspect my ear lobes, first right and then left. I hold as still as I can despite a slight cramp in one leg where its feet rest.

Our mutual inspection is interrupted by the chiming doorbell. The Xian leaps away and vanishes under my bed with a whisper of pads on wood. With a worried glance after, I run for the door, noticing too late that I am wearing only one shoe and that I still have jeans pulled on under my skirt and a tee shirt over my blouse. Given our current crisis, I don't want to keep my fellow Directors waiting, so, shrugging at my reflection, I open the door.

Toshi's usual casual elegance smells of bitter smoke. Although he smiles, the warmth is forced and a certain brooding shadows his eyes. Ash smears Tammany's clothing in odd places that she apparently couldn't dust off. She doesn't bother with a smile, but I'm not insulted. Qiang was her close friend.

Anton squeezes my shoulder as he goes by. The grin he gives my odd costume vanishes almost instantly. Only Vance, natty in a tailored linen suit, seems the same, but then he's seen much more death than the rest of us.

Perhaps because he's politely ignoring my odd state of attire, Vance is the first to notice that the Xian's cage is open and empty.

''Pardon me, Karen, but you did not lose the alien, did you?''

''No,'' I reply, toeing off my one shoe, ''I let the poor thing out. It's under my bed.''

"You have an alien under your bed?" Tammany asks incredulously.

"Yes," I reply with what dignity I can summon, "it ran there when the door bell scared it. Excuse me—I need to change."

Tammany manages something like a grin, brushing a hand along her mismatched, ashy slacks.

"Why? You look fine to me."

"May I set refreshments up in your dining area?" Toshi calls after me.

"Please," I answer and then close the door.

Sitting on the edge of the bed, I strip off my jeans and tee shirt. I'm straightening my skirt and blouse when the Xian's black nose peeks out from under the bed cover's fringe.

"You stay there as long as you want," I murmur softly, "I'll leave the door open for you if you want to come out."

The nose vanishes soundlessly and after sweeping a comb through my tousled hair I reemerge. The others are gathered around my oval pseudo-oak table, all but Anton, who is tending a makeshift bar at the kitchen counter.

"Drink, Kari?"

I scan the assortment and nod. "Peach nectar over crushed ice, please."

He makes a face but complies and, handing me the full tumbler, joins us at the table.

"I guess we all know why we're here," Toshi begins without formality. "Qiang is dead."

His voice catches but he pushes on, "And her lab is in shambles. All but one of the creatures that you four brought out of Lantic Labs are also dead."

The freedom with which he speaks assures me that a privacy curtain has been installed. Pushing back fleeting fantasies of revenge, I take a cookie from the tray at the table's center.

"How is the job of recovering Qiang's notes going?" I ask.

"Not as bad as it could be," Tammany replies. "Whoever bombed her lab was very careful, but she wasn't your average researcher. Even though they trashed her computer files, they missed her tertiary backup."

"Tertiary backup?" I repeat with a slight smile at the ornate phrase.

Tammany nods, "She had a fake cabinet under one of the counters in which she regularly stowed backup data. We got copies of everything but her last day's work."

The back of my neck prickles as I wonder if any of them have spotted my spice cabinet cubbyhole. Reaching for my drink to cover my sudden paranoia, I listen as Vance impatiently turns to Tammany.

"Well, what did you find?"

Tammany scowls and taps her datapad to life. "Qiang first confirmed that the creatures did not need whatever was in those IV drips that were attached to them when they were in the cages. By 'not need' she meant for immediate survival. She hadn't ruled out long-term deficiency ailments—things akin to scurvy or pellagra for a human—that might occur. Her next step was to see what they were being given and to try and guess how it might affect them."

"Why did she go to the trouble?" Vance asks. "We aren't planning to make pets of them, just keep them awhile."

"Precisely," Toshi's tone is icy, "and to keep them, we need to know what their former keepers were doing with them."

"Even more," Tammany says, "we need to know if these are the sentients mentioned in that message Karen showed us. We can hardly find a way to communicate with them if they are the equivalent of drunk or stoned out of their minds."

"Had Qiang arrived at any conclusions?" Vance asks, filling his tumbler from the bottle on the table in front of him.

"No," Tammany admits, "but she had asked if I would

have ready the files I'd copied from Lantic Labs. I had the impression that she wanted to cross-check her conclusions against their data."

"Do you have Qiang's files with you?" I ask, and when Tammany nods, continue, "We can run a check here—especially if Tammany knows what files Qiang planned to work with."

No one protests, so we adjourn to my home office and Tammany copies files onto my computer. The feeling of the computer humming beneath my hands banishes my last edgy desire to somehow murder the four people clustered behind me.

"That it?" I ask when Tammany steps back. "All right, let's see what she has here."

Three columns of nearly incomprehensible chemical formulas rise up on the screen in response to my requests, the symbols and superscripted numbers making them resemble arcane incantations rather than modern science.

"I recognize a few of those," Toshi volunteers. "That first column seems to be organic depressants."

"I recognize a few, too," Anton mutters, just loud enough for me to catch. "Isn't H_2O water?"

His flippancy gives me an idea and I command the computer to put the names of the various drugs next to their code. The columns squash and the print shrinks slightly as the screen reconfigures itself.

"Whew!" Tammany gasps. "If this is what those beasts were being given, they were doped up good."

"No," Vance says, "I don't think that they were on all of these. Karen, pull down the hypertext flag there."

I obey and a neat legend informs us that we are looking at a "blood trace analysis."

"I think," Vance continues, "that Lantic Labs may have tried these over time. Karen, page through and see if Qiang has a file on what was in those IVs."

Again I obey; catching on to Qiang's system quickly, I find what I want. The columns are shorter here, but contain several of the same drugs. A few new ones end the list. Once again, I have the computer flag the formulas with their more familiar names.

"Depressants, appetite suppressants, pain killer," Anton mutters half to himself. "I don't know what the last three are."

"More of the same," I say. "Why so many?"

After paging through both Qiang's and Lantic Labs' files we arrive at a working conclusion. Apparently, the Xian's body chemistry is enough like a human's that some drugs have similar effects. However, "similar" and "identical" allow for quite a bit of error.

"They must have multi-dosed them rather than risking their getting loose," Tammany hazards, "but why such concern?"

"Fear?" Vance suggests, "I don't see anything to be afraid of, but they may have known something we haven't discovered."

I can't help but remember that one of these creatures was last seen under my bed. Nor can I forget the gentle probing of its nose against my hair.

Shrugging, I stand, "Now what?"

"Now," Anton says, "now, Kari, it's up to you."

"Me?" I turn, expecting to find that he is joking, but his broad face is serious.

"You," he repeats. "You need to find out what we have here and how to talk with it."

"Me?" I repeat, looking at the others for contradiction and finding none.

"You."

THE XIAN'S BRASS EYES ARE FRAMED BY CURLING lashes as soft-seeming as velvet, but there is nothing soft in the way it clings to the carpet beneath my bed. After arguing with the others for over an hour, I had capitulated to their arguments. Now they want the Xian back in its cage and both of us relocated to a safer spot.

The way they see things is simple. If the creature we have taken from Lantic Labs is a sentient alien and potentially the first of its type off the surface of its planet, it is valuable. More than that, it is critical to uncovering a conspiracy that would make the collusion of Benedict Arnold with the British a mild prank. But before we can move on our suspicions, we must find out if this creature is a person or merely a curiosity.

None of Toshi's eloquent praise of my linguistic skills nor Anton's puppy-dog courtliness had moved me. Tammany's careful analysis of the vital factors assured me that I was most likely to find the answers we needed, but her rational argument did not sway me from my panicked conviction that this problem was out of my depth.

Only Vance did not join in the alternating rounds of cajoling and browbeating. Instead, he leaned his chair back against the wall and watched near motionlessly as the Xian crept from my bedroom and returned to its slinking inspection of my one-floor house. At last Vance straightened, his chair legs hitting the floor with a solid thump that sent the Xian fleeing back under my bed. Then he turned and said the one word that convinced me.

"Genocide."

He may have convinced me, but I have no comfort for the thoroughly spooked creature under my bed. Claws hooked into the pile of the carpet, it studies the group of us. No warning is growled, but the baring of its jagged jaw surfaces cannot be mistaken for other than threat. Its long tail stretches back from it, whipping careless hands that reach to grab it from behind.

"Damn you all," I curse, springing to my feet with an agility that would certainly have surprised my martial arts instructor.

The others all stare blankly at me from where they had been peering under the bed a moment before.

"Look," I say, "You've scared it. We could tranq it—if we were sure how much of just what it can take. Or we could subdue it—if we knew just precisely where its vital spots are."

Sitting back on her heels, Tammany nods. Toshi grimaces at the damage to his tailored suit.

"Yes," Vance prompts.

"So, get out of here," I continue. "I'll get it out somehow and you can move us tomorrow."

Anton nods and gets to his feet.

"Okay," he says, "that makes some sense. A couple of us should get her safe-house ready in any case."

"We're certainly not doing any good here," Toshi agrees. "If you think you can get it out, Karen, I agree."

"She shouldn't stay alone," Tammany protests. "If anyone is watching us, certainly this meeting will have aroused some interest."

"I'll stay," Vance says. "You three set up the safe-house. I'll dismiss the guard shift and take over myself."

"Is that wise?" Toshi asks.

"Is any of this?" Vance counters. "Yes, I think that it is. If you want to send a couple of fresh Knives, go ahead, but pick ones who know how to blend into the area. If suddenly it's obvious that we're guarding Karen's place, someone may decide to find out why. Agreed?''

The others all nod. Slowly, I do as well. As little as I want to be here alone with Vance and his Knives, I want even less to be alone. Someone killed Qiang and that someone was not me.

''What is this 'safe-house' you're talking about?'' I ask.

''Better you don't know exactly,'' Toshi says, ''not until you must. We maintain a variety of havens for our Knives when they're out on field work. We'll stash you and the Xian in one of these until you find what you can and we have a chance to see the reaction to the situation.''

''Fine,'' I say, a bit miffed that they won't trust me with the details.

Toshi bows coolly and leaves, trailed by Tammany (who doesn't forget to drop a handful of cookies into her pocket for later). Anton follows, giving me what is surely meant to be a reassuring smile.

When their vehicles pull away, Vance rises and walks to my patio door.

''I shall return within ten,'' he says and slips outside.

I slouch against a wall, nerves overloaded. Reason honed by a million puzzles pulls me to my feet.

''If we're leaving soon,'' I say to the invisible listener under my bed, ''I'll need to pack. Don't you think it would be nice if I had some idea of the climate I'm going into?''

There is no answer, not that I really expected one. Still, I keep up a stream of reassuring—I hope—chatter as I toss clothing and a few items from the spice cabinet into my smaller suitcase. My efforts are rewarded by a black nose emerging from between the fringes.

When Vance returns, his silent grace seeming more that of a dancer than a predator, the nose vanishes.

''All well?'' I ask, trying to be nonchalant.

''Maybe,'' he replies, leaning in my bedroom's doorway but not crossing the threshold. ''I will sleep on the sofa in your living room, if that is suitable.''

''Fine. Lift the kennel out of the way in there. I don't want to bump myself in the dark.''

''Very well.'' He moves to comply so readily that I feel a temporarily hostesslike impulse.

''Can I get you anything? Towels? Sheets? Coffee?''

''I would like a washcloth and towel,'' he says with the faintest courtly bow. ''I do not plan on sleeping very deeply, so I will not need sheets, but a pot of coffee would be much appreciated.''

After settling Vance, I retreat to my room, sleep tempting after the day's stress. Something undone nags at the corner of my mind, but I am nearly asleep before I realize what it is.

''You must be starving!'' I say aloud, sitting up so quickly that my nightshirt jerks at my throat. ''I haven't fed you since you got here.''

There is no response from the Xian, but I get up and toss on a robe, though the night is not overly cool. My nightwear is modest enough, but Vance's presence makes me nervous.

He only nods from where he slouches in one of the living room chairs. The vid is on in front of him with the sound low, although I doubt that the comedy is holding his attention.

''Forgot to feed it,'' I explain, opening a cabinet, ''I hope it eats tuna.''

Vance tilts his head back just enough to include me in his peripheral vision. ''There was food in the kennel, I believe.''

''Thanks.''

I find the packet of dry food and, sniffing it, decide to open the tuna anyhow. The Xian's funny jaw/teeth had seemed equipped for meat; however, I'm not sure. Qiang's files might tell more. For now, this could be a compromise. On a whim, I slice a few late tomatoes onto the plate next to the tuna, then shake out kibbles on the side.

Filling a bowl with water, I bid Vance good night.

Most certainly the only thing that saves my life when the explosion comes is that I am kneeling beside the bed, pushing the food underneath.

I feel the explosion's force before I hear it. Flattening quickly, I am not swift enough to avoid the minute slivers of glass from the shattered window. My cheeks prickle as if I'd brushed a stinging nettle and when I touch my face my fingers come away glossed with a faint sheen of blood.

No one comes in through the forced window. Perhaps the explosion is expected to have done the job. Perhaps the Knives are succeeding with their job. Speculating seems as foolish as waiting to see how long it takes for "Them" to come and check out their work.

Certainly, my neighbors will not investigate. A bold one might call the police. More reasonable is to expect that any who heard the explosion are cowering, hoping that they will not be next.

Only one thing is left then. Dropping to hands and knees, I crawl from the bedroom. In the peripheries of my shock, I realize that the Xian has chosen now to emerge from its hiding place and is trailing me. Perhaps my hands and knees posture finally makes sense, a reverse of all those cartoons where animals are drawn on two legs and in a human stance.

In my shocky state, this seems very funny, so I suppress little snorts of laughter as I crawl, trailed by my alien caboose.

The living room has been hit much harder than the bedroom. My pride, the old-fashioned floor-to-ceiling French doors, have shattered, occasional shards of glass hanging like jagged icicles from the window frame. The frames themselves have been blown in and open. From the darkness beyond the high boards of my wooden fence, I think I hear gunshots.

Vance is still sprawled in the same chair he had been

in when I had come through moments before, his head lolling toward me as if at the last moment he had tried to shield his face from the explosion. He is so washed with blood that his silvery hair seems pink. I assume that he is dead until his eyes open and his gaze rests on me.

His mouth moves, but no sound comes forth, only frothy blood bubbles. I can read his lips, however. They painfully shape the two syllables of my name.

Praying that the Knives are doing their job, I crawl to where I can hear him. An inky shadow, the Xian continues to trail me, suspiciously sniffing what the night wind carries through the shattered door.

''Vance,'' I whisper.

He focuses with obvious effort, ''M'car.''

''Your car,'' I interpret.

His fingers move in the general direction of the jacket he had hung neatly over a chair.

''The keys are there,'' I say, crawling to retrieve them.

Ugly thoughts, uglier memories play tug-of-war with my heart as I dig the ring out. The ring bears two keys and a gaudy red plastic gemstone. No mistaking this set for any other.

''I have them, Vance,'' I whisper. ''Any other ideas?''

''Get away,'' he says, grasping at the arms of the chair to push himself up. ''Safe-house.''

''Where is it, Vance? You certainly can't drive there.''

His eyes widen, ''Don't know.''

Again he tries to rise. This time I push him back—it doesn't take that much effort.

''You remember Mr. Allain?'' I ask softly.

Vance takes the change of subject with difficulty.

''Ben. Good man, got stupid, though,'' he manages, perhaps driven to eloquence by what he sees on my face.

''Not stupid,'' I whisper harshly, ''just idealistic. Was that worth killing him for? Was it? Don't deny it. I know.''

''Didn't kill him,'' Vance protests, ''Just let him die.''

''And that's all I'm going to do, Vance,'' I reply, crawling away, his keys knotted in my fist. ''Just let you die.''

SEVEN

MY SUITCASE IS BY THE DOOR AND I HAVE MINIMAL trouble getting the Xian into Vance's Gemster, but figuring out the complex control panel takes a moment that we don't have. A stranger in a dark grey bodysuit rises from the privet hedge that marks the property line between my house and my neighbor's. He's leveling something at me when I push up the power and smash into him.

His blood splashes almost prettily over the vehicle's ruby glowing plastic. I concentrate on steering and swallow the bile that burns my throat lining.

The Xian sits upright in the passenger seat, its posture reminding me of reprints I've seen of old record player advertisements. Even the black ears are perked at the same angle.

"You're enjoying this!" I mutter incredulously. "Don't you realize that we're about to be exploded or shot?"

No answer, but I've grown used to that.

"Where the hell do we go?" I growl, glaring at the sweeping radar. "No one is following us, but I don't think we can expect that to last. This car's too noticeable. I should have taken mine, even if it is less well equipped."

As if in response to my soliloquy, I notice an orange light flashing rapidly on the stereo. Wondering whether

I'm about to hear the latest popular song, I punch the "on" tab.

"Vance. Vance. Vance." Tammany's voice sounds tired.

I don't see a mike, so I try speaking to the air. "Tammany?"

"Karen!" She sounds relieved. "Where's Vance?"

"Dead." I feel certain of this. "The explosion got him."

"Oh. Did you get anything out of the house?"

"My bags, the computer files, and the other stuff I was planning on bringing with me."

"Okay, my readout says you're near the interstate. Go two exits and pull off at the restaurant there. It will be closed, but go around to the service entrance."

I wait, but she doesn't add anything before the radio goes dead. Cursing under my breath at all this cloak and dagger nonsense that doesn't even leave time for "Good luck," I follow Tammany's instructions. Everything, of course, is where she said it would be, and when I pull around back the only light is from a van parked in a loading bay. Anton gets out.

"Switch off the engine and those damn running lights," he orders, "and get out."

I do, reaching into the back for my suitcase. The Xian has sleeked its ears next to its head and is studying Anton suspiciously. When I open my door, however, it does follow me, lurking at my heels.

Anton is at least polite enough to come and help me with my bag, keeping his light held low enough to illuminate only the ground we're walking over. When he opens the back of the van, he finally gets a good look at my face.

"My God, Kari! What happened to you?"

"My goddamned house got blown all to hell," I reply, realizing with panic that I'm about to cry. "You expect me to waltz out of there without getting hurt?"

Gently, he helps me into the van. The Xian hesitates until I pat the seat next to me.

"C'mon, you, out there is not a good place to be."

It leaps up and slides under my legs to get me between it and Anton. Then it settles onto the floor by my feet.

"You've tamed it!" Anton comments, the supply locker into which he has stuck his head not concealing the surprise in his voice.

"'Tamed,' is too strong a word," I say, leaning back, "We seem to have reached an agreement."

"Whatever," Tammany says from the driver's seat. "Anton, look to Karen's wounds. We'll have to get started now."

"I'm already there, Tammany," he says kneeling next to me. "Hold still. This is going to hurt. I can't afford a topical until after I've pulled out the worst of these slivers."

"Great." I shiver, trying to distract myself by watching where Tammany is taking us. The night doesn't reveal much.

"You see," Anton says in that cheery tone dentists are particularly fond of, "I don't want the spray to anchor anything and this way you can let me know if I screw up."

"Er?" I grunt, trying not to move my face.

"The pain will tell you if I push something wrong."

"Er!"

After Anton has finished cleaning me up, I have energy to notice the interior of the van. Instead of the usual rows of seats and cargo space, the van has been outfitted as a miniature apartment. A couple of seats have been secured to a wall and made up as a bed. A refrigerator and microwave are anchored to the other wall.

The control panel in front is as complicated as the one in Vance's Gemster, containing a vid, fax/phone, and PC. I already know that the chest behind the driver's seat—despite its attractively stenciled checkerboard top—contains a hospital-quality medical kit. I suspect that the lockers under the bed are equally well-provisioned.

However, not until I notice that some of the computer disks from my office are stored in the dashboard racks do I get suspicious.

"Are we heading to that 'safe-house'?"

"Actually," Anton says with a mixture of pride and apprehension, "this is your safe house."

"What!"

"Karen," Tammany says, glancing over her shoulder, "we have had Qiang killed on our own grounds; you nearly killed—and Vance killed—in a residential neighborhood. This job is really hot and our best bet is to keep your friend moving."

"And me?"

"It seems to like you," she says, "and we still need proof that it is a member of a sentient race. Until then, nothing much that we do will make a difference."

"But who is coming after us?" I ask, dabbing my face with antiseptic cream from a container Anton hands me.

"We have suspicions, but nothing much more than we were conjecturing before. Xi-7 is valuable real estate and, apparently, there are those who believe that weakening the UAN is an acceptable risk if they can take possession. A few freelances hardly matter when the stakes are that high."

I watch the night flickering with neon through the front windows for a few minutes before speaking again.

"And what will you three be doing while the creature and I take the Grand Tour?"

"Making false trails, kidnapping a few folk who may know something, researching other sources," Anton says, "and trying to make it look like the Corp hasn't suffered from the loss of three Directors inside of a week."

"Oh."

I move to the passenger seat beside Tammany, not noticing that the Xian is trailing me until it lies down on my feet.

"I guess I'd better learn how to use these fancy controls."

Tammany drills me until I am perfect—which doesn't take long. A good memory is among my few virtues.

"The van is well stocked with food and stuff for both you and the creature there," Anton says when I'm satisfied I can handle the vehicle. "We've also made you copies of Qiang's files. Some are in very bad shape, but they're all we have."

"What do you want me to do?" I ask, "Whiz up and down the interstates until the solar converters die or a cop pulls me over out of boredom?"

"No," Tammany says, "I doubt that would help you learn much about the Xian creature. Even if it's as smart as Einstein, nonstop cruising should drive it buggy. From what I've sopped from the report the Survey team presented to the UAN, Xi-7 is largely undeveloped. A van is hardly the creature's natural habitat."

"Nor mine," I mutter in *sotto voce* protest.

"There's a large park system strung through this region," Anton says. "We thought that you could hide out in there for a few days. Camp. Take it easy. Get away from it all."

"Ah, a vacation," I manage a grin. "How long is a few days?"

Tammany shrugs and fumbles for the hot bottle of coffee next to the dashboard. "Don't call us. Turn your radio on at three-hour intervals. If we have a message we'll override whatever you have on and let you know. Otherwise, you just get off by yourself, don't let anyone get a good look at the 'doggie,' and try and figure . . ."

"Out if it's a person," I interrupt. "Yeah, I caught that part already. Every three hours—that's three o'clock, six, nine, et cetera?"

"Right," Anton says with a flinch at my nonprecise terminology, "0300 and then three-hour intervals thereafter."

"You sure don't want me to sleep much," I say, "but I'll manage. And if I need to reach you?"

"Harder," Tammany admits, "since we'll be being watched and we may be bugged or have spies in our compound."

She swallows more coffee and then turns the van down an access road. We are the only ones on the stretch and, oddly, I feel more exposed than when we were on the interstate.

"If you need to reach us," she says, at last, "simply radio from the van. You'll probably be in so much trouble that security won't matter."

"Thanks," I reply dryly.

"We'll be in touch," she promises.

After that we drive on in near silence. The hum of the van's engine is nearly inaudible and the stress and the hour catch up with me, so that my eyelids droop and my head lolls back against the headrest. Beneath my physical weariness, my mind races. Anxiety and exhaustion meld into nightmares that unwind along the black ribbon of the road.

When Tammany pulls off into a roadside rest area, I shake myself and realize that I am refreshed. The dashboard clock confirms my feeling that I have been asleep for several hours.

Contrary to my expectations, Tammany does not look tired. She gets down from the driver's seat and stretches her shoulders back, her eyes never leaving the diamond-studded darkness overhead.

"I love it out here," she says unexpectedly.

"Out here?" I ask, also climbing down. For a moment I wonder if I should leash my alien shadow, then fatalistically shrug. It has stayed by me thus far.

"Yes," Tammany answers, "I love the quiet places away from the cities. That's why I became a computer expert, you know, because I could work in my own places and send my work in without me. The plan seemed perfect, but then one never is ready for all life can throw at you."

''No,'' I agree softly. ''No.''

Anton drops from the van, walking stiffly and working his mouth as if he has discovered that something died within while he slept. After crossing to a water fountain, he joins us.

''You're on your own from here, Kari,'' he says, reaching to give my shoulder a squeeze. ''These public lands should be largely deserted this time of year.''

''How will you get back?'' I ask.

I see the glint of his teeth in his beard, ''Magic.''

Anton's ''magic'' proves to be two overland motorcycles stored in covered racks on either side of the van. Once the bikes are removed, the compartments are easily collapsed, altering the lines of the van so that it is a slimmer vehicle that I will take over.

Not content with this miracle, Tammany snaps out the maker's logo on the front grill and changes it for a competitor's. She has me help her stick striped mag lines a foot wide along each side and place opaque inserts in each window. As we do this, Anton switches the license tags and pulls different covers over the front seats. As a final touch, he flourishes a small plastic statuette of Jesus from his pocket and mounts it on the dashboard to the right of the driver's seat.

''There is a pull-down panel that you should use to cover the fancy control board when anyone is around or when you're not using it,'' he says, demonstrating. ''This isn't a perfect job, but if anyone saw us meet you—which I doubt—they won't have a make on a vehicle that looks like this.''

''And,'' Tammany adds, ''There are none matching this on our vehicle listings, so even if there are spies in the Corp, they won't be any help.''

''Thanks,'' I say awkwardly, too aware of all the reasons that I should hate these people and embarrassed that I am grateful to them. ''I'll try not to let you down.''

"We know, Kari," Anton says, straddling his bike. "For a Hand, you're really very competent."

"Thanks," I repeat.

Then, with a soft hum of electric engines, they are gone and I am alone except for a pair of brass eyes that glow from the darkness behind me.

EIGHT

THE WOODS, I FIND WHEN MORNING DAWNS OVER THE spot where I had camped in the dark, are largely pine and cedar with a smattering of hardwood deciduous trees. The latter have lost nearly all of their leaves, but those that remain are welcome splashes of yellow and red against the muted greens, greys, and browns that dominate the landscape. The van, I note, racing stripes and all, blends nicely into the terrain.

After the 9 A.M. radio check assures me that all is well, I go for a walk. Certain that I am the only camper in the area, I let the Xian out. It slinks from the vehicle with markedly less energy than it had shown the previous night.

The rumbling protest of my stomach against its "coffee only" repast reminds me of my duty.

"Damn!" I say as much to me as to it, "I wonder when you last ate? Your dinner last night was interrupted and I don't know what you were getting at the lab."

Clambering back into the residential portion of the vehicle, I start flinging open lockers. The Xian watches from outside, seeming distrustful of its safety among the swinging doors.

When I find a canister of dry nuggets, I scoop them out into a bowl by the double handful. The Xian's nose twitches, but it keeps its distance.

"Come here," I coax. "I don't think anything is going to blow up today."

When it doesn't approach, I carry the bowl over to it. Setting the bowl on the pine-needle-littered ground, I move a few yards away. Still, the Xian doesn't eat, although one would have to be less sensitive than I am to fail to notice the signs of hunger—slight panting, a gaze that cannot leave the bowl for more than a moment.

"Come on," I repeat. "What's wrong? You don't think that I'd poison you, do you?"

A conviction comes to me that this is precisely what it fears. Qiang's report had shown that the Xians were kept heavily sedated and God knows what else. Reluctantly, I ooch over to the bowl and lift out a nugget. It looks unappetizing—like dog chow—but the smell isn't too bad.

Bracing myself, I pop it into my mouth and chew resolutely. It tastes like stale bread and bland beef jerky. Overall, I had anticipated worse. Washing down the stuff with my cooling coffee, I toss a nugget to the Xian.

"Your turn," I say.

It snaps up the offering, but ignores the bowl. Even when I toss it another, it doesn't eat. Only when I trade off one for one will it eat at all. As breakfasts go, this is not the worst I've had, but some of the prison food could nearly compare.

Finally, we empty the bowl and I go in and refill it.

"If you want more," I tell the brass-eyed beast, "Help yourself. I'm full."

It studies me and then stretches out on its side in a sunny patch, its posture telegraphing pleasure, its sleek belly perhaps a bit distended.

"Full? Want some water?"

I fill another bowl, but when I come to set it down, the creature noses at my coffee mug.

"Coffee?" I ask, surprised. "Why not?"

I pour it a bowl, black. Although it whuffles on the steam as if blowing on the brew to cool it, the Xian seems to enjoy the drink immensely.

We sit for a while there in a kind of easy companionship that I have not felt since before I was nine and my cat died. Still, the experiences of the woman are master of the girl and eventually I rise. The Xian watches me as if uncertain why I have moved.

"Don't stir yourself," I say, "but I should turn on the radio and get a few things."

I do the former and once again "all clear" is broadcast—this time in the form of a pop song with grotesquely cheerful lyrics. A datapad is sheathed under the dashboard; a quick check shows that all the files from Qiang's research have been loaded into its memory. After refilling my coffee mug, I carry it and the datapad back outside.

As I am settling in with my back against a nubby cedar tree, the Xian gives me a look that is somehow reproachful. Leaning forward, I splash half of my mug of coffee into its bowl.

"Sorry," I say with a grin, "you didn't say you wanted a refill."

The haughty toss of the creature's thin nose seems to say, "You didn't offer."

Startled at the extent to which my current isolation is driving me to anthropomorphize, I quickly flip on the pad. The menu is now more helpful than when I first looked at these files. Clearly, Tammany has had some time to review them. Next to each of Qiang's cryptic numerical file designations is a parenthetical note briefly explaining what is in the file.

Choosing the one labeled as "Physiology," I settle back to read. Qiang's notes are pithy, almost cryptic, and loaded with abbreviations. As I read, my mind automatically analyzes various options for meaning, discarding those that won't work. I do this with such ease that the staccato text reads almost as if it was written in complete sentences.

Later it occurs to me that I am probably the only Director who could do this; one of Qiang's assistants might, if she had made any privy to her shorthand, but few others.

But I'm too busy soaking up what I can to be patting myself on the back. The physiology file is heavy going, but with file dips into the hypertext dictionary I am able to pad out my own observations.

My Xian creature, I discern from a few careful peeks, is female. Her companions were apparently another female and two males. Qiang's files curse that she cannot even estimate an age, but she thought from organ placement and bone growth that they were mature.

It—no—*she* has very odd bones. Qiang's scans found that the bones have unusual resiliency for support members. They are more akin to a multilayer cartilage than Terran bone. As with Terrans, teeth and bones are of the same basic material, but the Xian's bumpy ridges almost certainly replenish themselves.

Underneath Qiang's calm, clinical notes, I can sense a burning wish to dissect one of the Xians and see if her guesses are right. Unfortunately for her, she was just this side of too ethical to kill one of her test subjects. By the time there were ample corpses, she herself was too dead to take advantage of the windfall.

I scan past information on retractable claws in the feet, pleased to have deduced that already. The creature's fur, I learn, is quite likely to be very warm—Qiang had made some notes about the possibilities of further research into synthetic versions of the shaft structure—and also fairly waterproof. The tail is supple, she notes, and probably quite capable of being used as a limited bludgeon (but then anyone with a labrador retriever could have told us that).

Qiang was fascinated by the Xian's eyes, but had not gotten further than hypothesizing that the creatures had excellent night vision. Senses, from what I understand, can be quite difficult to test, because the subject must cooperate for a quick estimate. Even then, established standards help and Qiang had none with which to work.

Perhaps there is something in the pirated Lantic Labs files, but for now I realize that I am becoming a bit stiff. The wind through the pines seems much more inviting than a datapad and my charge seems to be awakening from her after-meal nap.

I dutifully work until the next three-hour check-in, then I put my gear back in the van and lock the vehicle securely.

''Want to go for a mosey?'' I ask the creature—deliberately avoiding the word ''walk'' with its associations of a leashed canine.

The Xian stands, stretches, shakes, and then blinks those weird eyes at me—does everything, in fact, but wag its tail.

''Fine then,'' I smile, pocketing the handgun that Anton had insisted I carry. ''Let's go.''

The woods are lovely, dark, and all the rest as we set off downslope, my feet slipping a bit on the pine needles. The Xian trots along at my side, dropping behind, never going ahead when the path narrows. Her ears are perked up, transforming her usually sleek head into something that reminds me of old Egyptian drawings of Anubis.

Despite remembering that the files had indicated that she was probably omnivorous, I get nervous when she starts to sniff a cluster of mushrooms and then a staghorn beetle.

''Listen,'' I say, ''I'm not sure that sampling the local flora and fauna is a really good idea. I mean, maybe you have some instinct about what's good for you, but this isn't your planet.''

The Xian lifts her head and stares at me, but I notice that she does refrain from eating anything.

We pick our way along, stopping to investigate a fallen tree, a stream bed that vanishes into a small, natural cave, a moldering stump, a nearly desiccated squirrel corpse. During all our wandering, I am careful never to lose sight of the van.

"I need a name for you," I say when we have returned to the van and are having coffee.

She tilts her head, politely perking one ear, and then returns to lapping her coffee. The bowl of food nuggets mixed with the remains of a can of tuna I'd opened for my lunch has been shoved awkwardly to the side now that she has finished eating. Fortunately, she had not insisted that I share.

"C'mon, you," I say when no idea for a name pops to mind, "let's go for a drive. I doubt camping in one place is a great idea."

As we cruise over the rough trail, I continue to muse aloud.

"I won't call you 'Subject D,' like Qiang's files," I say. "Bad enough that the UAN letters and numbers planets. And I don't really want to call you 'Blacky' or 'Lassie'—those just sound too much like names for a pet."

The Xian, as usual, is singularly unconversant, but I can tell when I glance over at the passenger seat that she is listening. Her eyes continue to stare out the window, but the ear nearest to me is upright and curved slightly, as if to catch my slightest word.

"Nice trick, that, always shows when you're listening. Might have helped with me and Will. Might not of, too, just to be fair."

As we drive, I recite a long string of common names, but end up discarding all of them. I almost settle on "Emily" for Emily Dickinson. There's something about my silent companion that reminds me of the reclusive Emily in her Massachusetts home, turning out sheaves of cryptic verse and gradually refusing to see anyone but her most intimate family.

But in the end I discard this too, recalling that the Xian has hardly chosen her solitude and that in normal circumstances she might be a gregarious pack animal. That certainly would explain her clinging to my heels these past couple of days.

Reluctantly, I return to descriptive names, considering

Inky, Jet, Midnight, Ebony, Charcoal, and Sable. Sable almost wins because the soft, dense darkness I associate with the word is so like the Xian's coat, but I decide that the sound is too much like my own surname to be practical—and in fact might smack of vanity.

Finally, imagination burnt, I settle on "Onyx"—short, sweet, and descriptive without being too belittling.

Getting the Xian to catch on to the idea that this word means her takes more work than I'd thought it would. As I check out the new area where I've parked the van—a sheltered hollow by another stream—I try to get her to understand. Every trick from the "Me Karen, You Onyx" routine to constantly using it when talking to her seems to have no impact.

I sigh as I settle myself into bed that night. So far, I haven't found any proof that Onyx is more than a really weird dog. Since she seems to lack both appendages designed to manipulate her environment and a means of abstract communication, the case looks pretty grim.

Maybe I deciphered that message wrong. Maybe it was a joke. Maybe the Corp is completely wrong about this one. Maybe.

But as sleep claims me, my new doubts come up against the chilling reminder that for someone murder was a reasonable price to pay to keep Qiang and the rest of us from learning Onyx's secret. If I don't want to be the next victim, I need to find out what they know before they find her—and me.

Despite both my apprehensions and my ambitions, the next week passes uneventfully. Onyx and I wander up and down the autumn slopes daily, sometimes for hours on end once I find that with her long nose she can always track us back to the van. I wear a belt pager with a read unit and flip it on for the three-hour check-ins.

Funny, I never realized how inane the lyrics to many songs are until I am forced to read them a few words at a time from an LED display.

We don't see anyone but an occasional camper, and I

prudently shift our site every day. The Corp does resupply us, but the drop is made first and then we are told the location through a few of the three-hour checks. One does not need to be an expert codebreaker to realize a pattern is developing when several songs in a row are about places. The scavenger hunt usually takes me a few days, but the stuff is mostly dry goods and nothing perishes.

I even get daring enough to allow myself a meal at a small diner that borders on a section of the parkland. An unusually brisk wind gives me ample reason to leave my cap and scarf on and I am careful to dress nondescriptly. Onyx, of course, stays in the van with the curtains drawn. Unlike a dog, she doesn't protest. In fact, she even stays away from the door when I am getting out. Somehow, I don't think that she trusts humans.

That makes her unquestioning trust of me all the more amazing, but she clearly does trust me. After that first shared meal of nuggets and coffee, she eats everything I give her without question. Sometimes she spits something out that is clearly not to her taste—after a slice of lemon meringue pie she drank down half a pot of coffee. She'll stare at me then while I eat my share, but it's a friendly thing, like one human might give another for liking squid or artichokes.

This bucolic idyll stretches on until the day that I see a pair of Chirr silhouetted against the purple-blue of an evening sky. One holds a set of binoculars up to its eyes. The other wears a camera looped around its neck, remarkably like the caricature of any human tourist anywhere.

Although the darkness had seemed like a comfortable curtain only a few moments before, I am not so naive as to forget that the Chirr are primarily a tunnel-dwelling people. Even where their modern cities are forced by rock to rise instead of burrow, the Chirr tend to build without windows. Their eyes process light differently than ours, so much so that their early peoples developed sunshades, tinted goggles, and contact lenses the way that humans developed warm clothing.

If either Onyx or I move, we will be seen. Stillness may keep them from scanning our location in more than a passing fashion. Onyx seems to understand that she must mimic my motionlessness, for she stays crouched by my feet in the stance from which she had been examining a passing woolly bear caterpillar, although the bug itself has long since trundled off.

Perhaps she recognizes the Chirr by scent or shape from her travel in the UAN survey ship. If so, she does not remember them fondly, for when the fitful wind brings the faint whistle of their chatter in our direction, she sinks lower to the ground.

At last, sufficient darkness has fallen that I believe we can risk moving—the Chirr can see in low light, not no light. Bending slightly and wincing at the protest of joints that have stiffened during our chilly wait, I brush my fingers across the silky fur between Onyx's ears.

"C'mon, girl," I whisper, "let's head back now."

She rises silently, only the slightest pressure of her body bumping against my leg signaling me that she at least understands what I want.

Knowing that I cannot hope to move through the woods with any speed or stealth, I turn on my flashlight. Carefully shielding the beam with my hand, I point it directly in front of me. Onyx, who has never before taken point, steps in front of me, so that she is just visible as a dense shadow at the edge of my light's pale nimbus.

I decide to trust her lead. What else can I do? Picking my way behind her, I listen for sounds of pursuit. My shoulders tighten against the impact of a bullet or club, but what comes lancing across the night is not at all what I expect.

"Directors Saber," cries a shrill voice, "we believe that you are there. Please, do not run from us. We mean no harm to you or to the being with you."

I pause. My name. They have my name. That means

either that one of them knows me well enough to recognize me in the dark or that Toshi's spy is still active. The number of Chirr who would know me is too few for me to feel comfortable with the former.

Still, even if they do have a spy in the Corp, might something be gained from speaking with them? Switching off my flash for the dubious protection that darkness offers, I stand frozen and indecisive.

Onyx walks back and bumps my hand with her nose. If we have been found here, certainly they must have located the van. I can think of several ways they could have managed. No matter how, we are found. If we flee, I do not believe that I am capable of surviving alone in the woods. I'm simply not Davy Crocket and it gets cold in these hills at night.

Hesitantly, I turn toward where the two Chirr are just visible against the gathering dark. Anton had mentioned that he believed some were sympathetic towards the Xians. Perhaps these are of that faction. If they are, they could be far more helpful than my co-Directors. Mind made up, I tap Onyx's nose.

''Come on, girl. Let's go see what they have to say.''

The image of a mushroom I had kicked open earlier, its insides aswarm with grayish worms, bursts into my mind. The image is so forceful that I do not doubt its meaning or its source, and I cannot believe that the minds of everyone else for miles are not blazing with this warning of corruption and rot.

Dropping to my knees beside Onyx, I whisper, ''Okay, then, let's get out of here.''

Crawling, I cannot use the flashlight that jolts uncomfortably against my hip. However, this awkward method of locomotion does help me keep track of Onyx and makes me less of a target. The Chirr have not called out to me but that once, and I begin to hope that they were guessing our location.

Concentrating on moving as quickly as I can on hands and knees—at least as quickly as I can without giving everything away by the noise—I pay little attention to where we are going. Grasping Onyx's tail between my fingers for a slickery second, I halt, rolling onto my side with the pleasure that can only come when constantly complaining knees, elbows, forearms, and hands all stop hurting at once. As I lie there on my side, feeling subtler aches beginning in my muscles, Onyx comes back a few steps and reclines sphinxlike beside me.

In the faint light of the crescent moon and stars, I can see that she is panting slightly. One of the things I have confirmed about Onyx is that like a terrestrial creature she pants either to dispel heat or from nervousness. Since the evening is rapidly becoming not just chill, but definitely cold, I realize that despite her steady silent companionship she is scared.

Barely pausing to consider the etiquette of my actions, I reach out and pat from the base of her neck along her spine. At first, she shudders slightly at the contact, but does not move away. After a few more caresses, she ceases to shudder. The nervous panting slows.

"Whoever they are, they really scared you, didn't they?" I whisper, more for the sound of my own voice than because I expect an answer. "You certainly found a way to let me know."

Onyx stops panting and angles her head to one side, ears slightly perked in what I've come to think of as her "attentive" pose. She makes no noise, as always.

"That was you," I continue, since she isn't answering. "I'm sure of that, but why didn't you ever do that before? Or perhaps I should ask 'What did you do?' "

Onyx settles her head down on her paws and studies me. As she seems relaxed and my muscles have largely stopped their complaining, I roll onto my back and study the lacework of stars and branches.

"Now what?" I say, "I'm lost, and even if you're not, I'm not certain that if we head back to the van we won't find more than we want, or get found ourselves."

I hear Onyx start panting again and catch a whiff of the apples and spice tinge of her breath.

"Easy, girl," I reassure, "I'm not going to turn us in. I'm just not certain how to find our way to any sort of safe spot here."

Silence. Not even cricket chirps, only a faint rustling of the wind in the highest branches of the tired trees.

"Damn! I hate talking to myself!" I say, sitting up with sudden vehemence. "I'm not made for decisions. I've never been good at them. The first decision I've made in twenty years I've all but blown off to go camping with an alien pup, and I'm not sure what's right or up or anything else these days."

I don't expect an answer; in a week Onyx has never given me an answer to any of the myriad questions I've posed to her. Anything more abstract than an offer of food or a walk has apparently slid right off that silk-furred skull. Even that increasingly unreal vision of that worm-infested, rotting mushroom could have been a projection of my own weary imagination.

So the last thing I expect is an answer to my panicked harangue to the indifferent stars.

In my mind, the image of the van appears. The perspective is strange—a great deal of detail is shown on the lower sections, almost none on the upper. The vehicle itself seems distorted, broad-based and squat. This picture floats in an isolated bubble of space I had not realized lay behind my forehead. Then, like the rapid dappling of an artist's brush, the surrounding details are filled in: a bent pine tree, a half circle of scrubby brush, the fire pit I lined with stones gathered at the creek at the bottom of the hill.

One does not need much imagination to recognize our most recent camp. Distantly, I hear Onyx panting again and reach out to pat her, forgetting completely this time how I had so carefully refrained from treating her like an animal.

"Easy, Onyx," I murmur, "I'm getting the picture—

the van, the camp. You think we should go back? Do you realize that the Chirr may be there?''

I try to project a picture of the Chirr as they had been on the roadside overlook, uncertain how much of my words she understands. Actually, if I wasn't tired, scared, sore, and hungry, I'd be delighted that we're communicating at all.

Whether from my words or my thoughts, the image she is sending changes. The Chirr are recognizable, though once again the perspective is lower than I am accustomed to. From this angle, the Chirr do not look so much like gophers in cute robes, but like chubby columns with protruding noses and long teeth that flash when they talk. As before, the picture acquires detail after a moment and the two Chirr are shown by our van, thumping ineffectually on the locks while shadowy figures I take for Onyx and me watch from the bushes.

''You're right!'' I say, ''I'd forgotten how well-locked that thing is. They may not have made it in yet. Maybe they'll even leave to get tools. Lead on, Onyx, that is, if you know the way.''

She doesn't move until I stand, but when I do she rises. I flip on the flashlight and follow her into the wood, toward our faintly possible refuge.

Sniffing along the traces of our afternoon's hike, she takes us along a twisting trail. Now that time is pressing, I impatiently reflect that this is a dreadfully inefficient way to guide oneself.

Onyx abruptly stops and stares back at me, her brass eyes bright in the flashlight's light. A blush warms me from collar to hairline. How much might she be able to understand of my thoughts? Discomfort prickles me and I find myself trying hard to think of nothing more than taking each step.

When we reach the van two hours later, I am so chilled and tired that not thinking is no longer an effort. Hearing the whistle of Chirr voices, I flip off my light and move from tree trunk to tree trunk, hoping that their mass will mask my presence.

The van is apparently still locked up tight and I allow myself a small sigh of relief. Several figures cluster outside: two Chirr, a su-ankh, and two humans. In my current state of mind, I envy their heavy coats and proximity to the fire first, and wonder who they are after.

Onyx crouches next to me, not protesting when I wrap my arm around her for warmth. Now that we have stopped walking, I quietly extract a small pair of bird-watching glasses from their case at my waist. As I do so, my hand bumps the nearly forgotten message pager.

Using both Onyx and the tree as shields, I review the messages that I had missed. The first, which must have come through a bit before I first spotted the two Chirr, is a song with a refrain about "Runaway! Runaway! Runaway!" Where had they wanted me to run?

The second message, which must have come while we were creeping back towards the van, is a pathetic entreaty from some forlorn girl begging for her guy to call. No mystery there.

I study my watch and check times. A new message is due fairly soon. Waiting for it and studying the area seem to be the wisest course of action. I hook the pager back onto my belt and raise the glasses to my eyes.

One of the Chirr might be Wheep, but the layers of cold-weather gear make a positive ID difficult. The two humans look like muscle; I've seen that stance in the Corp's own Knives. That doesn't mean I can dismiss them as dumb brawn. In fact, knowing what I do about our Knives, that would be the stupidest mistake that I could make.

The tall su-ankh is the only one I feel certain about. The angle of his head, his confident posture as he leans back against the van, the way the others defer to him all tell me that this is Chiron. His presence settles some questions for me. Recalling our interview in my office, I am positive that the purpose behind this visit is not one of which I would approve.

A faint vibration from the pager signals another message coming through. Shielding its glow with my hand, I read the lyrics: "Hickory, Dickory, Dock . . ." Staring down into the red glow, I fill in the rest: "the mouse ran up the clock. The clock struck twelve."

Twelve. They must mean sometime after midnight. That could be any time now or it could be at the other end of a long wait. A long wait seems unbearable. The light jacket that had been ample for a sunny afternoon feels thinner with every gust of wind, the fire circle up on the hill is hypnotically pleasant. I'm hungry and Onyx must be, too. For all her slimness, she eats far more than I do.

Biting my lower lip, I study the five people again. They are alert, but not tense. Waiting, but not with any particular expectation. One of the Chirr even seems to be dozing. The other is engaged in conversation with Chiron and one of the humans. Presumably, they are guarding against our return, perhaps expecting relief or reenforcement.

With a flash of unexpected anger, I realize that they consider themselves prepared for any threat that I offer. That they are not worried about the Corp bothers me less—I'm almost certain that they have a spy there, but they have dismissed me as a factor, possibly based on that interview in my office.

My arm tightens around Onyx, and she cranes her head around and blinks at me. I wonder if she is aware of my shift in mood, of my new resolution. I'm not going to wait for rescue. I'm going to get back the van myself and to hell with the consequences. I'm tired of being underestimated.

Deliberately, I weigh my options. There are five of them to me and—maybe—Onyx. We will have surprise, if we are careful, and some element of concealment. This latter cannot be counted on to last. The Chirr have superior night vision. I try to recall if the su-ankh do as well. It seems to me that they do.

I have the side arm that Anton insisted that I wear at all times. However, they are certainly armed as well—the humans are for sure. I can count on my first shots landing pretty much as I aim them. After that, the advantage will be theirs.

At a loss, I prod Onyx and we circle the camp with painful slowness. On the far side of the van a low-slung sporty two-seater is parked. No one is near it.

"I'll bet that belongs to those Knives," I whisper to Onyx. "It also tells me we'd better hurry. There's no way that all five of them got here in that. Someone has been here and left, probably to get gear to break open the van."

Onyx whuffles softly. A distorted image of someone I recognize as me sitting in the sports grav appears in my mind. A much more tidy portrait of Onyx sits in the passenger seat.

"Something like that, girl," I whisper.

I try and make a mental picture. "Actually, I had something more like this in mind."

Onyx's picture fades from my mind, to be replaced for a moment by a duplicate of the one I had constructed. Then that too fades.

I pat her and, taking a deep breath, I sneak from the wood line directly toward the two-seater. As Onyx slinks at my side, I can almost feel her alertness.

Once at the sports grav, I open the driver's side door, nerves atingle for the blast of some alarm. Nothing goes off, however.

Tsking to myself at the owner's carelessness, I quickly set a course in the car's autopilot. Onyx and I are running for the nose of the van as the sports grav rises into the air, backs up, and starts around the side on a course that should take it right through the midst of the cozy group around the fire.

I can't pause to hope that I had programmed it right.

My plan requires that we round the front of the van in time to take advantage of the situation.

When we duck around, the scene is quite satisfactory. One of the Knives is flat on his back, apparently out cold. His partner is jogging next to the driver's side door, her key card in one hand, shouting obscenities at the grav as if it will be offended enough to stop.

One of the Chirr, Wheep I am now certain, is scuttling out of the path of the advancing vehicle. Her companion has already gotten clear and is heading for the fallen human.

Only Chiron remains where I last saw him, leaning up against the side of the van, apparently oblivious to the fine chaos erupting around him.

At my side, Onyx erupts like a compact javelin ripped from the night itself. She streaks past me and at the somnolent su-ankh. Unable to fire my sidearm with her in the way, I pelt after, hoping she will succeed in moving Chiron from the van.

In the confusion that follows as I fumble to get my key card through the lock strip before someone notices and decides to shoot me, I know that I must be missing a great deal. One detail does brand itself in my mind. I am nearly certain that something shoves Chiron before Onyx reaches him. He is already falling as she leaps onto his midsection and knocks him to the ground.

But I do not take time to wonder what might have accounted for the odd motion. Once I have the driver's door open, I thump the ignition and yell for Onyx. She leaps over me and into her seat, her eyes so wild that they're almost round. Then I'm buttoning up the doors, keying the protective plates over the windows, and starting our rise into the air. Looking backward as we glide away over the dirt trail, I see a shower of sparks as the sports grav finally impacts solidly with a twisted juniper.

"Now what?" I mutter to myself.

Almost immediately, a distorted but recognizable portrait of Toshi, Anton, and Tammany floats into my mind.

"Becoming positively chatty, aren't you?" I chuckle, reaching out with my right hand to pat the still panting Xian. "Yes, I do think we should hazard contacting them."

My call gets picked up before I finish the code. Tammany must have been watching her board.

"Karen!" she says, her voice tense and tired. "We thought that you'd been taken."

"The van, not me," I clarify, nervously checking the scan for signs of pursuit, "and we got back the van."

"Ah," Tammany sounds impressed. I hear her relay my report to someone, then she's back.

"Can you meet us at Ben's?" she asks.

Ben's. My heart grows cold. Mr. Allain's. Except his house was sold. The Corp complex is too obvious a place for us to meet. That leaves one option, a place I have avoided since soon after his death. I lick my lips, my mouth suddenly dry.

"Karen?" Tammany sounds anxious.

"I'm here," I answer shortly. "Sure, I can meet you there."

"Fine, don't be seen," Tammany replies, "The rest is . . ."

"I know," I say, reaching for the toggle, "silence."

Once we're on the interstate again, I figure we have a measure of protection from casual assault. Even at night, the major roads are just too busy for trouble. Setting the autopilot, I merge us into the middle lane. Then I raise the scanner screen so that I can watch it from the back of the van and heave myself out of the driver's seat.

Now that the worst of the panic is over and I am warm, I realize that I'm starved. Onyx seems to divine my intentions and jumps down to follow me back. Dutifully, I reach for her food canister, but she is not finished surprising me this night.

The can floats past my hands and drops to the floor, then the lid wrenches itself off and the food nuggets start popping out a couple at a time. Onyx snatches the first few playfully out of the air before burying her nose in the canister.

My head reels and I stop to check that the beer can in my hand is still unopened. Deciding that maybe I don't want a drink after all, I set it back in the refrigerator and fish out a cold pack of juice instead. The sugars hit my system like a couple of shots of whiskey, chasing away a fog I hadn't even realized was congealed around my thoughts.

With my renewed acuity, I study the Xian. In her current pose, she seems more canine than ever, but I am certain about what I have just witnessed. I decide that the obligatory expressions of awe and amazement can wait until I've had a sandwich.

Only when I'm half through a roast beef and cheddar with horseradish and have set up a large pot of coffee do I allow myself to puzzle over Onyx's sudden ability to perform miracles. The object of my interest has finished her nuggets and the roast beef I tossed her and is now reclining luxuriously in the center of the floor, one brass eye watching me and the other marking the progress of the coffee.

I like her, I realize as I watch her. She's bright, tough, and resilient. But I have no more certainty than before that I can prove her personness. More than ever, I am struck by her alienness. The world as she experiences it is not my world, and I suspect that the world of the Chirr or even of the su-ankh would be familiar in contrast.

I've been puzzling over her, trying to define her people in terms that would fit what I know. Now I realize that I have been doing this in too closed-minded a fashion. Instead of looking for signs of language or tool use in her, I should be looking for ways to show how she does the things we do with our tools.

"Language," I say to the air, "is, after all, nothing more than another tool, one that's a bit less corporeal than a wrench or a screwdriver, but a tool nonetheless."

Onyx yawns at me, indicating the just-brewed coffee

with a clumsy toss of her head. When I don't get up, she rises and goes over to her coffee bowl and laps the empty surface.

"I get the hint," I say, "but you've gotten me curious. Can you fill your own bowl?"

She stops and stares at me. I repeat my question, trying to form a picture of the coffee pot rising into the air, floating over to the empty bowl, tilting, and then spilling a thin stream of liquid into the bowl. The effort to construct images that are both vivid and accurately representational makes my head ache slightly.

Onyx studies me and her empty bowl for so long that I am beginning to feel foolish. Then she shifts her attention to the coffee pot.

Just as in my vision, it elevates and drifts toward the bowl. Onyx is panting by the time she brings it into position and begins to pour. The hot coffee cascades down and some splashes up and onto her flank. She doesn't yelp, but whatever control she has over the carafe is lost and it tumbles to the floor. The soft flooring keeps it from breaking, but most of the coffee spills, soaking the carpet a darker brown.

I leap up and rescue it in time to preserve a mug for myself. With it, I toast Onyx.

"Amazing, girl, really amazing!" I smile. "I wish I'd had a camera set up, but I guess that there will be time for that later."

Onyx laps her coffee without comment, panting some between mouthfuls. When I reach over to check her damp fur where the coffee landed, she doesn't flinch and even bumps my hand with her nose.

"Feeling okay, Onyx?" I ask. "You seem tired. Doing that—whatever it is you do—seems to wear you out."

She bumps my hand again. I am saved from further speculation by the five-mile warning from the autopilot. Taking my coffee, I get into the driver's seat. Onyx heads for the passenger seat.

"Wait," I say, putting my hand back to bar her.

"You'd better stay out of sight for now. I don't know quite what to expect."

Or if I can trust the Directors, I add silently to myself, wondering if Onyx can pick up my concern and, if she can, if she understands any of the reasons for it. Whether or not she understands my words, she respects the barrier my arm makes and retreats to the back portion of the van. As I take the exit off the interstate, I hear her jump up onto the sofa bed.

Even though I have not traveled these roads for a longer time than might be considered decent given my destination, I know the way well. I have driven it in nightmare and fantasy too many times ever to forget.

Now I guide the van around the twists of the infrequently traveled road. When the lawns of the sleeping houses give way to trees and the trees to a spike-topped wrought iron fence, I mark the first half-kilometer and slow until I sight an angel, her face bent to regard an open book she holds in both hands. Then I make a sharp ninety-degree turn and hop the van over the twelve-foot fence.

The privacy field spits sparks around the van's edges—the van is wider than my little flitter—but nothing that will register with the security screens. Once over, I pause to nod at the granite angel. She doesn't return my greeting. She never does, but it somehow seems wrong not to acknowledge her. Formalities completed, I ease the van around a black basalt tombstone and head for Mr. Allain's mausoleum.

The area around the Grecian-style white limestone building is dark, but I do not doubt for a moment that the other Directors are or will be there. After parking the van behind an oak that offers some concealment from the main entryway, I step out. Onyx watches me impassively from her perch, her front legs matched in the sphinx posture she so often favors. Despite her stillness and composure, I imagine a question in the brass eyes.

"Yes," I say softly, "I do want you to come along.

I'd worry about you all alone and it's about time you had some say in these matters.

"Not," I add as an afterthought, "that you ever say anything."

Onyx doesn't surprise me. She leaps down and jumps to join me. As I lock the van, she looks side to side and then gestures with an awkward toss of her head towards Mr. Allain's mausoleum. I'm impressed despite myself. To me the structure cannot help but be unique, but rationally I know that there is little about it to differentiate it from the dozen similar buildings clustered on this particular slope.

The grass underfoot is icy and crackles under my feet as we walk to the mausoleum.

"I'm starting to envy your claws, Onyx," I mutter to cover my nervousness.

Like a scene from a low-grade horror film, the door into the mausoleum swings open before we reach it, and a shadow-cloaked figure beckons.

"Anton, cut it out!" I spit, hustling forward. "My nerves are shot already."

"Sorry, Kari," he apologizes, patting me as I go by. "The others are down below. I'll follow after I lock up."

"Right. Come on, Onyx."

With the Xian at my side, I walk through the tiny meditation chapel that fills the aboveground portion of the structure. A tight spiral staircase leads into the Allain family vaults. When I first came here, for the funeral of Mr. Allain's mother, I wondered how the coffins were even gotten down into the vault. That mystery was quickly solved—the vault holds only the cremated remains.

In the chamber Onyx and I enter, Tammany and Toshi sit on folding chairs around a card table. I cross to one of the chairs and motion Onyx to the other. She leaps up promptly.

"That's Anton's seat," Tammany protests.

I've been waiting for this and answer carefully.

"Would you ask Wheep or Chiron to sit on the floor?"

"No!" Toshi is shocked.

"Then why would you expect her to? She's a person, too, and with her height if she sits on the floor she can't see what's going on."

Tammany and Toshi exchange surprised looks and Anton pauses in his descent down the spiral stair.

"You have a point," Tammany admits. "Are you sure it's a person?"

"She," I correct. "Yes, an odd type of person, but most certainly a person."

I see them glance at each other, their disbelief obvious, and wonder at the strength of their doubt. Anton comes down the rest of the way and leans against the wall.

"What's happened while I was away?" I ask.

Again the quick glances.

"We had a conference with several—people—a mixed-race contingent. They showed us credentials that seemed to prove that they were members of the Xi-7 expedition."

"I ran a check later," Tammany cuts in, "and they did check out."

"They went to great lengths to explain that the creatures brought from Xi-7 could qualify as pseudo-sentient, but they did not fully qualify under the guidelines set up by the UAN agreement."

"Pseudo-sentient?" I echo. "What the hell does that mean?"

"Pseudo-sentient," Anton says, "is displaying behaviors that resemble sentience, but I figure you guessed that."

"Yes, I wasn't asking for a translation, but for how it applies to Onyx," I say dryly. "I see that Tammany has coffee. Is there any more?"

"Oh, sure." Tammany hauls a large hot bottle from under the table. "I have a cup somewhere."

"Two, please," I say sternly. "Onyx likes coffee, too."

Tammany hears the reprimand, but doesn't rise to it. She does produce two heavy paper cups.

"Black for both of you?"

"Yes, thank you." I smile formally as I take my cup. Onyx doesn't smile—well, at least I haven't learned what her smile looks like—but she politely takes a few laps from the cup Tammany slides across to her before settling back on her haunches.

"Very good," Toshi says, thrown off his stride. "I guess we should get down to business."

"Yes," I answer. "You were explaining the concept of pseudo-sentience."

Toshi nods sharply. "I think that you understand perfectly well, Karen. Pseudo-sentience is romanticizing impressions of a creature, choosing to believe that there is intelligence and rational, logical ability present, despite evidence to the contrary—something like the way some people respond to their pets."

"How do you judge the difference?" I ask.

"I don't," he chides, "but the UAN has set up guidelines developed by experts from the three races. These include such things as evidence of varieties of societies within the race, evidence of an ability to constructively manipulate the environment in which they live, and evidence of a language complex enough to convey abstract ideas."

Sipping my coffee, I nod, recalling my own similar criteria. Encouraged, Toshi leans forward.

"Have you proof of these for the Xian?"

"I was thinking," I answer, deliberately delaying a direct reply, "how unimaginative those criteria are, how very—for lack of a better word—human they are."

"Karen," Tammany begins, but I hold up my hand.

"No, listen," I say. "What those guidelines are saying is because we talk and build, because we define ourselves by our societies and racial subgroups, that if you want to be acknowledged as on our level, you must do as we do."

"That's pretty harsh, Kari," Anton says. "I mean, they had to decide some way to judge."

"Yes," I concede, "and part of why I'm so harsh on

them is because I was just as limited in my way of thinking when I started. Now, now I'm just plain scared, because despite these limiting guidelines the UAN team managed to figure out what I have figured out, and then coolly used the Xians' differences to disguise the fact of their sentience."

"Whoa!" Tammany says. "Karen, I think you need to slow down. I follow what you're saying about a cover-up—that message you deciphered implied as much—but are you saying that you've got proof that the Xian over there is not 'pseudo-sentient'?"

I draw a deep breath, "Yes, but it's not going to be easy to prove before a judicial board."

Toshi puts his head in his hands, "Somehow, Karen, I'm not surprised. Before you start the explanation I can see you're about to launch into, let me warn you that the people who are going to have to be convinced will have been inundated with stories about counting horses who are alert for cues from their trainers and about sign-language-using apes who were actually not talking—as the UAN defines it—but were again taking cues from the scientists studying them."

"What you're saying, Toshi," I translate coldly, "is that someone—or someones—has indoctrinated you and before you'll help me prove the Xian's case to them I have to prove it to you. Fine."

They all stare expectantly at me. For a choking, burning breath of time I remember how much I want to kill each one of them. I avoid looking at Mr. Allain's urn, atavistically fearful that I'll see his ghost regarding me with reproach. The gaze of a set of pyramidal brass eyes reminds me that there are others who have their ghosts.

"Very well," I say. "In short, I have no proof that would stand up against the guidelines that you have presented to me."

"Then what?" Toshi starts to interrupt, but I stop him with a quick gesture.

"Give me a chance to finish first. The evidence of culture is impossible for me to obtain, especially with one specimen. Right?''

Three nods, one brass stare.

''That leaves, essentially, language and what is termed 'manipulation.' As you've probably noticed, Onyx is the silent type. As far as I can tell, she doesn't talk with verbal components, not even whines or grunts. Her throat isn't even designed with more than a rudimentary voice box. She's quieter than the average Terran creature.''

I gulp my lukewarm coffee. Tammany refills my cup without comment.

''That leaves us with 'manipulation.' Interestingly, the word in English probably has its roots in the Latin word for 'hand'—an appendage that humans, Chirr, and su-ankh all have. In fact, the su-ankh have hands in excess of ours, but that doesn't make us less sentient. Yet, under that definition, Onyx is suffering from a real deficit. She simply doesn't have hands. Her feet are neatly equipt with retractable claws, but they do not have anything like fingers and her tail is not prehensile.''

''Sounds like you've closed all the options, Kari,'' Anton says. ''Where's the rabbit?''

I smile. ''No rabbit, Anton, just a Xian. The answer is simple and obvious, once you know it. She both talks and manipulates her environment with the same organ.''

''Her tongue?'' Tammany guesses.

''No,'' I shake my head, ''with her mind.''

A chorus of questions, protests, and demands erupts. I wait until one question wins out over the others.

''How do you know?'' Toshi exclaims.

''I'd like to say that I deduced it from the available data,'' I admit, ''but it's more simple than that. Onyx showed me what she could do.''

''Can you—I mean she—show us?'' Toshi demands.

''That is up to her,'' I say. ''I only learned some of this earlier today. She doesn't have much reason to trust virtual strangers.''

This said, I give Onyx my full attention. An idiotic

impulse urges me to say something like "Speak, Onyx! Speak, girl!" I restrain myself, recognizing the edge of hysteria fraying my mind. Today has been too long and too stressful. My body cries for the rest it has earned. Rubbing a hand across my face, I struggle to compose myself.

"Onyx," I say, staring into eyes that seem as alien to me as they did the first time I saw her, "Onyx, today you—did some things, put pictures in my mind, picked up the coffee pot."

I hear Toshi clear his throat. A blush burns my cheeks. I know I sound unhinged, but doggedly I continue. I focus on Onyx, trying to make a picture in my mind to match my words.

"Show them you understand me, girl. Pick up your coffee cup and hand—I mean give—it to me."

The world becomes those brass eyes; then an image forms in my mind, barely a sketch, but the meaning is clear.

"That's right, Onyx. Can you do it?"

The image flickers out, leaving me with a weird sensation of emptiness behind my forehead. I hear Onyx's breathing increase, and then her half-filled cup rises about three inches above the card table and drifts over to me. I open the fist I hadn't realized that I was clenching and wrap my fingers around the cup. I am aware of it settling into my grasp as an intangible competing force releases it.

Grinning foolishly, I shove the cup back to the Xian and look at each of the Directors in turn.

"Well?" I challenge. "Communication? Manipulation?"

"Seemed like it to me," Anton says, his eyes wide.

Tammany nods, "And to me. Amazing!"

"Yes," Toshi agrees, "but a limited sample. All she did was respond to a direct request. There's no evidence of reason in that. Moreover, although the apparent telekinesis is fascinating, we'll need to set up controls against fraud.''

''Shit!'' I respond, my exhaustion getting the better of me. ''You're a real bastard, Toshi. Forgive me, but your carefulness just doesn't impress me right now. I'm so damned tired that all I can think is that you're a calculating, cold-hearted prick who's so determined to cover his worthless ass that he'll fuck over the people he claims to be helping.''

Anton's eyes, when I look up from the table, are wider still, even impressed. Hissing his breath through his teeth, he thumps Toshi on one indignantly stiff shoulder.

''Kari's got a point, Toshi,'' he says, ''and she probably doesn't even know the latest news.''

''What?'' I ask. ''What have I missed while I've been camping?''

Tammany reads off her datapad, ''Based on the Survey team's reports, the UAN has announced that Xi-7 has no indigenous sentient species. A multispecies colonization effort will be mounted immediately. The Survey did note that several of the indigenous species were quite intelligent, if not sentient or rational, and as much might serve as . . .''

She pauses and I growl.

''As either potential hazards or,'' Tammany pauses, ''pets.''

NINE

I WAKE UP THE NEXT MORNING DISORIENTED, KNOWING only that I am neither in my bed nor in the van. The sight of Onyx asleep on a heap of blankets across the chamber brings my memory into focus.

I'd blown up after hearing the UAN resolution and eventually the others had ruled that nothing more productive was going to get done until I had a chance to sleep. The question of where Onyx and I were to go next—my home and the Corp Complex still being unrealistic options—had been settled before our arrival. No one asked how I felt about it, and I was too mad to comment, so with little protest we were settled into Mr. Allain's family crypt.

Waking up there was less eerie than might be imagined. After the people I'd shared cells with back in prison, the urns of ashes made comparatively unfrightening roommates and I couldn't shake the feeling that Mr. Allain was watching over me.

Rising, I make my way to the washroom Anton has jury-rigged in one corner. He'd even managed running water by tapping into the cemetery's sprinkler system. Refreshed, I make coffee. The smell brings Onyx around and she lies on her pallet, her nose wrinkling appreciatively.

"Good morning, partner," I grumble, splashing some

into her bowl, "Does Madame want her coffee in bed or will she come and get it?"

In answer, the coffee bowl skids across the marble floor to the edge of her pallet. I chuckle despite myself.

"You're crazy," I say, "You know that."

She blinks at me as if to say, "Me? You're the one hiding in this hole full of dead people's ashes. I know that there are beings who want me dead; therefore my behavior is sensible. But you share coffee with me and chatter at me in a friendly fashion and have tried neither to kill me or to drug me. Therefore, I like you. I think that we are becoming friends."

At least that's what I want to believe she is thinking. She could just as easily be wondering where her lunch is or computing the trajectories of space-going vehicles.

As I make us both some food—breakfast being most definitely on my mind if not on hers—I make a mental list of questions for Tammany, who is due to arrive fairly soon.

She comes tripping down the stairs about an hour later, a covered case that I assume contains her datapad in one hand.

"Good morning, Karen," she says. "Good morning, Onyx."

I give her a mental "plus" for that.

"Morning, Tammany," I answer. "Coffee?"

"Please," she says, taking a seat. "Sleep well?"

"Like the dead," I deadpan with a glance at the urns.

As she groans at my joke, her coffee cup slides across the card table to rest before her.

"Uh, thank you, Onyx," she says with a nod for the Xian.

Two pluses. And two for Onyx. Smiling, I refill my cup and Onyx's bowl. As I'm seating myself across the table from Tammany, the bowl floats up to an unoccupied place and Onyx leaps up onto the chair. After tidily lapping up a small spill, she looks expectantly between us.

Tammany shakes her head as if to clear it.

''Well, I expect that you both have a lot of questions.''

''Yes,'' I agree, then a sudden worry intrudes. ''Are we safe? How did you get here?''

''In a hearse,'' she says, obviously delighted to be asked. ''How else does one come to a cemetery? Seriously, it was very carefully set up. Unless someone tapped into our communique to you last night, this should stay a safe place. Only Toshi, Anton, and I know you two are here. Toshi is so worried about a spy at the Corp that he's been working only with me and Anton on this project. This way, we know where the leaks have to start.''

''I know I was sharp with him last night,'' I say, hating myself for even coming this close to apologizing, ''but he really irked me by how he took Onyx's demonstration.''

''Understandably,'' Tammany soothes, ''he's been trying too hard since back before Ben died. Then when Rhys died, he lost the person he was relying on for group orientations of the Knives. Vance took over some, but he is—I mean was—such a lone wolf. He'd work with groups, but didn't like it. Then when the explosion got Qiang, well, Toshi's been a wreck since. I think he really regrets . . .''

She catches herself and goes on, ''Regrets trying so hard to coordinate both Hands and Knives.''

She sips her coffee and busies herself pulling out her datapad. I watch, wondering how much Onyx is following and finishing Tammany's altered sentence in my mind. I would bet anything that what she had nearly said was that ''he really regrets setting things up so that Ben Allain would die.''

Inchoate anger rises to choke me and I am purely glad that she had caught herself in time. If she had openly admitted to knowing about the circumstances surrounding Mr. Allain's death, I would have had to try and kill her. I might even have managed, and that would be a pity, because I need her—or rather Onyx does. And if I am sure of anything I am sure that Onyx needs me to help her gain her freedom just as I once needed Mr. Allain to help me earn mine.

"Where should I start?" Tammany asks.

I swallow my anger and concentrate on the problem before us.

"You said that the UAN Council passed a resolution on setting up colonization on Xi-7. You didn't give any specifics."

Tammany nods and starts pulling information. I notice, however, that she barely refers to her screen.

"The resolution was passed quickly in order to take advantage of a generous proposal by—do you care to guess who?"

"StarUs?" I say with a half-smile.

"Your point. The main colony ship will not depart for some time yet, but a set-up team consisting largely of members of the original survey crew will precede them."

"When do they leave?" I demand.

"That, unfortunately, is privileged information. There have been mutters of dissatisfaction about how quickly Xi-7 was ruled open."

"When do they leave?" I repeat.

She laughs, "The best that Anton has found for us indicates that they may go as soon as within a week. I'm inclined to doubt that they could be ready that soon—interstellar operations aren't mounted that quickly."

"Maybe this one has been in the planning for a lot longer than that. The deception regarding Onyx's people wasn't decided on whim."

"No," she admits, "I know. What next?"

"Was anything said publicly about the Xians who were brought here?"

She shakes her head, "Not specifically. Some of the reporters apparently picked up information that native life-forms had been brought in on the survey ship, and these were asked about. The answer was general—that yes there were some, but that they were currently in quarantine. Plenty of holos were available and these seemed to satisfy curiosity.''

''Hmm, any action from Lantic Labs?''

''None publicly, but their parent company is clearly involved in this. We did learn that Chiron holds a large block of stock in StarUs and from what you have reported he's been very active in this entire affair.''

''What does StarUs have to gain from this?''

''That,'' Tammany answers with a quick fidget on her datapad, ''is what Toshi and I have been sweating over. Without Qiang or Ben, we spent a great deal of time running down blind alleys. Once we figured it out, we felt really dumb.''

She turns her screen so that I can see it, then quickly realigns it so that Onyx has a clear view as well.

A lovely 3-D star map sparkles at me. Even though I realize that the sparkling isn't strictly accurate, I find myself grinning at this unexpected evidence of Tammany's imaginative side.

Touching the screen, she highlights one star; then she touches two more.

''This is Sol system; these two are the Chirr and su-ankh main worlds.'' She taps a few more stars. ''These are worlds that now have UAN settlements. You'll notice that the bulk are over nearer to the Chirr and su-ankh worlds; this is, of course, because they have been space-faring for far longer than we have.''

''Right, they met after both were space capable. Then they found us when they headed this way.''

''Hold that idea and watch,'' she says touching the screen. ''This is the Xian home world. Note that it is nicely in position to facilitate advancement into 'unknown territories.' ''

''Yes, that seems obvious.''

Her grin is rueful, ''It is, once you look at it that way.''

I'm opening my mouth to speak when the conversation takes an odd turn. A duplication of Tammany's map appears in that space behind my eyes; it is an odd, but for me somewhat familiar, experience. Tammany looks so shocked that I wonder how I must have looked when Onyx sprang this method of communication on me.

The mental map sparkles and then the Xi system is unhighlighted. Slowly, an inchworm of light draws a pattern showing the relationship between the Chirr and su-ankh worlds and the Sol system. Perhaps Onyx adds some nonpictorial prompt to her display, but I have no trouble understanding what she is driving at. Apparently, neither does Tammany.

"She's saying that our system is in a very similar expansion pattern to the one that the Xi system is in!" she gasps. "Damn me for not noticing! The three home worlds were so much the constant in our plotting that . . . damn!"

Her voice fades off in amazement, whether at Onyx's ability or at her own blind spot I cannot be certain.

"This would imply, at least," I say as Onyx's map fades from my mind, "that Terra could have faced the same situation that Xi-7 currently is in. I wonder why the more aggressive approach to Xi-7?"

"There are lots of reasons," Tammany says, ticking the points off on her fingertips. "We've already noted economics—if they were stopped from exploiting this position thirty or so years ago, this one may seem irresistible. The new UAN members—us—aren't likely to oppose a good argument for taking the territory."

"Yes," I agree, "there must be something different about Xi-7 that lets the argument that there are no sentient races there hold water."

Another picture forms in my mind and, presumably, in Tammany's. This one shows on one side a picture that, though distorted by a shorter perspective, I recognize as a city street. This picture shrinks and scritters to one side; in the space made vacant in my mental screen, a rich, verdant scene appears.

My first impression, that this is the park where Onyx and I camped, is immediately quashed. This is too green.

Quickly I realize that none of the plants are familiar. Most are too squat. That tree is oaklike, the flower geranium-like, that shrub briarlike, but there are no oaks, no geraniums, no briars.

Into this scene trots a creature I think is Onyx. Then I notice that this Xian has a white streak on its forelegs. Its eyes are more silver than brass. She (I feel the pictured Xian is female) is trailed by a half dozen little ones. These are also predominantly dark coated, but with variations in their markings.

The Terran scene fades completely to make room for the Xian to lead her patrol through the greenness. They pause at various points. Several times she levitates a stick or rock to draw the young ones' attention to it. Gradually, I realize that this is a school session, but it is being conducted in complete silence. There are no yips or whines, nor do the young cavort or fail to attend to their teacher.

At last, she leads them into a natural-seeming vale, shaped like a soup bowl, with a pool at its heart. Here in the open, a mist is falling. The teacher steps to one side and the students go tearing down the slope to splash in the water. Turning, the teacher walks over to join a small group of adults. Here I see some variation. One is nearly fawn-colored and has startlingly blue eyes. Another is half again the teacher's size and more heavily furred.

The scene fades as the adults begin a game that involves shifting rocks in a complex pattern both above and on the ground. Only their eyes move, although perked ears and thumping tails reflect their enthusiasm for the game.

I shake my head as the vision breaks. Onyx is panting hard, the apple smell of her breath heavy in the closed crypt. Hurriedly, I fetch her some coffee and a saucer of food nuggets. Pausing to fill my own cup, I turn to Tammany.

"Did you see that?"

Her dark face is still laced with enchantment.

"Do you think that's what Xi-7 is like, Karen?"

"Well," I say, filling her cup, "that seems a good guess."

"Then I can see why this cover-up was possible. If that scene Onyx showed us is as representative of Xi-7 as the city street is of Terra, then the obvious marks of 'civilization' aren't there, and the less obvious signs can be overlooked."

"Or glossed over," I agree.

I look over to where Onyx is busily lapping coffee. She's panting less and seems to be recovering more quickly. Tammany follows my gaze.

"Can that be a natural ability for her race?" she asks, "I mean, making those pictures seemed to wipe her out. Lousy communications system if it exhausts the user."

"Yes," I agree hesitantly, "but she is communicating with not one but two aliens. That must be more difficult."

"Er . . ." Tammany mutters, suddenly absorbed in her datapad, "I just remembered something from when I was looking at the preliminary breakdown of . . ."

She trails off, not seeming to realize that she has stopped talking. While she is occupied, I get up and stretch. My fingers almost brush the ceiling when I stand on my toes. Onyx watches, I'd like to think with amazement. She seems less tired.

"Recovering, girl?" I ask softly.

"Why do you do that?" Tammany asks, looking up sharply from her screen.

"What?" I say, completely confused.

" 'Girl,' " she says. "You call her 'girl,' like she's a dog or something."

"I do, don't I?" I answer, a blush spreading over my face. "I wondered why she wasn't answering to her 'name.' I must be confusing the hell out of her."

Tammany smiles and goes on with her computer work. After a few more minutes she looks up.

"I thought so!" she crows, "Look at this. I couldn't believe that someone on the Survey team didn't learn about these psionic abilities we've seen in Onyx. They couldn't very well bring the Xians here and keep them as 'animals' without some way of regulating how they used them."

"I'm with you," I say, recalling the pathetic creatures strapped in their cages. "What did you find?"

"I pulled the list of the drugs that Qiang found were being given to the Xians. Remember the depressants listed on it?"

"Yes."

"I ran a scan through my Physician's Desktop and got everything classified. Then I ran a search for anything listed as particularly good at shutting down mental activity without also shutting down the body. A few matches came up. I pulled the entries for each one and found that each had in some way been used in work for controlling erratic psionic manifestations—usually poltergeist activity in children. I'll need a larger data bank than this one to check further, and we've got some great classified stuff back in the Corp libraries. I'll bet you dimes to donuts that we'll find that the Xians were being doped up to suppress their natural abilities."

"No bet," I say. "Donuts cost too much. I wonder if Onyx is still recovering from that crap."

"Possibly. Lots of drugs take time to build up in the system and almost as long to flush out. That would explain why she gets worn out like that after 'talking' to us."

She grins and I can tell that she is still rather bemused at the situation. I know what she feels. Telepathic "dogs" seem like something out of a bad Disney movie.

"Now what?" I ask.

A picture, a bit rough at the edges but clear enough, immediately appears. A Survey ship against the stars, heading toward a green ball. The perspective is all wrong, like a child's drawing of a house, but the meaning is clear.

"You want us to take you home, Onyx?" I ask.

Then, for the first time, awkwardly she nods her slender

head. As if a bridge has been built between us, something in me shivers into being at that moment. I realize that, no matter how high the odds are against us, somehow I am going to find a way to take Onyx home.

TEN

"THAT'S IMPOSSIBLE!" TOSHI ROARS FROM HIS END OF the table in the secured conference room.

More chairs are empty than even at our last meeting, but a new one is filled. Onyx sits primly in the chair beside me, her tail wrapped around her feet. As usual she is silent, but her slender head darts back and forth, following the conversation.

"What's impossible, Toshi?" I ask sweetly. "That Onyx is sentient? That the UAN plans, if not genocide, at least systematic displacement of another race?"

"No!" he growls. "This crazy idea you have about somehow going to Xi-7."

"Crazy?" I tilt my head to one side, deliberately mimicking Onyx. "Maybe, but let me play the prophet, Toshi. Not only am I going to give this project my best effort, but you and all the resources of the Corp are going to help me to do it."

Anton looks startled, but Toshi's eyes narrow dangerously. Only Tammany remains neutral, but I suspect that she is suddenly suspicious. I am sorry to have to sacrifice our newly blossoming accord this way, but I need all of the Corp's resources available to help Onyx; and, with the UAN colonization plans getting set at record speed, I do not dare wait long enough to let the others come over to my point of view.

They will not have the weeks in the van and mausoleum with Onyx that I have had, weeks during which my initial affection has become tempered with respect. As the drugs washed from her system, Onyx began to communicate more freely. She has begun to augment the detailed pictures by single pictures that, rather like ideograms, stand for ideas. I'm amused that she represents me as a vaguely female figure, seated, with hands wrapped around a coffee mug.

"We're going to help you do this?" Toshi repeats. "How can you be so certain?"

"Simple. I'm going to make you."

Toshi starts to laugh, but something in my expression stops him. Tammany's chocolate eyes are thoughtful. I believe she may have guessed, but then she's always been the smartest of us. Anton looks suspicious and somehow hurt. I suspect I've destroyed some cherished illusions.

"Make us, Kari?" he says, his tone mingling hurt and indignation. "I don't know what I wonder more—how you're going to do it or why you feel the need to coerce us."

"I'm going to ignore your second question, Anton," I say, "because you know damn well that we don't have time to work this out. I'm going to start with how."

Drawing a deep breath and wrapping my fingers around my mug, I smile tightly.

"I know that you all—along with Vance, Rhys, and Qiang—collaborated to let Mr. Allain die."

They stare at me; not one bothers to protest or deny. Then Anton leans back in his chair.

"How long have you known?" he asks, almost conversationally.

"More importantly," Toshi interrupts sharply, "how can you prove it?"

"Do you think I care to give everything away so you can put some of our teams to work on defusing it?" I laugh with real humor. "No, I'm not stupid. I have evidence and I've arranged that if I don't check in, my evidence will go to interested parties. My death would count as not checking in. I don't suppose that I need to state that.''

''I suppose that asking you if you're bluffing is useless,'' Tammany says. ''Isn't it?''

''I would say so,'' I agree, happily.

Toshi glowers at me, ''There is no way that you can prove what you're alleging, Karen Saber.''

''There is no way that I should even know about this,'' I counter, ''is there? You would have been too careful about covering your tracks. Therefore, if I know, it follows that I must also be able to prove what I'm saying.''

''Toshi, finding out if she's bluffing will take time,'' Tammany says, as if I'm not there, ''and if she is not, she can get us involved in some very ugly proceedings. Do you know what the end result would be if the three of us were under criminal suspicion?''

Toshi, I could swear, blanches. Then he recovers, arrogant as ever.

He folds his arms across his chest and snarls, ''Karen, as the remaining Director, would have full control of the Corp and its resources.''

Tammany nods and toasts me with her mug, defeat graciously accepted, ''Yes, that's right. And we don't want anything to happen to the Corp, do we?''

''Hmm,'' Anton says, ''Well, I guess it's a good idea we were all planning to go along with what you wanted, Kari.''

''Yes,'' Toshi says sourly, ''I guess it is, isn't it?''

''Great!'' I beam, affecting a manic cheerfulness to cover a confused sense that there is an undercurrent that I'm missing. ''We're going to need to find out several things. First of all, we'll need to get to Xi-7.''

Silence reigns for a tense moment.

''There are a few options, as I see the situation,'' Toshi says, as if sudden concentration on the problem will erase our disagreement. ''The best would be to have Onyx's sentience acknowledged by some highly visible members of the UAN Grand Council, preferably by a mixed-race contingent.''

''Agreed,'' Anton says, ''but the difficulty is that the UAN Council is not headquartered on Terra. If we're going to try and take a commercial trader to them, we're going to have a hell of a time explaining Onyx.''

''Yes,'' Toshi agrees, ''so that option seems out. We'll need to get Onyx recognized by the contingent here on Terra or find our own way to get her home. Anton, last time we discussed your work, your cover was still intact at StarUs.''

''Still is,'' Anton says. ''You want me to check on the progress of the colony ships.''

''Right,'' Toshi agrees, ''We may be able to use that as a timer for our own actions. However, we can rule out hitching a ride—life-support is too carefully monitored.''

''Which means,'' Tammany says, looking up from the datapad over which she has been busily working, ''that we need a ship and crew. I have a couple of leads here. Unfortunately, our best bets are going to be Chirr ships, since they have the most extensive merchant fleet.''

''Unfortunately?'' Toshi says, one eyebrow raised at this apparent racism.

''Yeah,'' Tammany sighs, ''I hate veggies and all Chirr ships are vegetarian only. Oh well, I'll keep looking, but they'll be the best bet.''

''And who will work on the diplomatic connections?'' I ask, suspicious of this sudden flood of cooperation.

''I think that leaves you and me,'' Toshi says. ''The Corp has some contacts and we'll split the list and work through.''

''Very good,'' I say, ''Just as long as the list doesn't include either Chiron or Wheep.''

''No,'' Toshi grins, ''but I was going to suggest that you talk with Shi Freesh. We've been keeping an ear out for any sign that there were malcontents among the Survey team members. Freesh most certainly is one. He may even be the one who drafted that note.''

I nod thoughtfully, ''Is he that obvious about being unhappy with the situation?''

''No,'' Tammany cuts in, ''not at all, but we took Anton's lead and kept an eye on him. I acquired the preliminary rosters for both the returning Survey ship and the colony ships. He's not included on either of the rosters.''

''Indeed,'' I say, ''that does seem promising. I'm glad that you folks have everything so well organized.''

When we leave the meeting, Onyx and I walk toward the Corp Atrium, our current hideaway. There is a certain logic behind this location. Although he did not wish to incite vengeance by firing anyone, Toshi has sent into the field those operatives he suspected of being responsible for leaking information.

Onyx and I arrived here in complete secret, apparently never detected in our mausoleum refuge. If we are located here, it will indicate that there is still a weak spot within our organization. Another advantage is that Onyx can move about within the Atrium with some freedom. From ''conversations'' with her, I have gathered that the Xians are largely an outdoor people. The structures they construct are little more than sleeping and storage dens. The concept of living indoors, as many humans and Chirr do, is clearly alien to her. Even the few days we spent in Mr. Allain's crypt were enough to make her nervous and excitable.

She seems to like the Atrium, although I get the impression that she is amused at the concept of constructing a structure that serves to bring the outside indoors.

In the days that come, I discover that although Onyx's and my job had seemed very easy when Toshi had posed it during our conference, it is proving to have all sorts of difficulties. Shi Freesh doesn't answer any of my calls and refuses to see the Corp emissary I send to him.

One afternoon, as Onyx and I are watching snow form on the glass ceiling overhead and luxuriating in the humidity of the Atrium, Tammany comes to call. I fill her in on my latest rejection, while she listens sympathetically.

"If he's as disconnected from his support system as Anton believed, he could be a bit more cooperative," I conclude. "We could help him."

Tammany chuckles, particularly smug because her ship search is going well.

"No, really, Tammany," I protest, "I don't exactly blame him for being careful, but getting an appointment with an alien scientist when you can't tell him why you need to see him and you don't even dare tell him who you are is impossible."

"Yes," Tammany answers, ill-concealing her mirth, "it must be. In fact, I'm sure it is."

"You knew it would be like this!" I gasp, open-mouthed in amazement. "You and Toshi set me up!"

Tammany nods, "Not exactly 'set you up,' but we had tried to get an appointment with Shi Freesh while you were still out in the woods and he refused. We hoped you'd have more luck—after all, you're the word wizard."

"Damn you both," I say with something like affection.

We are reviewing various strategies when Onyx joins the conversation.

The image she sends is of me inserting a letter into a courier's pouch like those I have been using (the notes are written with ink that fades rapidly after being exposed to light. Not only does this destroy the messages soon after they're read, but it effectively keeps them from being photocopied). Once the pouch is sealed, she comes over and rubs her head, especially the underside of her jaw, along the pouch. The pouch is then delivered to a courier and her picture fades.

I turn to Onyx, who is staring expectantly at me.

"That's a neat idea, Onyx," I say. "Do you think he'll understand the message?"

She nods, perking her ears for emphasis.

"You're certain," I interpret for Tammany.

Tammany, in turn, is looking at Onyx in confusion.

''Didn't she include you in the image?'' I ask.

''She did, she did,'' Tammany affirms, ''but I think I failed to get the message. What's with this jaw rubbing?''

I laugh, ''Not jaw rubbing, Tammany, scent marking.''

She still looks confused, so I explain.

''Lots of Terran species use it. To oversimplify, the creature produces an individual scent recognizable to other creatures. These scents can be so specific in some cases that individual members of a school of fish or a pack of wolves can be identified by their scent. I'd noticed that Onyx scent-marks things wherever we've holed up—probably she can navigate in the dark by these landmarks when there's not enough light. And my guess is that her people use such marks to augment their telepathic communication—especially since Onyx, at least, resorts to sound only as a last resort.''

Tammany looks overwhelmed. ''So Onyx wants to send a scent message to Freesh in the hope that he'll clue in on what you need to see him about.''

''Exactly,'' I frown. ''It's a risk, especially if anyone else with the capacity to 'read' Onyx's message is around when he gets it, but we need to take the risk. Anyhow, according to what we've learned, he's either breaking custom or is being reprimanded, because he's been living apart from any Chirr except for his immediate family group.''

''We'll have to hope that he takes his mail on his own and that the members of his family are loyal to him,'' Tammany says. ''We may be short of time. Try Onyx's idea.''

The next morning, I draft another letter and present it to Onyx, who, for good measure, rubs herself along both the page and the courier pouch.

Our answer comes within an hour of the courier's departure. Onyx and I are involved in the laborious and largely futile process of teaching her to read. Although she spontaneously creates ideogramic pictographs, she cannot seem to grasp the relationship between certain letters and corresponding sounds. The process is complicated by the fluid values of many letters.

I think we're both grateful when an outside line signals. Onyx flops to the floor when I rise to flip open the call, but at hearing the voice at the other end, her ears perk up.

"Directors Saber," says a voice with the unmistakable chirp of a Chirr vocalizer, "this is Shi Freesh. I was foolish not to take the scent of your message sooner. May I come to see you?"

I blink a few times in surprise, checking to see that the view screen is indeed off.

"Yes, of course. How did you know who sent the message? I know I didn't sign my name."

There is a trill, then, "Of course, but the one message led me to sniff for a second and I found you. Foolish of me not to so check before, but yours are a nose-dead people. I had not even imagined such a variant in communication."

"I see. We can meet, but I would prefer that your coming here is not obvious. I will connect you to Toshi, but first one question. Have you spoken to anyone?"

"No one," he assures me, "not even when I was ignoring your messages. I knew they could be sensitive."

Alerted, Toshi arranges for Freesh to be spirited to meet us at the Corp Atrium that afternoon. The Chirr is still portly after the fashion of his kind, but his black and white fur seems to have lost some of its luster.

"Discoverer Freesh," I say formally as he hops into the Atrium, "thank you for coming."

"We are pleased to learn of your role in these activities," he replies, equally formally. "We were saddened when report was given that the Xian animals had been killed by a disease. I was suspicious as well, for they had been healthy when they left Xi-7 in our ship. I knew that a disease from one of our races would need to be highly adaptable to strike an alien metabolism so swiftly, and in such a case major health warnings should have been issued to all the races.''

''I see,'' I say, nodding. ''The announcement must have been made after the Xians came to leave the Lantic Labs facility where they had been held, and their captors lost hope of regaining them alive.''

''So I gathered when I asked questions, before I was informed that my curiosity exceeded my place.''

Without comment, I note that Freesh has just used the singular pronoun with extraordinary frequency for a Chirr. Uncertain what significance this might have, I file the point for later reflection and indicate where Onyx rests on a garden bench.

''This is the only Xian that we are certain survived this 'plague,' '' I say. ''She has permitted me to call her Onyx, since I am unable to grasp her own name.''

Freesh hops over to her, his tail curling in the dirt behind him in what I believe is a mixture of anticipation and fear.

''Onyx,'' he whistles in panlingi, ''we are pleased to meet you.''

She graciously dips her head. Freesh's tail curls into a little spiral and then relaxes.

''Directors Saber, I must be abrupt. We are aware that there is a risk in our involvement with this matter.''

''You are aware of a risk?'' I say, the shifting pronouns making me dizzy.

''Yes,'' he replies sharply, ''isn't that what I said?''

I smile a touch sourly and reply deliberately in his home world's trade pidgin, ''We believed so, but we are aware of the shortcomings of mechanical translation. We wished to be certain.''

He taps his tail along the floor in laughter.

''We understand,'' he says. ''We will attempt to be clear.''

''Let me offer you a seat,'' I say, suddenly aware that my behavior has been less than courteous. ''Then we can talk about risks and why they need to be taken.''

Freesh accepts a padded footstool, and I roll a cart with a variety of refreshments into his easy reach and pull up a chair on the other side.

"Please continue," I say, "and we will attempt to answer your questions."

Freesh nods and pours himself some cranberry juice. Snapping through a stalk of endive with one bite, he appears to meditate before speaking.

"We wish to ask you how you became so involved in this issue," he says, "but we suspect that this would open a discussion largely philosophical in nature. Therefore, I ask, when did you personally become aware that there was going to be an attempt to defraud the Xians of their world?"

I blink. For a moment, I honestly can't remember a time before I lived in hiding with my silent companion. There is another Karen Saber, solitary, set on one self-destructive goal, but she seems a stranger. Then I remember.

"There was a coded message," I say, "brought in by clients who thought it might be related to problems they had been experiencing with internal espionage. I deciphered it and from what it said, combined with information one of our operatives had acquired, we deduced what was happening."

"And you decided to interfere?" Freesh whistles, amazed. "You must have known that the Terran government and the UAN Council were in some accord on this."

"Still," I say, remembering that meeting, "some of us felt that it was the right thing to do. Others thought that there might be profit to be made."

Freesh considers this, his attention momentarily distracted by Onyx levitating a jelly roll over to her. She unrolls it telekinetically, licks off the jelly, and bites into the sponge cake. Freesh takes the display calmly enough to confirm that he at least suspected something about how the Xians functioned.

"We do not classify science as you Terrans do," he

says, startling me with his change of subject. "I am learned in areas that your people would call biology, anthropology, geology, and physics. I was among those who first encountered the Xians and I was among the first to experience their novel method of communication. But for all my knowledge, I was ignorant of the one science that might have saved Onyx's companions—politics."

I laugh dryly, "That seems to be a universal science."

Freesh nods, "I will not tell you here of Onyx's world, but it is an untame and verdant place, one which would never have evolved your people or mine. But we can tame such a world with tools and machines and the combined lore of the three races. The challenges that would have killed our primitive selves are nothing to us now. There is variety there and beauty, and there is also an atmosphere we can breath with little trouble."

"And it lies in an expansion path," I add.

Freesh's white whiskers curl. "What?"

Instantly, a star field appears in my mind and, apparently, in his. Onyx runs through the routine, highlighting the planets in relation to each other. The star field fades and is replaced by a grotesquely oversized version of what I recognize from the news as a Survey team camp geodesic. The ground around it is trampled and a shuttle is awkwardly parked off to one side.

"Yes, Onyx," Freesh replies, "we understand better now why this plan was so attractive. There is great wealth and great promise both in the planet itself and in its potential role as a gateway."

He curls his tail tightly around himself before continuing, "The message you found was left, I believe, for me by an ally in the Chirr UAN delegation. Because of my protests that the Xians were intelligent, I was forbidden a place on the commission."

"Preexisting bias?" I guess.

"Yes," he says. "The message, what did it say?"

I quote from memory: "Tests prove unquestionably that the alien animal is intelligent. DuPoy orders information suppressed for good of UAN. Selected resistance suggested.''

Freesh chitters something that his translator ignores.

''Yes, I believe that was meant for me. After the committee refused a place to me, StarUs graciously made opportunities available for me at one of their facilities. I accepted—space exploration is fascinating, but the stipend between voyages is not large and my clan claims my salary during the voyage.''

''You believe that StarUs offered you the job to keep an eye on you?'' I ask, resolutely not venturing into the tantalizing puzzle of Chirr economics.

''Indeed,'' he answers with a gusty sigh. ''My UAN delegation ally has not communicated with me in some time. Perhaps he did not believe that I was of his mind when I did not reply. Perhaps he too has been won by the benefits of concealing the alien's sentience.''

''Why didn't he write to you in your own language?'' I ask, suddenly suspicious that this is all an elaborate trap.

Freesh taps his tail, ''When you read our languages, clearly you see them in transliteration. Our script is closer to braille than to anything you use. It was designed for use without light. Had he written to me in that fashion, the fact that the message was from one Chirr to another would have been obvious. We are more common on Terra than we once were, but the pool is still quite small. Therefore we adapted a game to our purposes and agreed to pass messages in this cumbersome fashion.''

''I see,'' I reply, temporarily satisfied.

Onyx yawns widely enough to show the black roof of her mouth. Amazed despite myself at how well she is learning to adapt human gestures, I return to our immediate problem.

''Discoverer Freesh, we are committed to a dual course. One, we wish to publicly expose the fraud the UAN Council has accepted. Two, we wish to take Onyx back home, where she will have both a chance to survive and a chance to warn her people.''

"Admirable," Freesh says. "How will you do this?"

I smile mysteriously, "We are working on both goals. What I need to know is whether we can count on you in your role as a member of the Survey team to support us."

He bobs his head, "I will send to you some suggestions for how to help Onyx prepare for an interview—if through some miracle you do manage to get one."

"Then we're committed. I'll make certain that the other Directors are notified. I suspect Toshi will want to arrange some protection for you."

Onyx looks at Freesh.

"You're welcome," he whistles. "I only wish that I could be certain that my assistance will be of any use."

I smile reassuringly, hiding a growing conviction that this is a more complex problem than I had imagined and the fear that we cannot possibly succeed.

ELEVEN

ONYX AND I ARE IN THE ATRIUM SHARING COFFEE AND playing chess when Toshi comes running in.

"Karen!" His words tumble over each other in excitement. "We have gotten an interview with the UAN Terran commission. We called in some favors and went over DuPoy's head—indicating that we had some information that would effect the colonization attempt. DuPoy will be there, but he won't be the ranking official."

"Wow!" I say, glancing to see if Onyx is following this. "Those must have been some favors."

"They were," he replies a bit smugly, "but I think the final point in our favor is that the haste with which this expedition is being put together is creating all sorts of expenses that weren't apparent when StarUs first made their generous offer. There has been some grumbling, and with the stories that Tammany has been feeding the tabloids . . ."

We both laugh.

"This is great, Toshi," I say. "Onyx is communicating more fluidly now and you should take time to play chess with her. She sees possibilities for the knight that I keep missing. It must be the influence of that 'float stone' game her people play."

"We'll bring a set," Toshi says. "Something showy may be just what we need. The appointment is for the three of us and Freesh. Tammany will keep things running here and Anton's in deep at StarUs. He sent word today that he thinks there will be a major announcement soon about the colony ships' departure."

When he leaves, we return to our game, but I find that I am too nervous and excited to play well. Onyx checkmates me in two moves, making a show of tipping over my king with her right front paw. She's begun to use various gestures now, something I take to be her meeting us halfway because neither in any of Freesh's visual records nor in her own pictures do any of the Xians use their digits for manipulation if a telekinetic touch can do the job.

For me, I'm learning that attempting to shape pictures in my mind as I speak—something like running a comic strip—does seem to help her comprehension. I honestly am not certain that she understands more than a couple dozen words as sounds, but she is becoming more adept at picking up my mind pictures.

The next morning, Toshi and I dress formally and get into a Corp limo. Onyx doesn't wear any formal attire, but several weeks of good feeding have made her coat shiny and slightly rounded her body so that she is no longer slat-sided. She wants to sit in her usual front seat, but Toshi waves her to the back.

"Look out one of the tinted side windows, Onyx," he says gruffly. "This isn't a time to risk you being seen."

She leaps into the back, taking the seat behind me. Toshi takes the passenger seat, tucking a briefcase containing a chess set and a few other pieces of paraphernalia at his feet.

For the next twenty minutes or so, I concentrate on city driving. Despite continual improvements in public transportation, the number of private vehicles on the road never seems to diminish. About halfway to our destination, flashing lights against the overhanging buildings alert me to an accident ahead.

"Take this cross street," Toshi says. "We'll lose less time than if we wait to get around this mess."

Seeing the traffic backup building in front of us, I nod agreement and swing the limo around. We go a few blocks before the street is blocked by a trash-collecting truck. The overseer looks almost too lazy to punch the buttons on her control pad. Cursing under my breath, I size up a narrow side street and turn down it.

We've not gone very far before I realize that we don't want to be here. When the first person steps out of a doorway, I slow automatically. By the time the second and third have emerged, I realize that we're in trouble.

Glancing in the rearview, I see several more people have emerged. All are human. All show a bulk that suggests body armor, and all carry weapons. The first person to emerge takes a central position, apparently secure that his backup is sufficient to make me slow down. Just in case I haven't caught on, he raises the hand that isn't aiming a high-caliber pistol at the windshield.

Next to me, his upper body immobile above the wrists, Toshi is sliding a hand gun from the glove box. His eyes forward, he studies the gang leader.

"When I say so, floor it," he says in Japanese.

I don't bother to signal that I understand, my full attention on the gun aimed at my head.

"Now!" he says.

With a show of confidence that I don't feel, I press the accelerator. The scene before me fragments with motion. Vaguely, I am aware of people tumbling out of the way of the unexpected assault. The vibration of rounds impacting on our armored sides is only a dim tattoo. The one thing I am certain of is that the leader's gun is torn from his grasp microseconds before Toshi's bullet pulps his head.

I feel the jolt of our air cushion passing over his body as I frame a vivid "thank you" to Onyx and see the steaming coffee bowl of her reply.

Most of my attention is reserved for getting the limo,

which had seemed streamlined in comparison to the bulky van, through alleyways never meant for traffic. Certain that the gang members must know the layout better than I do, I drive as quickly as I dare, scattering litter and crated goods.

Coming to a blockade of crates and garbage, I try a maneuver I've only seen on film. Wondering if it really works, I run us with the limo's air cushion against the edge of the buildings and up. Somewhat to my surprise, it does work. We clear the pile of crates and get a few meters further to a relatively open space before I feel our spent momentum dragging us down.

As we thud—upright—onto our air cushion, I hear a strangled protest from Toshi.

"Yes, Toshi?" I say, sparing a glance to the side.

He is clutching his gun with both hands, his face pale. "Karen, the limo wasn't made for that."

"It worked," I comment, seeing with relief the flow of traffic at the alley's end, "better than a bullet in my head."

A picture of the gang leader with his weapon steady on me appears in my mind.

Toshi starts, then collects himself. The picture vanishes from my mind, but I suspect detail is added to his, for he grunts and turns to Onyx.

"Yes, I did seem to put Karen at risk," he says, "but I felt that the windshield was adequately reinforced to protect her even if he did have a chance to fire."

Another pause. I ease us into traffic and head for the UAN Tower, wishing Onyx was including me in her communication. Whatever she's showing, Toshi doesn't like it.

"Don't you accuse me!" he snaps. "Yes, I did open a shooting strip, but only on my side of the window."

I can't resist cutting in, "Be certain to shape a mental picture, Toshi. She's still not too good with words."

He growls, but, I suspect, complies. After that there is

no further conversation until we arrive at the imposing tower of stone and glass that is UAN Terran headquarters.

The building is like nothing else on Earth, built from a su-ankh design by Chirr architects. It is both official headquarters for the UAN and a visible symbol of the pact between the three races.

Su-ankh are amphibious, so they don't view the elements like humans or Chirr do. This structure reflects something of their philosophy. From the center of an artificial lake twists a tower that reminds me of nothing so much as a DNA helix.

The base is made from enormous blocks of rough metamorphic rock. The metal and glass that rises above shimmers like an oil slick in the demands of changing light. Midway up the tower's height, the building abruptly vanishes and is replaced by a curtain of water that mimics the helix curve before melding to rise again as apparently unsupported steel and glass.

The entire effect is weird, lovely, and impressive—precisely, I am certain, the designer's intention. Even today, which is wintery chill, tourists of the three races wander the lakeshore, taking pictures and tossing bread to the inevitable ducks and seagulls.

Normally, I would pause to admire the Tower, but today our business, combined with the gang's assault has immunized me to beauty. Stopping the limo near a gazebo-like guard-post bearing the legend "For Official Use Only" in a shifting collage of languages, I wait until a young man with the perpetually cheerful smile of a professional tour guide emerges. Only the way that his right hand never strays from the vicinity of his holstered weapon reveals that he is quite probably as deadly as one of our Knives.

"How may I help you?" he asks politely, his pale blue eyes widening slightly as he notes the fresh firearm scars on our paint work.

"My name is Karen Saber," I answer through the limo's external comm unit. "We have an appointment with Councilor DuPoy."

The guard touches a throat mike and relays the information. Reading his lips is difficult because he is subvocalizing most of his report, but I do catch that he has mentioned the damage to the limo.

With a warm smile, the guard returns his attention to us. "You are expected. Please wait one moment while I open the entrance. Enjoy your visit."

"Thank you," I murmur, not really caring if he hears.

From within the gazebo, the guard does something, and what I had taken for a decorative chunk of basalt rises about a meter into the air and then shifts to the left. The space it has vacated now reveals a large, well-lit tunnel. Waving to the guard, I take the limo forward, down, and under the lake.

Although there is no need to hold my breath, I find that I do, a reaction that's not unreasonable given the surroundings. Most Terran tunnels that go underwater are constructed to distract the traveller from recalling the tons of water pressing in on all sides. The su-ankh either are arrogantly confident about their design or have a different value system, with peace of mind secondary to aesthetic considerations.

I suspect a bit of both might be closest to the truth. The entry tunnel we traverse is made of a substance so clear that it might as well not be there. The direction we need to go is marked by pale pink lights. Following them, our limo hums along across a brightly lit lake bottom tenanted by myriad exotic swimmers.

"Hey!" Toshi exclaims, "Not all of these are Terran creatures. I'm certain that fuschia thing with all the fins is a su-ankh salome."

"I'm driving," I protest. "I can't sightsee."

Instantly, a portrait of the water dweller in question winks into my mind and then winks out.

"Thanks, Onyx. You may be right, Toshi, but I don't know much about alien fish."

"I don't either, really," he says, "but think about the engineering involved in creating all of these habitats under water without any cross-contamination. I'm impressed."

I smile, "I suspect that we may get a tour, Toshi."

"Yes," he says, suddenly serious, "and they may try and distract us or even woo us with some marvel."

A guard, apparently underwater, is waving to us from straight ahead. Obediently, I angle away from the pink lights over toward him. When I stop, I decide that like the tunnel this room is a carefully engineered illusion, but I still need to resist the urge to take a deep breath before opening the limo door.

"Karen Saber? Toshi Van Druuik? I am directed to tell you that your vehicle will be taken care of for you here. You and your companion are to take the lift to the first floor, where a reception committee will meet you."

"Thank you," I answer, smiling slightly as I note the guard's studied lack of curiosity about Onyx. "One question, if you might?"

"Yes, ma'am."

"Did a Chirr called Discoverer Shi Freesh come through? He was to meet us here."

"Yes, ma'am. He arrived just before you."

The lift proves to be a showy Chirr grav disk that wafts us up on a cushion of air. I jump when it starts and Toshi chuckles, but I notice that his hand tightens around the decorative bronze handrail in the center. Onyx flattens slightly to keep her balance, but appears unimpressed.

I barely have time to collect myself against this deluge of strangeness when the disk becomes the floor of a column of swirling mist that blows away as the floor locks into place beneath our feet.

The promised reception committee is waiting and with them is Freesh. The Chirr scientist is splendid in a beribboned dress version of the many-pocketed vest that he usually wears. The biggest change is not to his attire, but rather to his demeanor. Normally hyperactive, today he is almost frenetic. He hops forward almost before the lift disk has snapped into place, his whiskers curled forward in greeting.

"Karen, Onyx, Directors Toshi! I am pleased and relieved to see you. We had begun to worry that we were going to go into this meeting alone."

"No such luck, Freesh," I assure him, noting the escort concealing smiles.

A somewhat prim woman with a Hindu caste mark steps forward and bows.

"I am Anna Pradesh. I am honored to escort you to your meeting. May I know if any special arrangements need to be made?"

I shake my head, "Not as long as there is a chair that Onyx can see from. We have our gear with us."

"May I have your word that none of you are carrying any prohibited weapons?"

Smiling slightly, for I am certain that we have already been scanned in every way possible, I answer for all of us.

"Nothing we weren't born with, just as Director Van Druuik agreed in advance."

Ms. Pradesh bows again and motions for us to follow her. With a burst of insight, I realize that she is nervous. Hoping sincerely that she is merely overwhelmed by the honor of escorting the diplomatic party representing an alien race, I give Onyx a quick pat and then try hard to feel impressive.

The conference room we are escorted into would be generic except for two features. One is that the furniture is clearly designed for members of the three races; two, the walls are falling curtains of water. The air is extraordinarily fresh, without the canned feeling even the best climate control can give. Toshi glances around, clearly impressed.

"Be hard as hell to snoop this place," he mutters. "I wonder if we can contact their designers?"

"Later, Toshi, we're on," I whisper, too aware of the stares that follow us around the room.

"I know," he smiles and I realize that he does indeed, but has calculated his comments to make our entry appear as casual as possible.

Trying to seem as if I meet with aliens on a daily basis, I allow Ms. Pradesh to show me to where a group of chairs have been reserved at the end of an oval table. Only when Onyx leaps into the seat to my left and Freesh hops onto the ottomanlike seat to my right does the truth hit me.

I do meet with aliens on a daily basis! With that realization, much of my nervousness leaves me and I am able to study the select group gathered around this table.

The group is not large and I immediately recognize the two human members. One is Pavel DuPoy, the UAN councilor who, if we are correct, has been collaborating to conceal the sentience of Onyx's race. The other is a slender Finnish woman with hair the color of beaten silver. Her name is Aino Rand and for five years she has been the UAN Ambassador on the su-ankh home world. That she is here so soon after her highly publicized retirement says something about how seriously this matter is being dealt with.

I do not recognize the Chirr representatives, but from the little I catch of the whistles and clicks they exchange with Freesh, the smaller one with the snowy fur is also a member of the Xi-7 Survey team. The other, a stout individual with patchy brown and grey fur, is apparently a diplomat.

The last two members of the group, excepting Pradesh and a few other staff members, are both su-ankh. One has iridescent blue scales and green eyes. The other has gold eyes and white scales that blush gradually more pink until by the end of the creature's tail they are blood red.

For this last member, I do not need a name plate. She is the Honorable Kwan Yin, UAN Senior Ambassador on Terra. Remembering the source of the name she has adapted for her own, I feel heartened, believing we will find justice here.

Some of my optimism diminishes as Kwan Yin calls the meeting to order with a rap of her left upper talon against a crystal bell.

"We are here to answer allegations of misconduct regarding the alleged sentients of Xi-7."

She speaks in panlingi, her words echoing in English through the translator jack in my ear. For the rest of the long meeting all conversation is accompanied by the ghostly echo of a translation. Thus everyone is assured of understanding something even when speakers are not fluent in panlingi and so lapse into their native tongues.

"First, we will hear from Toshi Van Druuik."

Toshi stands, bows stiffly from the waist, and links his hands behind his back. With poise I respect even as I envy it, he addresses the councilors.

"Several weeks ago, the organization of which I am a Director was contacted and asked to decipher a message that had been found on the client's property. At that time, it was believed that the message might be related to some industrial espionage the company had been suffering."

He goes on recounting our work up to this point. The account is vague at points, for example when mentioning exactly how we acquired Onyx, but is truthful to a fault.

When he finishes, Kwan Yin taps her crystal bell.

"Any questions for this person?"

When there are none, she says, "Next, Karen Saber will prove to us that this Xi-7 entitity is sentient."

That's it. As I rise I notice that the posture of the audience has shifted. The white-furred Chirr looks at Freesh, then at DuPoy. For a moment, I think she is going to speak, but she settles back.

Clearing my throat, I begin, "I don't really know what you expect me to do. I'm not a scientist and you should be talking to Onyx, not to me. I can tell you how to do it and even translate, sort of, but I don't have any idea what proofs you expect."

There is a rustle of comments, then Kwan Yin says, carefully, "We may speak with this Onyx?"

"Well," I say, "You can speak and she'll understand some of it. From what I've learned, her form of communication isn't verbal."

"No?" Rrufeep, the brown and grey Chirr, asks. "How then?"

"By mentally transmitted pictures," I answer, aware of incredulous stares from several of the councilors, "Wait. It isn't that crazy, but she does seem to need some time with a person before she can—or will—talk to them."

I turn to Onyx, "Onyx, I believe that you know some of these people."

The picture she sends me is absolute blackness. Puzzled, I look at her. Painstakingly, I frame a picture of the members of the group that I believe Onyx should recognize.

"These, Onyx."

Again the blackness. Then against it, she sketches flat representations of the white Chirr, DuPoy, and Freesh. Beside these she adds the Scout Survey ship. Then again, deep blackness.

Toshi leans forward to look at me.

"She seems to agree and yet to disagree at the same time. Strange."

"What charade is this?" Rrufeep exclaims. "You will not convince us in this fashion. We need incontrovertible proof."

"Calm down," I demand, "Calm down! No other race has faced review under such abrupt circumstances."

"You assume much, human," Kwan Yin says softly, "but you are liaison for this creature. I will follow your suggestions for now. Do not be too outrageous."

"Fine," I nod sharply. "First of all, this meeting started with too many assumptions."

I hear Toshi hiss but push on.

"We all assumed that we know each other and in a way we do—by reputation. But the most important member of this group is at a grave disadvantage. Onyx knows nothing of the UAN, of your honorable selves, and you certainly don't expect her to read the nameplates. Why don't we introduce ourselves?"

A startled silence meets my suggestion. Sighing again, I act as if I hadn't noticed. I smile.

"Let me start. I am Karen Saber, Allain Corp Director. My specialization is translation and related matters."

For a moment, I don't think that anyone will accept my lead. Toshi is stirring to his feet when the lithe white su-ankh rises.

"I am called Kwan Yin, as my personal name does not shape well to mouths shaped not like ours. I am the principal UAN Ambassador of the Terran conciliate."

The blue su-ankh rises almost before Kwan Yin has taken her seat, "I am called Sango. My position is Curiosity."

I feel my eyebrows creep up to my hairline, "Pardon?"

The elegant salamander head tilts to one side and a pearly film slips across the green eye. Sango considers, then tries another term in his own language.

This time his position is given as "Investigative/ Comparative Anthropologist." I nod, wondering if Onyx is making anything at all of this.

The next person to rise is Rrufeep.

"We are Rrufeep, currently released from clan obligations to represent the Chirr in the UAN Terran conciliate."

"We are Ooohoop," says the white Chirr, the translator struggling to render the double whistle of her name. "Until a short time ago, we served as senior Discoverer on the UAN Survey ship *Blue Jay*. Currently, we are preparing to return to the home world and clan obligations. This hearing delays us."

DuPoy and Rand introduce themselves with admirable brevity that DuPoy, at least, must have borrowed from the aliens. I've heard him on video and he must love the sound of his own voice. Heavens knows, no one else could.

While Toshi and Freesh introduce themselves, I mull

over Ooohoop's answer. Clearly, she wants to get home without delay. I wonder if what drives her is a personal or public consideration.

Toshi seats himself and Kwan Yin says softly, "Now, may we continue with this hearing?"

I am starting to reply when the words are strangled in my throat by a sending from Onyx.

The image is of a velvet meadow carpeted with a plant the rich yellow gold of a setting sun. Into this walk eight Xians, each as midnight black as Onyx. They meet in the center of the golden meadow, their noses nearly touching, a black star against the blazing sun.

Under the table, I gently stroke a panting Onyx, shaken by the beauty of the vision. Around the table, I see what I believe is a reflection of the same awe. In this spirit of relief and relaxation, Ooohoop's words shock me.

"What is the point of this display?" she whistles indignantly.

"Point?" Toshi says, "Display? What the hell?"

"These psionic pictures," she clarifies. "Why do you make them?"

"Me?" "Us?" Toshi and I blurt simultaneously. Then I laugh.

"No, no. We aren't doing anything. Onyx was simply introducing herself."

Ooohoop titters, "You think us so simple, human Directors Saber? You arrange this circle of friendly introductions and then plant the 'introduction.' We know rare humans have such abilities. You cannot fool us so."

Support comes from an unexpected source.

"No," Aino Rand says, "I am one of these human talents, Ooohoop, although my abilities are limited. However, I can confirm what Director Saber says. The sending came from Onyx."

"That proves nothing," DuPoy says. "The creature could have been trained to send a set message at a given signal."

I look helplessly at Toshi and Freesh. Onyx's panting

is subsiding, but to those of us who know her, clearly the multiple sending to unfamiliar minds has tired her. I hope she's up to the hours that this meeting is certain to run.

Kwan Yin waves all four hands outward in a sweeping gesture, "I must rule with DuPoy. Although we have evidence that Onyx has psionic abilities, we do not yet have evidence that she can use them with independent volition. Let us continue."

For the next several hours we argue, debate, and demonstrate. The Survey team's classified report is accessed and we adjourn for a few hours to study its contents. While we review it, Onyx sleeps.

Freesh chitters angrily as he recalls the initial drafting of the report during the voyage to Terra. "Over-ruled! Over-ruled! We were time and again while the Xians were drugged, so that even those who were in doubt were finally forced to admit that there was reason to report them as nonsentient. Matters were made worse in that much of the Team was enthusiastic about the wealth of the planet and the apparent ease of colonization."

Glancing at the clock, Toshi stretches, "About time to get back and try again, folks. We'll push the comparative biochem again and let Onyx keep showing them how well she, at least, fits their criteria."

"We fear," Freesh says, "that in doing the latter we defeat ourselves. The most private space for any person is the space between their ears; the second is the space around their bodies. This is what makes the Xian's abilities so terrifying. They negate both regularly."

"Then," I say, "even if the Xians didn't have such nicely positioned real estate there would still be a reluctance to admit them."

"Yes," Freesh answers, "I think so. I know so."

Onyx studies us as we somberly head out. As usual, I wonder what she is thinking.

Almost before we settle into the conference room, Toshi, bless him (bless him?), is ready to launch into a second explanation of how Onyx and the other Xians must have been drugged so that they could neither communicate nor manipulate their environments in any purposeful fashion. DuPoy and Ooohoop are obviously ready to counter with their established arguments that the "specimens" were sedated to prepare them for travel. Kwan Yin, however, cuts the debate off before it can warm.

"Hush, hush," she hisses, "we have swum in these waters before and they are no fitter for the exertions. During our private conference, Sango noted that the eloquence of positions on either side matters not, so long as one single point remains in question."

Sango picks up the thread. "What is essential to establish is the question of whether this Onyx is capable of independent thought, reasoning, and decision, or whether she is dependent upon some outside agent—most likely Director Saber—for some signals or coaching."

No one protests, though Rrufeep twitches his tail restlessly. Sango continues.

"I have proposed to Kwan Yin that Onyx be given an opportunity to be tested without her guardians present. Only in this fashion will a control on the data be established."

Toshi leaps to his feet, "Honorable Kwan Yin! I must protest. We have told you of the murder of Onyx's companions and the state in which we found her. We cannot leave her without protection!"

"I guarantee her safety," the su-ankh says frostily, "and this building is well guarded. She should be safe."

"We only propose a brief test," Sango adds. "You have demonstrated the Onyx is capable of playing chess. We propose that she play a game with me. I am not unskilled and will choose an opening not at all like any of those used in your demonstration games. In a few games, her reasoning ability should be established, at least to the point that we can order a delay on the colony ships and send a new set of orders to the Survey team."

Aino Rand nods, "Su-ankh take promises seriously, Director Van Druuik. One of their most respected philosophers has said that 'Promises are the only constant in the shifting realms of existence.' You may believe that Kwan Yin and Sango will do their best to keep Onyx safe.''

''There were su-ankh on the survey team,'' I protest, ''and yet the Xians were abused.''

''Then they were not given the su-ankh's promise,'' Rand states. ''I know Mimir, one of the members of that Team. If she had given her promise she would have personally stayed with the Xians until they returned home.''

A picture blossoms into our conversation: Onyx across a chessboard from Sango. She is playing black and the picture fades with the white king tipping over.

Sango hisses with bright laughter, ''Onyx accepts the test then. Arrogantly! I am delighted to give my promise here.''

DuPoy and Ooohoop have stayed quiet throughout this discussion, but they listen carefully as, with Rand's help, Toshi and I hammer out the best protection that we can for Onyx. No one will be permitted to watch the game, even by video, to reduce the chance that Onyx could telepathically reach out for coaching. The game, however, will be played on a computer board that will record each move and the time in between them.

Impulsively, I kneel and squeeze her before I leave. ''Good luck, girl,'' I whisper.

The picture that she sends is of a bowl and a mug of coffee side by side, their steams wreathing to intertwine. Then I am cleared away with the rest. The last sound I hear is the click of chess pieces being set up on a board and Sango asking Onyx, ''Black or white?''

TWELVE

WE RETIRE TO THE SAME SMALL CONFERENCE ROOM where we had been before and I kick the table.

''Easy, Karen,'' Toshi chides. ''Onyx knows what she's doing. This is such a perfect solution I only wonder why we didn't come up with it earlier.''

''We did,'' I remind him sourly, ''and discarded it as too dangerous for Onyx. Damn! Damn! Damn!''

I kick the table again. Freesh chitters anxiously.

''Calm, Directors Saber. Calm! We dig not tunnels to these people by breaking their furniture.'' He pats the stool next to his own. ''Come. I will distract you by correcting your use of our trade language.''

Reluctantly I do as I'm told. Miraculously, the lesson in chirps and whistles does distract me somewhat—I only check my watch every few minutes. Toshi alternates between drowsing and hammering fiercely on his datapad. If the shrillness of my conversation with Freesh annoys him, he's apparently willing to suffer through it.

However, my patience wears out despite Freesh's distraction.

''It's been a half hour,'' I announce. ''They should have come for us by now. What's happening?''

''Chess,'' Toshi says wearily, ''is a slow game. Doubtless, Sango is trying some difficult or obscure strategies to keep from the accusation that Onyx could be being fed the data.''

''Hmm,'' I growl and let Freesh continue his lessons.

''It's been an hour,'' I announce thirty minutes later.

''Karen . . .'' Toshi is beginning, when Freesh makes a silencing gesture. We freeze and the plump Chirr hops over to the door and stands listening. I strain, but hear nothing. Only when the Chirr signals for the door to open and is refused does the vague worry I have been nursing crystalize into panic.

''What did you hear?'' I demand.

''Many footsteps and raised voices,'' he replies.

Toshi, meanwhile, is kneeling by the door, investigating the lock.

''Sealed from without,'' he announces, ''but I may be able to open it. First, Karen, you get on the comm and ask some questions. I'll reserve the questionable methods of getting this open until we're sure that we need them.''

''Fine,'' I say, keying on the comm.

''And, Karen,'' Toshi warns, ''be tactful. We don't want these people to become angry at us or to realize that we're suspicious.''

''Of course.''

I shift my attention to the comm and signal the central conference room. After an appreciable delay, it is answered by Anna Pradesh.

''Ms. Pradesh,'' I say calmly, introducing myself, although the view screen makes that unnecessary, ''Director Saber here. We were wondering about the progress of the chess game.''

She licks her lips. ''It is progressing, Director. I can't offer any details of course. The game is being played in private.''

''Certainly, I hadn't forgotten. After all, no interference was the purpose of this particular trial. Onyx must be doing wonderfully well if she has held her own this long against an experienced player. Perhaps we should call the point settled.''

"Perhaps," Ms. Pradesh blinks, "but I am not qualified to decide that matter."

"No," I say, "you are not. Kwan Yin is, however. May I speak with her?"

Again the blink. Either Ms. Pradesh has eye trouble or she is very nervous. I'd bet the latter.

Blink. "Kwan Yin is not available."

"I see." Counting to ten by twos, I control myself, "No doubt she is resting or involved in some important business. Very well."

"I will relay your thoughts," her hand reaches for the cut tab.

"Ms. Pradesh? One more question."

"Yes, Director Saber?" she asks warily.

"Why is the door to our room locked?"

"For your safety," she replies with a flutter of eyelashes.

"From outside?" I counter, leveling my tone to neutral at Toshi's warning gesture.

"Yes, Director, that is standard procedure here."

"I understand," I smile sweetly. "Thank you so much for your time and please relay my message to Kwan Yin."

I let her cut the call off before I wheel to Toshi and Freesh. "She's lying! Something is wrong!"

"Of course," Toshi agrees urbanely. "We knew that before you called. Now we know that whatever it is is serious enough to merit both lying to a visiting diplomatic party and imprisoning them. Under those circumstances, I think we are quite justified in letting ourselves out of here."

Freesh clicks an agreement that the translator gives as "Okay."

I nod sharply, "Can you do it?"

"I believe so," Toshi's blue eyes narrow. "I will need quiet and access to our in-room terminal."

I collapse back onto a sofa, sipping ice water. Freesh crouches by the door, one petal-like ear close to the surface. Toshi puts his datapad next to the in-room computer and begins doing incomprehensible things. All I know is that he is not decrypting the lock code, but rather accessing a series of—I suspect—secured files.

Several aeons pass in this fashion, although my watch stubbornly assures me that only five minutes have gone by. Then Toshi pockets his datapad and leans back with a grunt of satisfaction.

"It should open any moment now. Freesh, you might want to stand away."

"What did . . ." I begin, but he waves me to silence.

"Wait and see," he promises.

A few anxious minutes later there is a discrete buzz, then the door swings open. In rolls an automated cart of the type I've seen in a few of the better hotels. It bears a steaming coffee urn, a basket of sweet rolls, and a pitcher of orange juice.

Freesh hurries to block open the door while Toshi scoops up the butter knife and drops it into his pocket.

"Room Service," he explains as we sprint out of our former prison. "The standard programming in those includes a 'wake-up call' that permits that cart to open locked doors. The idea is that the guest awakens to a hot breakfast delivered without fuss. I'd noticed that the Tower was using them earlier and bet that they hadn't wiped the standard programming just because no one here is likely to want breakfast in bed."

"Cute," I acknowledge. "Damn! I'm all disoriented. Which way do we go?"

"Here," Freesh whistles, waving us after him. "I recall and, in any case, I can hear something in this direction."

We pad after him and fortunately no one intercepts us. I can feel the damp air when Freesh gestures us to a halt.

My ears are not as good as the Chirr's, but then the people arguing aren't making any effort to stay quiet.

". . . ripped out!" says a male voice. "Certainly, we must assume that it is dangerous. The building must be cleared."

"No," Kwan Yin replies, "it may escape in the confusion. I advise that you simply increase precautions and continue searching. Where can it go?''

''Director Saber called a few minutes ago,'' says Anna Pradesh. ''I believe that they are becoming suspicious.''

''As well they might,'' DuPoy says, ''since they must have known how vicious that creature could be.''

I glance at Toshi. They must be talking about Onyx, but vicious? Anything but. I start to move forward, but both Toshi and Freesh indicate that they want to listen further.

''Keep them in their room,'' Kwan Yin orders, ''and request that Ooohoop and Rrufeep do the same. Ask Aino Rand to come to me. I will need her advice. You, DuPoy, are free within the building, but do not leave.''

''Yes, Honorable,'' he says.

''Shall I report search progress to you?'' asks the male voice—a security chief I'd guess.

''No,'' Kwan Yin says, ''Report to me only when the Xian is found. Otherwise, use your discretion or consult with Pradesh.''

''Yes, Honorable.''

Five breaths to let him retreat and then I poke Toshi.

''C'mon,'' I breathe, ''we've got to be open about this.''

Reluctantly, he trails me as I round the corner and march up to the startled Pradesh and the impassive Kwan Yin. DuPoy is gone; he must have left with the security chief.

''Greetings,'' I say stiffly, trying to project indignation without words. ''I have come to find out the results of the chess game.''

Some emotion shivers across Kwan Yin's shiny, smooth skin and snaps the end of her blood red tail.

''You have that right,'' she says. ''Come. Touch nothing.''

We follow her into the conference room. The chess board sits on the table, a game still set up, but the results are the last thing I care about.

Sango sprawls awkwardly on the floor by the table and there is no doubt that he is dead. His slender throat near the base of his jaw has been ripped open and a substance other than human blood has leaked out. His green eyes are coated with a milky film.

"Damn," Toshi whispers. Freesh chitters something that the translator doesn't accept, but from what I catch it has to do with collapsed tunnels and crushed bodies. I merely stare.

"Your 'friend' did this," Kwan Yin states.

"How do you know?" I reply. "Did you see it happen?"

"No, but . . ." Kwan Yin begins, but I interrupt.

"I know, I know. But no one else was in the room. Sango has been bitten and Onyx is gone."

"Well," Kwan Yin admits, "that is my thinking."

"And the motive for this action?" Toshi asks, recovering smoothly.

Pradesh indicates the chessboard, "From what we can tell, Sango was playing White, Onyx—appropriately—Black. White has checkmated Black. Our theory is that when Onyx lost she became enraged and charged Sango, who, caught off guard, was easily slain."

"Strange," Freesh says, hopping to where he can see the board, "that the creature who could play such a fine game—White did not mate easily—would then lose her temper so easily. Odd indeed. And odd too that a crime of such passion would not even unsettle the board."

"I don't know," comes a voice from the doorway. "I once played chess with a woman who played a fine game most of the time. One game I maneuvered her out of a bishop she was counting on. She surrendered the piece to me only after biting it in half."

We turn and Pavel DuPoy is behind us.

"In half?" Toshi asks.

"Well, the upper part from the lower," DuPoy says amiably. "It was a cheap plastic travel set. I'd come to report that the Allain Corp delegation wasn't in their quarters. I see they're here.''

''Yes,'' Kwan Yin says dryly.

''Then you don't need to know,'' he turns to leave.

''We will, of course, not be returning to our quarters, but will be assisting in the search for Onyx,'' Toshi says.

''Of course,'' DuPoy says, ''but of course.''

When he is gone and Kwan Yin is distracted by Pradesh arriving with the message that Aino Rand awaits her in her office, I whisper to Toshi, ''That was too easy.''

''Yes,'' he agrees, ''This isn't good. I need to talk with Tammany. You see, I suspect that if Onyx were here DuPoy would be more upset that we're out and insisting on helping.''

''My thoughts exactly,'' I say, ''and that gives me an idea.''

''An idea?'' Freesh says. ''Good, we need many of these.''

I quirk a smile. ''Sorry, just one. Toshi, do what you can about talking with Tammany. I'll meet back with you after I talk with Aino Rand.''

''Aino Rand?'' he says turning.

''Yes, Aino Rand,'' I say. ''I have a thought.''

The guard at the door to Kwan Yin's office refuses me entrance. I expected this and even as I argue with him the bulk of my attention is centered on something I've never attempted with anyone but Onyx.

''Aino Rand,'' I shape, building up a picture in my mind of the serious, silver-haired diplomat, dressing her as I had seen her last. The guard holds his place, but the door flies open from within and from her seat to the side of Kwan Yin's desk Aino Rand gestures for me to enter.

''Director Saber,'' Rand says, ''come in, please.''

When the door is closed, she continues, ''Your method of contact was—curious. For how long have you known that you were psionic?'

I blink, ''I'm not. I just learned to concentrate to talk

with Onyx. I figured that what worked with her would work with you.''

For a moment, Rand looks offended, then a smile brightens her angular features. ''It did. It did. Now, what may I do for you?''

I bow to Kwan Yin, who has watched this byplay with bubble-eyed amazement.

''My apologies for disturbing your meeting, Honorable, but I believe that Aino Rand can help locate Onyx.''

Rand is quick to see the direction of my thoughts.

''You want me to track her by psionics—telepathically.''

''Yes,'' I answer. ''That way, if she isn't inclined to come out on her own you still might be able to talk with her.''

''She hasn't attempted to contact you?'' Kwan Yin says.

''No, Honorable,'' I say, ''and that puzzles me. I want her found so that this problem can be resolved.''

After some discussion with Kwan Yin, Rand agrees.

''The range of my ability is quite limited,'' she explains, ''and is not really suited for finding something that must have experience shielding its thoughts. Therefore, I want you to walk with me and call for her. It may be that in finding you near, Onyx will give something away and I will be able to sense that.''

''Sounds good,'' I agree. ''Let me go and fill Toshi in, then I'll be back.''

Toshi is just clicking off his datapad when I find him and brief him on my plan. He nods.

''Good, be showy about it. I've spoken privately with Tammany and she agrees with me that—''

''Stop,'' I say, holding up a hand. ''I don't know how well Rand reads minds or if she'd even care to read mine, but the less I know at this point, the better.''

Toshi smiles and nods, ''Good thinking, Karen.''

As I'm heading back to join Rand, I pass DuPoy. He smiles without warmth and slows.

''I understand that you've come up with a creative way to locate the Xian creature,'' he says. ''I hope that Rand does not wear herself out.''

I turn to meet his gaze, wishing that I *could* read minds.

''It's a great deal of work, I know,'' I reply, ''and considering the best we can hope for is a murder trial, I suppose a fairly painful job.''

''Murder trial?'' DuPoy says, arching an eyebrow. ''Those are for people. We shoot dogs—alien or not.''

He is gone before I can recover from my shock; with a sensation of dread, I hurry to meet Aino Rand.

Our quest is fruitless, garnering little more than stares from UAN workers of the three races, all too well trained to comment. Aino Rand is shaking by the time we finish, but puzzlement rather than irritation dominates her mood as we return to Kwan Yin's office.

''Nothing,'' she tells Kwan Yin, between sips of a hot su-ankh beverage, ''nothing. Chief Teissech cleared each section as we came through and we used a map of the Tower that included all service crawlways and cubbies. Not only didn't I sense anything—which is reasonable—but the investigative team that went with us to look for more mundane evidence found nothing.''

She drains her cup and refills it before continuing.

''I knew one of the members of the search crew—a su-ankh named Horus. He had been on my staff at the Consulate on your homeworld. If Horus the Hawk could not find any sign of a creature who had never been in this building before today, I wonder what route it took to escape.''

''Hmm,'' Kwan Yin meditates, then shifts her attention to me. ''Director Saber, have you seen any evidence of peculiar transportation methods used by the Xian while it was in your custody?''

''No, *she*,'' I say, stressing the pronoun, ''did use telekinesis, as demonstrated earlier, but I never saw her move anything much heavier than ten kilos. She never levitated or teleported or anything like that, just walked. And the people who were holding her and her kin had them strapped into their cages, which wouldn't have done much good if they could teleport.''

''Until the drugs took effect,'' Kwan Yin reminds me. ''You did indicate that they had been drugged.''

''Yes, Honorable,'' I reply, ''they had been.''

''A shame that your Allain Corp scientist who did the tests is no longer alive,'' Kwan Yin comments. ''She could have been very useful to this investigation.''

I find myself devotedly agreeing, a curious sensation given that recently I would have given much to see Qiang dead.

Unbidden, another question nags at me. Might this mess have been avoided if Vance were still alive? He would never have agreed to leave Onyx alone without having a tracer put on her. Would our labs and my house have been sabotaged if Rhys had been alive to direct security? I've been patting myself on the back for allowing Toshi, Tammany, and Anton the chance to help Onyx and me and thus to redeem themselves for Mr. Allain's death, but have I created this situation by my own actions?

''Director Saber? Karen?'' Aino Rand's voice pulls me from my revery.

With a flash of panic, I wonder if she is recovered enough to read my thoughts.

''Sorry,'' I muster a grin, ''woolgathering. This has been a hell of a day.''

Kwan Yin dips her head in agreement. ''Your colleague, Van Druuik, has petitioned that your delegation be permitted to leave, and I have agreed on the condition that you report finding Onyx to me immediately.''

I sense that she still suspects that Onyx may be able to teleport—a talent claimed by certain rare su-ankh as the logical extension of an amphibious nature. If Onyx has departed the Tower in such a fashion, she may come to us.

''I understand,'' I say, rising. ''Thank you, Honorable,

and thank you, too, Councilor Rand. I am sorry we weren't more fortunate in our search."

"We will meet again to resolve this issue," Kwan Yin says, her inflection giving me no clue as to whether she means this as threat or promise. "Good day."

Toshi and Freesh are waiting for me, but we save talking not only until we are clear of the UAN Tower but also until we have met with Tammany and a Corp van at an underpass in a small park.

She sniffs us for bugs, turns the limo over to a Knife. The entire exchange takes less than a minute and no other vehicles pass us. Once we're out of the congested areas, Tammany puts us on autopilot on a major interstate.

"Where are we going?" I ask.

"To get Onyx," she says, "I hope."

"What!" I exclaim.

Freesh chitters amusement and Toshi smiles.

"You asked me not to tell you earlier," he says, "but I suspected early on that Onyx was not in the UAN Tower as soon as we saw the murder site. The whole thing was too neat. When I remembered our brush with the gang earlier and DuPoy's lack of protest over the chess game, I felt certain that I was right. I let you go on with your search both on the off-chance that Onyx was there and as cover. If DuPoy and his allies believed that we thought Onyx was there, then he wouldn't look for us to be looking elsewhere."

"And," Freesh chitters, "you impressed both Aino Rand and Kwan Yin because of your eagerness to help rather than to argue. This is good."

"But where is she? And how did you find out?"

Tammany laughs, "Where? StarUs, we think. How? When Toshi filled me in, including his suspicions that Onyx had been removed from the UAN Tower, I set one of the Hands to work on tapping the oversight satellite that is geosync over the Tower to provide data for circumstances precisely like this one."

"Of course, that data is not meant for public use,"

Freesh says, shaking the tip of his tail at her like an admonishing finger.

''No,'' Tammany agrees, ''but we felt that building security had to have been compromised and, even if it had not, only a fool would have removed Onyx in a fashion that could be seen by internal security—active or passive. So we went to the top.''

I groan at the pun and she grins before continuing.

''I couldn't do the tap myself—we're so damn short-staffed—but the Hand I put on it was good. He got in and I had him download us a picture of all the action around the UAN complex from the time the chess game started through the present. Next, I set a couple of Hands on getting the ID on every vehicle that left the place and running it through our link with Vehicle Registration.''

''Again, illegal!'' Freesh whistles, manically delighted.

''Hey, pouch brother,'' she says, ''it was for a good cause.''

''These Hands,'' Toshi says, worry thinning his blue eyes, ''are they clean? I'm still worried about a leak.''

''Clean or no,'' Tammany replies, ''there won't be a leak. I've Knives watching them, just like Ben did back when we pulled the Sahara bit.''

Toshi seems satisfied, so I am, though the job they refer to is unfamiliar to me.

''How did you find Onyx?'' I prompt.

''Well, most of the vehicles checked out as pretty unpromising and I was wondering if we would need to start checking pedestrian departures, when one of the Hands came up with a service van with a StarUs registration. Funny thing was that its paint job claimed that it was from a stationery supply company.''

''Sloppy, sloppy,'' Toshi murmurs.

''Hey, they're amateurs,'' Tammany says before going on. ''We traced it via satellite. When we were sure it was heading to the main StarUs shipyards, we made some calls and set up this rendezvous.''

I nod, "Did you get through to Anton?"

"Yes," she says. "He's checking things out and should contact us before we get there and tell us the best way to get in. That's why we're driving down—speed wouldn't serve us as well as information will."

Toshi yawns, "I'm beat."

"Me, too," I admit, "but I'm too nervous to sleep."

"A field op can always sleep," Toshi says, tilting back his seat. "Try and learn a new skill."

"Go, sleep," Freesh assures me, "Tammany, too. Chirr sleep differently than humans and this van drives itself. I will wake for crisis or call if either comes."

Tammany agrees so readily that I, too, lean my seat back. Maybe because I've missed my usual allotment of coffee or maybe because I'm wiped out, the gentle hum of the van along the interstate gradually lulls me under.

I'm dreaming that Onyx and I are back camping in the park when the sounds of conversation bring me around. At first, I let them mingle with the last rags of my dream, then I hear Anton's voice and shake myself alert.

"...her, but it doesn't look good," he is saying. "There's a parking area by the StarUs airfield where employees who are flying on company business can leave their vehicles. I'm leaving my flitter there for you. No one should notice and if you use the East entry the electronic guard will put you through. I'll try and keep anything bad from happening until you get here."

He clicks off and Toshi notices that I'm awake.

"How much of that did you catch?"

"Enough. He's found her and he's worried." I stretch, fumbling for a hot bottle that Tammany holds out to me. "My question is, why is DuPoy doing all of this? He as much as told me that Onyx was dead meat if she was found. Why sneak her away?"

"I think that I know," Tammany says, winning a look of surprise from Toshi. "I did a deep background check on him before this broke. He's in bad trouble financially—a love affair that went bad and a couple of poor investments. My guess is that he stands to gain financially the longer Xi-7 is open, but that cash will be slow to materialize.

"On the other hand, Onyx is a commodity that he can sell right off, and from what Anton was saying, apparently he's found some buyers in the biological sciences. My guess is that the price was higher if she was alive upon delivery. How long they keep her alive will depend largely on whether what they want to learn they can learn from a corpse."

Freesh whistles, "Yes, yes. I can see this happening. I know the scientific community. A first publication will count for much in prestige and position. Since Onyx's clanfolk were killed and their bodies destroyed and the chances of others coming from Xi-7 is now unlikely for several years, Onyx is a valuable asset."

"Can't we go any faster?" I plead.

"No," Toshi says, "we can't without attracting attention at this point. We're just going to have to sit back and trust Anton."

Trust Anton. Trust Toshi. Trust Tammany. And somewhere in StarUs's sprawl is Onyx. Is she thinking "Trust Karen"? Dear lord, I hope so. The alternative is that she is dead or doped or so tormented that she trusts nothing.

We speed along and day shifts into evening and into night. Beneath the orange backglow of a cloudy urban sky, we change our van for the modest flitter that is part of Anton's cover here at StarUs.

Tammany is sliding into the driver's seat when Anton comes trotting across, opens the passenger door, and gets in.

"Hi," he says. "Tammany, we don't need to go in. Onyx was moved a half hour ago. I put a tracer on the vehicle."

"Where did they take her?" I demand.

He grins, "This airfield. No plane has lifted, so we still have time. Pile into the back of the van and I'll get us through the checkpoints."

While we pile, he pulls ID data from the flitter. I hold my breath when we come to the gate, but Anton gets us past the checkpoint easily. Ignoring the marked lanes, he cuts across the runway toward a small hanger beside which a beige pickup truck with a covered back is parked.

"That's the truck they took her in," Anton says unnecessarily. "I told the gate we were meeting them, so I don't expect any pursuit, but it's anyone's guess if they're still there."

"Or if the gate has called ahead," Toshi adds, leaning forward as if that could hurry us faster. "Be ready to hit the ground running."

"Be there, Onyx," I plead silently, "We're almost there. We haven't forgotten you. Just hold on."

I keep up my silent prayer as Anton jerks us to a halt, leaving the van to block the hangar doors.

"Go around left, Tosh," Anton calls. "I'll cut right."

I'm following Anton when the hangar doors slowly begin to rise. From inside, there are shouts of surprise.

"Through here!" I yell and run in, trusting the others to follow.

There are four people within. One, a stocky woman in chocolate brown coveralls, throws herself on the ground and rolls under the light plane that is parked in the middle of the hangar. Guessing that she's the pilot and that the three indignantly advancing on me are Onyx's captors, I dismiss her and continue towards the plane.

"Onyx! Onyx! I'm here, girl!"

"What is this intrusion?" demands a gangling black man, striding to intercept me.

His companion, a short red-haired man, seems less confident, but blusters, "This is a private facility!"

The third member of the group, a woman in a lab coat, her long brown hair twisted in a bun, keeps splitting her attention between the plane and me.

Deciding, I angle myself at her, beginning to run.

"Onyx! Onyx!"

There isn't any yap of welcome, but, then, I didn't expect one. Instead, a cup of coffee steams into my mind, just before the woman's long hair comes tumbling down. She cries out, and I dodge between the two men and past her.

There are shouts behind me. I spare a glance to see Tammany floor the red-haired man with an impressive clip to the jaw. Toshi flips the gangling man down and twists his arm behind his back.

I jump inside of the plane's cargo hatch, confident in their ability to secure things behind me. Onyx is there, crated, but otherwise unrestrained.

As I crawl in beside her, she perks up her ears and projects a picture of herself apparently deep asleep while the cage is hauled from building to vehicle and finally to the plane. Although her rib cage rises and falls evenly, her image shows me her eyes slitting open like stained brass to watch her captors.

"You played dead—or at least asleep!" I answer, "Smart. That way they didn't bother to dope you."

She shows me an image of DuPoy forcing something into her mouth and squeezing her nose until she had no choice but to swallow or suffocate. The backdrop is sketched in but lightly; still there is enough detail for me to recognize the UAN conference room where Sango had been killed.

"You'd already been drugged once," I amend, "so it was easier for you to convince them that you were asleep, even with lots of movement and rough handling."

She nods. Before we can talk further, Anton has climbed into the cockpit of the plane and is flipping switches. Outside, I catch fragments of conversation between Tammany and Toshi. It's rather terse, but the basic import is that they're going to leave Onyx's "owners" tied up in the hangar and park both vehicles inside. With luck and the pilot riding along to make sure that we are cleared for departure, we should be able to make our escape by air.

"Won't they be able to trace us by the van's registration?" I ask.

"They'll know who did it," Toshi says. "We were seen and didn't term the witnesses—though we did give them a hit of Oblivion. Anyhow, who else would snatch Onyx? The van doesn't matter."

"But they won't trace us through the van," Tammany adds, without moving from where she crouches with a gun to the back of the pilot's neck. "I worked up a fake registry. It's listed as belonging to StarUs. Let them puzzle it out."

"Where are we going?" I ask as the plane lifts and heads purposefully into the night sky.

"To a shuttle field," answers Freesh, who has been so quiet that I had forgotten him—which says something about these last few days. "Tammany has made contact with some Chirr merchants. We are going to keep our promise and take Onyx home."

"But what about Sango's death?" I sputter in amazement.

"If we make it," Toshi says, "we'll drop a message capsule coded for Kwan Yin only. It will explain everything we know. That will have to do. Terra isn't safe for Onyx and I suspect it isn't too safe for us if we continue to pursue this."

"And we will," Anton promises. "We must if the three races are to continue in peace."

I reach to unlatch Onyx's cage. "The four, now."

THIRTEEN

THE SHUTTLE PORT ISN'T ANYTHING LIKE WHAT I'D EXpected. It does have its own airport and ample parking to accommodate a variety of traffic. It does have crystalline control towers that oversee the comings and goings of the fat-bellied shuttles that commute between the two space stations and orbital space craft.

Educated about space travel by videos that showed clear, clean landing ways filled with purposeful, organized crowds, I am utterly unprepared for the chaos of a working port. The entire sprawling area resembles a commercial airport on a major holiday. Flitters dodge each other on poorly marked roadways; members of the three races hurry about on foot or on zipbikes. No one seems to know where they are going—or rather everyone knows where they are going and is taking the most direct route there.

I had been worrying how we were going to get Onyx to our shuttle without being seen, but my worry evaporates. In this mess, we'll be lucky to stay with each other.

Onyx agrees to return to her crate. Freesh squeezes in with her. Then we toss a tarp over it to conceal our cargo. By the time Anton comes whistling back from disposing of the plane, Toshi has found us a redcap disk, onto which we slide the lot. Tammany pushes the controls and the disk hovers.

"Let's flank the redcap," Anton suggests, "so we'll

stay together. Our shuttle is in the cargo loading area and is waiting for us. They have a takeoff window set for forty-five minutes from now—so we have time.''

''Maybe'' is Tammany's sole comment as she commands the redcap to follow her. I share her feeling. Forty-five minutes seems little enough time to get fifty feet, much less halfway across this mess.

Anton and Tammany lead the way with a casual purposefulness that tells me that they have been here before. Toshi trails the redcap with the introspective expression he gets when plotting something. Only I seem to have wonder to spare for the colorful mass of human, Chirr, and su-ankh.

I can remember, if dimly, when aliens belonged to the pages of fiction and sensational newsrags. Oddly, even though I am so nervous that my heart threatens to stop every time anyone wearing a UAN uniform or looking even vaguely official goes by, I realize that I am happy. Silently, I promise myself that I will come back and take a tour in one of the squat, bubble-topped vans that lumber around the periphery of the action, extolling the marvels of progress to the people clustered inside.

The cargo areas off the main concourse are marginally less chaotic, perhaps because the tourists and liner passengers have been siphoned off into other sections. The top-heavy cargo flats, giant cousins to our little redcap, offer their own threat, barreling down corridors and roadways with the same ''I'm bigger so clear out of my way'' arrogance that the Mack trucks had lorded over the interstates of my childhood.

I'm relieved when Anton says, ''That's it. Bay C8. That must be one of the crew waiting for us.''

A somewhat chewed-looking Chirr, golden brown and fluffy like a teddy bear hamster rather than prairie dog sleek, hops out to greet us.

''Hey, Allain Corp group. Four humans, one Chirr, one animal.''

"Yes," Tammany says, as Freesh emerges from the crate, "I made our reservations. Is all in order?"

"Yep, your luggage came separate and is already loaded," the Chirr says, studying Freesh with amusement. "We are ready to leave as soon as you are on board. You are speaking to Tsi tss Whoop. Humans have used the nickname 'Pooh Bear' without causing offense."

"Thanks, Pooh Bear," Tammany answers, with the faintest of smiles. "We'll hurry now."

The shuttle is a neat, aerodynamic shape, painted blue and gold in the elaborate swirling patterns the Chirr favor. Its interior is divided into three sections: a cockpit, a passenger section, and a cargo hold. More cargo can be stored in the belly. The bulkhead between the cockpit and the aft compartments is down, but the cargo area is accessible. Toshi and Tammany move back to check our gear.

Anton stretches out in one of the window seats and loosens the collar of his shirt. After considering, he shucks his jacket and stows it under the seat. Much of his corporate look gone, he sighs happily.

"Much, much better. Be good to lean back for a while."

Freesh, contrary to my expectations, since he is almost certainly the most experienced space traveller among us, seems agitated.

I pause from collapsing Onyx's crate for storage—she's already jumped up to the window seat across the aisle from Anton and is studying the shuttleport—and look at the Chirr.

"What's eating you, Freesh?" I ask, aware that the idiom won't translate.

His whiskers don't even curl as his translator gives him an altered version, although I have learned that this is his idea of a good joke.

"This vessel, or precisely the one this shuttle belongs to, if it is the one I know of, we have fallen into notorious company. The Tsi clan has a dubious reputation."

"So, what do you expect?" Tammany says, coming

forward and slouching next to Anton. "Given what we need carried—fugitives—and where we're going—a restricted planet—you didn't think we'd be going Trillium Lines, did you? The Tsi clan considers the *Shadowsweep* their finest vessel and their token to respectability. It can accommodate aliens. Its captain and crew are the diamonds in a very rocky clan. Besides, if they didn't come cheap, they were at least reasonable."

"You can stay behind," Toshi reminds him, settling in behind Onyx. "No one's keeping you. We trust that you won't say anything to DuPoy or Ooohoop or their lot."

Freesh hops back at the suggestion that he stay; at Toshi's reminder of our adversaries he takes one of the remaining seats. Toshi drops something over the seat into my lap.

"If you would stop gawking long enough to review this, Languages Expert, I would be grateful. It's the message we plan to leave for Kwan Yin."

Sticking my tongue out at him, I run the message through my datapad. After changing a few words a translator program might have problems with, I hand it back.

"Looks good," I'm about to return to sightseeing when Onyx puts a thought into my head, "Oh, and code it for either Kwan Yin and Aino Rand. Rand's on our side in this and if something happens to Kwan Yin or she feels too strongly that she has to be fair, it's wise to have a partisan on Terra."

"Good thinking," Toshi says, accepting the message.

"Onyx's, not mine," I clarify, then resting my chin on the Xian's glossy head, I cheerfully watch the *Shadowsweep*'s crew getting us ready for departure.

Even if I hadn't known that the Chirr were family oriented, I would have suspected that the *Shadowsweep* was a family business. The Chirr who hop about stowing gear and goods all share Pooh Bear's fluffy golden fur and portly build. They should be easy enough to tell apart, however.

One has milky white ears and tail, which I think are

natural variations in shading until I see a second Chirr with similar patterning, this time in a loud, unnatural violet. The shuttle pilot, who is also the ship's captain, I learn later, has shaved the thick fur around her eyes and ears, presumably to accommodate the earphones and goggles she wears almost constantly. The remaining crew member—and second in command—has jetty black fur and wiry whiskers, which he twirls almost constantly. He is a Tsi by marriage to either Pearl or Violet.

We clear the shuttle port without any complications, the vessel's internal stabilization so well calculated that the sensation is less violent than many flitter rides.

My vague feeling of disappointment dwindles as Onyx and I lean to stare out the window. She is as excited as I am. A constant thread of tiny pictures runs through my mind as she indicates a cloud bank, a city grown small, a distant airplane, stars glimmering through an atmosphere grown thin and fragile above us.

I listen, squeezing her shoulder to let her know that I understand her. More than once, she snakes her head back and meets my eyes with her bright brass triangles, sharing with me a feeling that at last all is well.

Trouble comes almost as soon as we dock. Tsi Grrfu (whom Anton privately dubs "Gerbil") tells the Captain as we are unloading that there is a message for "our honored passengers."

"Who is the sender," Toshi asks when the captain relays the word, "and does the message indicate any one of us in particular?"

"The sender is one Chiron," Grrfu answers after a pause, "and he asks for any of you six, each by name—if Onyx is the name of the unnamed member of your group."

"We're tagged," Anton swears. "Any thoughts?"

"Ignore it," Tammany advises, tossing luggage to each of us. "He has no jurisdiction over any of us."

"Hmm," Toshi says, but refrains from further comment until we are in the passenger hold and Pooh Bear has discreetly withdrawn. "I'd like to know what he has to say. He's influential—we ignore him at our own risk."

"I'm with Toshi on this one," I say.

Onyx watches without comment, but her ears had flattened at Chiron's name. Tammany nods, letting herself be convinced.

"Okay, Anton?"

"I'm with you all on this one." He taps the comm. "Captain, we'll take the message in here."

When the message comes through, the screen is dead, flat silver. Then DuPoy's face appears. He smiles.

"Because my associates and I would not wish this information to be intercepted by the wrong people, I have security-sealed it. If you are the people I intend this for, you should have no difficulty opening it."

The screen lapses to flat silver.

"Your department, Kari," Anton says.

"Thanks." I pull up to the table and study the silver screen. "It can't be too difficult to figure out, but practically impossible for anyone else."

"Something even Onyx could get?" Tammany asks, her face wrinkled up with doubt.

"No," I shake my head, "I'm guessing that he knew that she'd be with us. Now, the key can't be our names—they're in the routing instructions, so that's too easy."

Curious, Onyx has come over to watch, standing with her paws on the table top. Absently, I reach to rub one of her silky ears. With my other hand, I awkwardly drum the table with the screen stylus. Idly, I wonder if Tammany thought to pack me a keyboard.

"What do we know that DuPoy does too?" I muse. "Or, more important, what is it that he would expect us to know and to think of in these circumstances?"

"Easy," Tammany says, "something to do with Onyx."

I nod agreement, "Yes, but what? DuPoy's not a scientist of any sort, is he Freesh?"

The Chirr, who has not yet recovered from finding himself on a merchant tramp, fans out his ears thoughtfully.

"No, I don't believe so. An administrator and a diplomat," he wrinkles his nose as if the last word doesn't quite convey his meaning. "A manipulator."

"Good," I respond. "Then that rules out most of the technical information."

"The results of the chess game?" Toshi offers.

I start to try that, then, "No. Tammany and Anton weren't there. It's too much to expect that we would have told them."

"You haven't," Anton comments.

I grin briefly, my thoughts running over the problem like my fingers do over the furry smoothness of Onyx's ear. It is in an interruption to that smoothness that I find what I believe is the answer. Each time I stroke her ear my fingers meet the tiny knot of scar tissue where the plastic ID chip had been punched through the skin.

"Onyx's ID number!" I exclaim, "That's just the sort of thing some form jockey would commit to memory and just the type of thing he'd expect us to know."

I quickly pull my datapad and scan my files. They come up blank—Onyx had been a unique problem to me from the start.

"Do any of you remember it?" I ask.

Heads shake around the group.

"Perhaps in Qiang's files?" Anton suggests. "She was working with the larger group."

"I don't have those on my datapad now," I confess. "I off-loaded them when Onyx and I came back to civilization."

"No problem," Toshi says confidently, "We brought copies of all her data. Which bag is it in, Tammany?"

Her dark eyes widen, "They're in the cargo hold."

"What? Why?" Toshi asks amazed.

"It was cheaper," Tammany explains, "and the Tsi assured me that we could have any of our gear within two hours. It seemed good to me."

Toshi growls and I close their bickering out, aware that the files may as well be on Xi-7, trying to remember the numbers. Beside me, Onyx studies the blank screen. Mentally, I shape an image of the heavy clips that Tammany had cut from the ears of the Xians soon after we removed them from Lantic Labs. I struggle to make the image sharp, remembering that the same number had been coded on each of the holding cages as well.

Onyx moves and looks at me. Then quickly the picture in my mind grows sharper, even if the perspective is distorted. Every detail is there and I bless the systematic pedantry of the scientific mind when I see that the ID numbers are repeated on each of the restraining bands that circle the Xian's limbs. Onyx's number is X74(FA).

"We got it!" I crow and scribble the characters on the screen.

"Good memory, Kari," Anton applauds.

"Not me, Anton," I smile, squeezing Onyx, "Her."

DuPoy, lounging behind a polished walnut desk, stares directly into the screen without his usual insincere smile.

"Hello, let me be brief. You have something I want. I have something that you do not want me to have. I'm willing to trade."

"What the hell?" Anton says.

"Hush," Toshi answers.

DuPoy continues, "To be direct. It is very romantic to spin stories about people with secrets or whose pasts are shrouded in mystery. It is another thing to have one of those pasts. Each one of you has a 'colorful' past. In fact, those pasts are part of the incentive that Ben Allain used to recruit you."

Freesh looks as if he is wondering if it is too late to get a shuttle to the surface. I am simply shocked. I knew that the other Directors had secrets, but I had never seriously suspected that any of the other Directors shared my shady past.

Tammany is sitting very still. Anton has paled beneath his beard. Toshi is blanched, his expression identical to the one that I had glimpsed during the conference during which I had threatened them with exposure of their complicity in Mr. Allain's death. I begin to understand why gaining their cooperation had been comparatively easy. None of them would have welcomed queries into their pasts.

The corners of DuPoy's mouth quirk as if he knows the impact of his words, "Before Ben Allain died, copies of his documentation regarding your backgrounds were obtained. Of course, upon his death, as he promised to you, the originals were destroyed. However, what I have is convincing."

He pulls a datapad and touches the screen, then looks up, "Because I care about keeping your good will, I will not offer any of your own backgrounds as proof. Instead, appended to this recording are some very neat facts about Rhys Martine. Review or not as you choose. Return Onyx to me and drop your interest in this affair or I will make certain that your histories go precisely where they will do you and Allain Corp the most harm.

"I know what ship you are traveling on. If you do not contact me with what I want before the ship leaves system, I will carry out my plan. I hope to be speaking with you soon."

The screen goes blank. Then the words "Message Ended" march across the silver screen. This fades to black.

In that brief time, I watch fear, horror, disbelief, and finally stoicism parade across my fellow Directors' faces. Freesh peeps something about needing to check his quarters and leaves us alone to consider DuPoy's threat.

"Shit!" Anton curses. "How the hell did he . . ."

"Did he?" Toshi asks. "He could be bluffing."

"No," Tammany says, her eyes wild, "no one knew but Ben. No one even knew that I had anything to hide. But if you want proof, we can continue with the file and find out what scummy secret our friend Rhys was hiding."

"I don't want to know," I say flatly. "It won't help us to decide. DuPoy doesn't strike me as someone who would bluff on a pair of deuces. If he doesn't have what he says he does, he has something."

For a long moment we sit silently. Then Onyx drops from where she has stood with her paws against the table and our problem comes into focus as she moves and deliberately stares into each of our faces. I don't know what message she sends the others or if her silence is as eloquent for them as if is for me.

"I won't turn her over," I state. "I can't. We've gone through too much to get this far. And she has her rights."

"What if we overrule you?" Toshi says coldly.

"You'll have to do it permanently," I answer. "Remember, I have some leverage of my own. Kill me and you'll find Mr. Allain's murder under investigation. Do you think that DuPoy would withhold his information when he could reveal it under cover of being a good citizen and ruin the Corp forever?"

"Damn!" Anton hisses. "We're squashed. Kari . . ."

"I'm set here, Anton. The rest is up to you three."

The intercom comes alive and a computer voice announces, "Thirty minutes to out-system departure window."

I deliberately rise and walk to a couch built into the wall near a viewport. Noting a drink dispenser, I go and pour two cups of coffee. Onyx jumps up next to me and laps from hers. Watching the Earth slowly turn below, I shamelessly eavesdrop on the others.

"DuPoy has the connections to have gotten even Ben's private documents," Tammany comments. "If he's working with Chiron, money would not have been an object."

"If we go along with Karen to Xi-7," Toshi states, "we're ruined. If we don't, DuPoy has a hold over us. I don't believe for a minute he'll turn over everything he has."

"Then let's go for ruin," Anton urges. "Something good may still come from this. Maybe in the long run the act of helping Onyx will be remembered longer than the—other.''

Tammany grunts and crosses to the coffee dispenser. Leaning against the wall next to it, she casts a speculative glance my way. Aware of her attention, I steadfastly ignore it. At last, Tammany speaks.

''There has to be a way to pull at least a partial win from this. DuPoy has us scared, but we can defuse him. We're good at what we do.''

''With time, I'd agree,'' Toshi says. ''We could steal the data or even kill DuPoy, if that would help, but we have something less than half an hour.''

Suddenly he laughs so strangely that I turn to look. A cool glint of merciless glee is lighting his blue eyes.

''Defuse,'' he says.

''Toshi, have you flipped?'' Anton asks.

''Yes,'' Toshi answers. ''There are basically two ways to deal with an explosive device. What are they, Anton?''

''Basically,'' Anton says carefully, his expression showing that he is worried for Toshi's sanity, ''either the device has to be altered so that the explosion won't happen or the explosion has to be set off in a controlled fashion so that the force will not do the planned harm.''

''Right,'' Toshi says, ''Now . . .''

''Wait!'' Tammany interrupts. ''You're not suggesting we broadcast our dirty secrets so that DuPoy can't use them against us, are you? That would be just as bad.''

''Not quite,'' Toshi says. ''We tell only one person.''

''Kwan Yin!'' Tammany's smile is stars against her dark skin. ''And we don't tell her anything about us. We simply send a copy of DuPoy's message along with the message that we've already drafted. Whatever happens after that, DuPoy's bombshell will have at least lost the impact of surprise.''

''Shock,'' Anton says, ''may still be there if she learns the truth about us. However, it's the best of a bad situation. Kari?''

"I can have the message updated well before we need it," I stop, wanting to thank them, not sure how.

Onyx, apparently, has no doubts. I'm excluded from whatever image she sends, but nearly identical smiles soften their faces.

The computer voice—almost certainly a synthesized translator of less high quality than the ones the UAN staff had provided for Toshi and me, Tammany and I agree—leads us through the steps to ready for departure.

Fifteen minutes before we leave, the Tsi captain sends Kwan Yin our message. After that, we simply wait. In many ways, there will be no returning from this trip, at least not to the world we had known. Craning my neck to get the best angle through the viewport, I wonder if that's such a bad thing.

FOURTEEN

THE *SHADOWSWEEP* IS A FASCINATING SHIP, AT LEAST for me and Onyx. Once we have cleared the solar system and begun the long coast to the Xi system, Tsi Captain invites us all to tour the ship. One tour is enough for the others, but Onyx and I repeatedly ramble through the corridors.

Most, outside of those in the passenger areas, are rounded tubes only high enough for a Chirr, so I need to crawl on hands and knees or waddle like a duck. No one laughs at me, at least to my face, so I crawl along happily. Onyx, of course, can move as freely as a Chirr, but she usually paces along behind me, for once the taller of the pair.

We visit the bridge, the tiny medical bay, and the larger lounge and living areas. Chirr seem to lack the human need for privacy, so there are no large sleeping areas. Instead, padded cubbies are set in odd, unused corners. Pooh Bear sleeps in an air duct to a currently sealed hold area; the captain prefers a space on the bridge where a new computer terminal doesn't fit quite snugly with the rest of the equipment. I don't ask where Gerbil and his lady friend sleep, though perhaps the Chirr wouldn't find the matter indelicate.

I do a lot of climbing around, for curiosity, for exercise, and not the least because the mood in the passengers' quarters grows increasingly tense as the days pass. DuPoy's message may not have worked the way he intended, but it has had an effect. Before, I would guess that each of us believed that the past was behind us. Now it has returned. I, at least, alternate between moods of burning shame when I contemplate my partners learning what I am capable of and equally sharp fear as I wonder what they have done.

The small lounge with its cupboardlike private berths doesn't help much. Anton and Tammany both have sedatives issued to them and spend long hours drowsing between meals. These provide little relief, for Tammany carps continually about the vegetarian menu, rhapsodizing about steak or ribs with the eloquence of a greeting card poet.

The food doesn't bother me. It's a bit bland at times, but it's well balanced for our needs by Violet, who has a background in alien physiology. I don't dare touch the sedatives—coffee is about as strong a drug as I dare, so I fill the hours with taking language lessons from Freesh, building an image vocabulary with Onyx, or playing games.

The four of us who are steadily conscious join a running chess tournament with Pearl, Tsi Captain, and Pooh Bear. Other times, Toshi and I play a traditional Japanese holiday game that I'd taught him when we first met. Time passes, but the tension builds.

Freesh doesn't help. Neither one of the Allain Corp nor one of the Tsi, he is given to fits of moodiness followed by frenetic activity. The more I learn of the finer points of Chirr trade pidgin, the more I suspect of the cultures and languages that underlie it. Given this, Freesh's lapses into the first person become not merely puzzling, but foreboding.

One evening (for us humans, that is; the Chirr don't seem to have the same biochemical links to day/night cycles), things come to something like a head. Anton and Tammany are between pills. The combination of coffee and lingering sedatives has made Tammany bitchy and Anton incoherent.

"Are you going to finish your soup, Anton?" Toshi asks.

Shipboard life has revealed him as fanatically tidy. Right now he's collecting dinner plates. Anton continues to draw lines with his spoon between the green floret islands in his cream of broccoli soup.

"Anton! Are you finished with your soup?"

"Of course he is," Tammany snaps, pushing Anton's bowl out from under his spoon. "Who couldn't be finished with this slop!"

"I," Freesh announces, standing on his chair and drawing himself up straight, "am tired of your complaining. The Tsi have served you well and finely. If Chirr choose to eat growing matter rather than flesh, this is our choice. If you choose to travel with them, you should be respectful."

The room falls dead quiet. Violet, who had been entering with the next course, swiftly retreats, leaving the kelp and leeks casserole on the serving cart by the door. Tammany stares up at Freesh, her mouth dropping open as she realizes that she has genuinely angered the little scientist.

"Hey, Freesh, I'm sorry," she starts, but he isn't ready to be easily soothed.

"Sure, sure," he chatters, hopping down from his seat and across to the casserole dish. "Prove! Prove!"

Rolling the cart across the room, he seizes her plate and heaps on the green mash, complete with a generous helping of the golden brown crust. It actually smells pretty good, but Tammany's attention isn't on the meal, but on the chattering Chirr.

"Have some lovely sipple juice!" he shrills, pouring her glass full of an iced juice that tastes like a cross between yams and cherries. *"Bon appétit!"*

The last is shrieked in French. The translator, which had been struggling to manage his tirade, seems relieved. Then, after a pause during which the little machine processes that this was not the dominant conversational language, it translates the words as "Chow down!"

I can't help giggling nervously, but that is the one noise until Tammany lifts her chop sticks and starts to eat. After the third bite, she sips the juice and manages a weak smile.

"Delicious," she whispers, "Really. Please join me."

Anton, who has finally noticed that his soup is gone, ladles out servings. We pull up to the table, all but Onyx, who takes her bowl on the floor.

After a few bites, Freesh gives an ear-splitting whistle that I recognize as a wail of despair. Then he leaps from his seat and hops out of the lounge and into his cubby. The privacy lock seals behind him with a hollow pop.

"Shit!" Anton curses, the last of his fuzziness vanishing. "What is eating him?"

"It can't just be my bitching," Tammany says. "Can it?"

"No," I say, "I don't think so. I'd need to ask Pooh Bear or one of the others, but I think it has to do with his clan."

Onyx, meanwhile, has wandered over to Freesh's sealed cubby. I see the doorbell tab flicker as if depressed. There is no response. Then Onyx sits down and freezes, her long nose tilted up; her brass eyes staring at the closed doors as if she can conjure them open.

Perhaps she can, for after the uncomfortable stillness of morgues, the cubby opens and Freesh hops forth. His ears are curled close to his head and his tail drags behind him. Even his whiskers are limp. He looks like a battered child's toy that has been left forgotten on some closet shelf. My heart twists with pity.

"Hey, Freesh," Tammany says softly, "I'm sorry. The chow's good."

Freesh looks up at her with visible effort. He whistles acceptance and droops once more. Onyx shifts to look at him and he hops slowly forward and onto his chair. Then he looks at each of us.

"I, also, am sorry," he says, "but also I have been advised that I must explain myself for this to be sincere."

"Advised?" Tammany asks. "By the Tsi?"

"No," Freesh says, "by Onyx. She is not easy to understand, but I believe this is what she meant."

I steal a glance at Onyx, but she laps her sipple juice and gives nothing away. Anton rubs his temples as if his head hurts.

"Please," Toshi says, positively courtly, "continue."

"A Chirr is a social creature," Freesh says in a flat mockery of his usual pedantry, "more so than a human, generally speaking. Many of your cultures glorify loners, those who can do without connections. Chirr find this not only an unattractive concept but somewhat unbelievable. Because of our capacity for cooperation, we are superior in many ways to the other sentient races. For example, we are the finest builders and spacers."

Anton growls and Tammany gently slaps his hand. Freesh doesn't even seem to notice, protecting himself in his role as the Discoverer lecturing to novices.

"Chirr have become great because of our ability to cooperate, but our need for our group alliances is also our greatest weakness." He pauses and waggles his tail tip. "Now, don't believe that a Chirr cannot survive alone. A Chirr who is secure in its alliances to family, clan, over-clan, and world is capable of long periods of solitude. Far more vulnerable is a Chirr disowned by any one of these groups; and, because of inter-relationships of these groups, disownment by one may lead to weakening of ties with others.

"When I protested against the treatment of the Xians, I was given warning. When I met with you people, I was reprimanded. When I persisted, Wheep cut me from the over-clan. I am certain that because of my departure with you, Ooohoop will recommend that I be cut from my clan. What my immediate family will do, I cannot be certain."

"Certainly, they won't disown you!" Toshi protests.

Freesh looks at him, narrowing his eyes within their

patches of black and white fur. If he had ever looked comical, that memory is lost in the tragic dignity of his position.

"I," he says, pausing to draw attention to the pronoun, "I hope that they do. Otherwise, the entire family faces the penalties of clan displeasure. I may believe in the wisdom of my position, but I cannot ask my kinfolk to suffer for what may be a futile cause."

"So you're on your own," Anton says, "with nobody, and all for Onyx and the creatures of Xi-7."

Freesh nods. "Yes, and that is why I became insane at the way you humans are tearing into each other and your own selves over events that are past—in many cases long past. Yet, I cannot have you believe that I support the Xians in complete disinterest. I am not a sacred person. I do see what letting this happen to the Xians will do to the fragile peace of the UAN."

"Which is?" Tammany says, her lips tight as if she is waiting for an answer she already knows.

"Ultimately, it will destroy it," Freesh says, "That is why we cannot let this happen. If the Xians are destroyed or even if they are merely shunted aside, we are helping create a guilty secret that cannot fail to create war, if not in our lifetimes, in the lifetimes of our children."

Anton leans his head into his hands with a groan. Given that this is the most thinking he's had to do since our voyage has started, he may feel that his thought processes are dragging like booted feet slogging through a swamp.

"I can't handle this," he mutters so unintelligibly that I wonder if Freesh's translator can make sense of the sounds. "First save a couple of critters, then save a race, now save the fucking UAN! I'm just a poor Knife. I can't handle this."

"Cut the nonsense, Anton," Tammany snaps unsympathetically, "You aren't 'just a poor Knife' and you never have been, no matter how much you want to fool yourself now. Straighten up and face facts. Anyhow, weren't you the one who dragged us all into this?"

I rub my chin, quietly assessing her quick recovery from the steady diet of sedatives. Either she has a fantastic metabolism or she's been only pretending to take them. What plans might that active mind have been evolving as she lay in her solitary bunk? What webs might she have been weaving? What conjectures might she have reached?

Anton has sat up in response to her command. His neck is held stiffly as if the act of keeping his head upright hurts.

"Yeah," he says slowly, "Guess it was my idea to start with. Kari's work just gave me a chance to broach the subject to the rest of you. But . . ."

He flaps his arms out at his sides, "It's gotten all so damn big. Too big for private folk like us."

"Connection can be frightening, young human," Freesh says. "Your Christians speak of the impact of a sparrow's fall. Ecologists have long seen that the removal of a rock or tree may shift an entire ecosystem as the change is adapted to, but these are little things when compared to the games that sentients play."

"For want of a nail a shoe was lost
For want of a shoe a horse was lost
For want of a horse a soldier was lost
For want of a soldier a battle was lost
For want of a battle a kingdom was lost
All for the want of a horseshoe nail."

Toshi falls silent as we all turn to look at him. Uncharacteristically, he blushes.

"Well, that says it all, even if it is a nursery rhyme. Shall we get down to business?"

I nod, "Maybe we'd better let Tsi Violet know all's clear in here. She hopped out rather fast before."

"And maybe we could have dessert," Tammany says with a small smile for Freesh. "Her dried fruit cobbler is divine."

Dessert cleared away, we pull our favored seats into a

loose ring in the lounge. Onyx floats coffee around to everyone as the rest of us pull out datapads and notes. For the first time since DuPoy's attempt at blackmail, we are again a team, and it feels good.

I'm not the only one who feels the change. Anton has lost his hangdog look and has somehow found time to trim his beard and mustache so that he looks vaguely Mephistophelean. Tammany sits by Freesh, deliberately showering him with attention. He in turn whistles frequent laughter. Toshi is cool and razor sharp, assuming for the first time a conscious role as group leader.

We plan late into the ship's night and resume over breakfast in the morning. No effort is made to keep our work secret from the Tsi. Soon members of the crew are drifting in and out, listening and suggesting.

Their knowledge of ships and ship limitations is invaluable to us. We learn that quite possibly we will be expected by the UAN Survey group, since a small ship dedicated to engine space, with minimal crew and cargo, could beat us to Xi-7.

Freesh contributes his knowledge of the Survey team and typical procedures. Onyx supplies information about the planet and her people in vivid images that I convert into words we can work with.

As the others slowly shape plans from this data, I translate, not just clarifying Onyx's images or the Chirr's comments when electronic translation falls short, but between my fellow humans as well. Smoothing out connotation and denotation, idiom, neutralizing jibes and slights—both intentional and unintentional—I feel more a part of the Corp than I ever have before.

By the time Toshi calls for a recess, promising to ground the first person "who so much as thinks about the problem" over the next four hours, I'm drained and want a drink more than I have in at least ten years. Onyx, too, is tired. Although she appears fully recovered from the debilitating effects of the course of drugs, she still seems to find communicating with aliens, especially in groups, tiring. I don't blame her given how I feel and I at least speak all the languages.

Squeezing her around the shoulders, I invite her to a run through the ship. For the next several hours, as we crawl and slide about the miniature corridors, I meditate on the fact that in just two days we will be on her world. There all of us, humans, Chirr, and su-ankh, will be the minorities, and an entire population of quite possibly angry, and certainly justly indignant, telepathic and telekinetic aliens will have us at their mercy.

In that view, Onyx again seems as strange and incomprehensible as she had at our earliest meetings. I wonder how she really sees things with those strange brass eyes. Does she hold any resentment for the deaths of her companions? After what she has seen, does she view the UAN races as threats or friends? Somehow, I know that even if I knew how to ask these questions, I would not ask.

FIFTEEN

OUR ARRIVAL ON THE FRINGES OF THE XI SYSTEM IS AS unceremonious and unnoticed as we could wish. At least we hope so. No one meets us or hails us. Although Tsi Captain has commanded radio silence, she keeps either Pooh Bear or Pearl scanning for signals to us or to others.

Using a combination of scanning and system maps that she will not say where she acquired, Tsi Captain brings us in toward Onyx's home world, keeping every bit of solid matter she can between us and the presumed watchers.

Although the view from the bridge screen is breathtaking, I'm too nervous to enjoy the complex choreography of the inner planets and the asteroids around each other. Maybe I've seen too many science fiction thrillers, but I keep expecting some vast armada of heavily armed ships (never mind that even if the UAN gathered all its armed ships together they would hardly make a decent fleet) to emerge from the shadow of a planet. My intellect and my emotions aren't cooperating. After two days of my fidgety presence, Tsi Captain gently but sternly restricts me to the passenger quarters.

In our quarters, things are readied for our departure planetside. After considerable debate, we have decided that we will set down the *Shadowsweep*'s shuttle some distance from the UAN encampment. Based on his experience, Freesh believes that they will have returned to the same spot as their first camp—the expense of labor and materials to set up a new camp would be prohibitive, especially given that the site had been chosen initially as a near ideal location. Even if they have moved, we should be able to locate them because of the standard practice of setting up a relay satellite in geosync above the base area.

When we find them, the plan is to make contact with some of Onyx's people, set up a demo that will force the Survey team to accept the Xian's sentience, then record the whole thing for arbitration back on Terra. Finally, we ship off into the velvet sky, problem resolved.

I don't doubt that I'm not the only one who expects this simple plan to fail. The question is, not knowing the UAN team's state of readiness and information, how can we plan?

We will, as Freesh puts it, "Tuck it in our cheek pouches and hope."

No one bothers us as we come in system; the ship we see sweeping a regular orbit around the planet apparently doesn't notice us. Still, Tsi Captain decides to be careful and choose an orbit where a small moon will provide the *Shadowsweep* with some shielding from groundside scanners. Of course, this means that our communications once we're downside are going to be limited.

"We will do what we can," Tsi Captain promises. "Pooh Bear and Grrfu are working on a means to use the Survey team's satellite without being detected. We will send Violet to pilot our shuttle and stay on the ground with you. If we hear nothing from her in two sun cycles, we will send help."

Toshi thanks her. Then the time has come to leave. The *Shadowsweep* has actually come to feel homey during our voyage, so that it is with something of a pang that I watch her recede behind us. Onyx ignores the ship, watching with fixed intensity as the blue-green sphere of Xi-7 grows larger in the port. She's silent as ever; nevertheless, her impatience is almost audible.

"See if she'll sit away from the window," Tammany says, looking at the slender black bowstring of Onyx against the port. "I've some coffee here in my hot bottle."

I don't even try.

"She won't, Tammany. She's coming home at last, a place she may have thought she'd never see again. Coffee is a pretty poor substitute for that feeling."

"I guess I'll never know," Tammany says so softly only the translator I wear from habit catches the words for me. Then she makes herself busy tucking away the coffee.

"We'll be landing in a few minutes," Anton's voice comes back from where he's copiloting for Violet. "Batten down the hatches and secure all personal possessions. There's a storm in the area we're heading into. No danger, but things may get bumpy."

It does, but no worse than the regular suborbitals and is, in fact, a lot smoother than the ride in the plane we'd "borrowed" from StarUs. Onyx is so determined not to leave her post at the window that I finally give up trying to strap her in and just wrap my arm around her lean middle. Her fur is dense, and beneath her springy rib cage, I can feel her heart racing furiously.

The storm gives us plenty of concealment from any naked-eye spotting, and the clearing Violet and Anton have chosen for landing in is outside of what Freesh says are the usual security scans for the Survey camp.

We land fairly smoothly, aware all at once of the world around us. With the engine noise reduced to a dull hum, we can hear the driving rain against our hull. The same rain reduces visibility to a Monet-like blur, but one thing shouts for our attention.

"My lord!" Tammany says, almost in awe. "It's so impossibly green!"

"Not impossible," Freesh lectures. "This planet's overall climate is warmer than most regions of Terra. There is a higher proportion of oxygen than what either

Chirr or humans are accustomed to. This may leave you feeling a bit heady, but should also increase your endurance somewhat. Su-ankh, interestingly, have enough compensating mechanisms within their systems that they adapted without any apparent effect. The gravity is within Terran ranges—you might notice a difference in a lab, but I doubt you will in practice, especially after all the time on shipboard.''

''Damn rain!'' Anton says. ''Coming all this way and then having to wait for the rain to stop seems somehow unfair.''

Freesh looks surprised. ''Waiting is hardly practical, Anton. In this region, at this time of year, the rain may continue for some days.''

''Great,'' Anton answers. ''Great.''

I hide a smile, since I'd read what Freesh had given us on Xi-7 while Anton was doped up. Onyx's water-shedding fur makes a lot more sense now.

''Come on, Anton,'' I say, opening a locker where wet weather gear is stored, ''you won't melt.''

''No, but I bet you will,'' he grumbles, stepping into the vac-suit-like overalls and pressing the front seam shut. ''Just leave the ruby slippers behind, okay?''

Freesh studies us with open-eared amazement. His only concession to the rain is an enormous wide-brimmed hat, almost like an umbrella perched on his head.

''You humans complain about rain excessively,'' he says sternly. ''The water content bears little that can harm you. Unless the Survey team has been sloppy, the life-forms—even the microscopic ones—on this planet simply have not had time to adapt for successful forays into human physiology.''

''Sorry, Discoverer Freesh,'' Toshi says lazily, ''we're not the explorer types, just a bunch of Knives and Hands out to save the Universe from the forces of Evil.''

He grins then, brightly, and while Freesh sputters for an appropriate reply, Tsi Violet whistles back that she is ready to open the shuttle door.

Toshi and Tammany insist on going out first and checking that nothing large and toothy is waiting for us. In my opinion, that's pretty useless, since anything stupid or mean enough to hang around after a shuttle landing isn't going to be dissuaded by the weapons they caress so nervously. In fact, whatever it is is quite likely to be part of the Survey team.

But I sit on my protests and hover in the doorway, my fingers lightly brushing the top of Onyx's head. She is a mad quiver of excitement, but I hardly wonder why she is waiting with me for the "all clear." We've been together through so much now that I can hardly imagine not having her around.

I guess that's why when she abruptly gathers herself and shoots out into the rain like a bolt of oily lightning, I just stand there and let her go. Only when she has vanished into the tangled tree line do I realize that she is gone.

"Onyx!" I call tentatively, then louder, "Onyx!

Toshi and Tammany come thudding back across the wet meadow. I feel Anton's hands on my shoulders and realize that I had been about to run after Onyx. Instead, he pulls me back and I slide against the wet threshold and thump down hard on my tailbone. With the pain singing in my ears, a moment passes before I can sort through the conversation.

"She took off?" Toshi is repeating for the third time when I finally get focused.

"Yes," I answer for Anton and Freesh. "She lit out when you and Tammany were up by the nose of the shuttle."

"When we had rounded it, actually," Tammany notes thoughtfully. "She waited until she would no longer be in our line of sight. Then she ran off."

"What are our chances of tracking her?" Anton asks Freesh and Violet, although from his expression he knows the answer as well as I do.

"Not good," Violet replies. "The growth is thick,

darkness is falling, and we know too little of the life-forms here to hope that infrared could sort her signature from the rest. Even if she has remained in range, the task would be formidable.''

''We've got to find her,'' I protest anxiously. ''We've got to.''

''Kari,'' Anton says soothingly, stepping out into the rain, ''she's fine. This is her world. She probably couldn't resist the urge to go out and make sure that it is really here.''

''Maybe,'' I say, far from convinced.

Seeing that I'm not going to tear off into the gathering dusk, the others quickly start setting up shelters. Despite Anton's reassurances, by full dark Onyx has not returned. Apprehensively, I pace the palest edge of the halo of light from our camp. Above the murmur of the others' conversation, I listen to the dripping jungle, to the shrill cries of insects or birds, to the squeak of branches against each other. Errant raindrops cast some of our light back at us, and occasionally I believe that I see the steadier glimmer of eyes.

The others are starting to turn in, anticipating the next day's contact with the UAN team, when without warning I walk out of the light and into the tangle. My eyes have adjusted enough that I don't crash into the larger trees, but I snag myself continually on vines and branches. Come morning, I will be easily tracked.

Making my way foot by jolting foot, I listen for the others, but I am not immediately missed and might not be for a while. I know that I couldn't explain to them why I am doing this. I'm not completely sure myself, but as I make my halting progress my mind centers on a simple thing. I need to talk to Onyx and ask her, ''Why?'' Why did she run away? Why now and not in the morning? Why didn't she tell me or take me with her? Why?

The question becomes increasingly important the longer I walk, beating like a mantra into my head. Cloud cover and forest canopy have removed all but the faintest light, so I guide myself by instinct and that single word.

Of course, the inevitable happens. Fumbling around in the darkness, my feet go out from under me and I fall, landing hard on my already sore tailbone. Cursing, mostly to keep from whimpering, I slide out the pocket flash I hadn't been using for fear that the others would see it. In its tidy light, I take a look at what I've gotten myself into.

I've fallen at least four meters into a hole that fortunately contains a liberal padding of sopping plant matter. Standing on shaky knees, I move to inspect the walls. Neither rough nor smooth, they show no evidence that the pit was dug. Comfortingly, they are not smooth enough for this to be a regular runoff channel. Tentatively, I decide that I'm in a sinkhole, or maybe in one of those pits left when a really big tree falls down all at once.

My rain gear is keeping me from getting too uncomfortably wet, but I'm rapidly becoming hungry, chilled, and tired of the dark. Grabbing a double handful of the silver-green vines that trail down from above, I tug experimentally. They seem sturdy enough—until I'm about halfway up. With little warning, they break, sending me tumbling to the bottom again.

This third jolt to my abused backside is more than I can handle; to my embarrassment, I start to cry. Damning myself for my stupidity in setting off by myself without a comm or rope or anything that would be useful, I sniffle back the tears.

I'm considering whether trying to get out again is worth the effort when my light reflects off something on the pit's upper edge that had not been there before.

Bright and brassy gold, they give back my light in angles that glow in a Picassoesque conception of a cat at night.

"Onyx?" I whisper, wanting it to be so, so much that my heart actually hurts and my breath comes fast. "Onyx?"

Miraculously, a picture forms in my mind, ''Woman with Coffee,'' her ideogram for me.

''Yes, Onyx,'' I call, not caring who hears, ''it's me.''

''Woman with Coffee?'' the image comes again. ''Tree hole in the ground?'' The pictures come first separately, then together, splitting so that the first is below the second.

''Yes, Onyx,'' I answer, ''I'm down here. Can you get me out?''

My hair and loose fringes of my clothing drift upwards in an eerie tickling as she tries to telekinetically lift me. Then they drop back.

''I'm too heavy,'' I tell her. ''You'll need to get help.''

She vanishes, Lassie from an old film, but what she brings back are not the other humans, but instead a half-dozen Xians as oil black as herself. Ringing the pit, their eyes are glowing fragments of an antique bracelet.

I pivot slowly, wondering where to orient myself for the rope or ladder. Then, just as I am considering the possibility, I start to rise into the air. The sensation is not precisely pleasant, more like being tugged by a bunch of small clamps that pull me haphazardly into the air. I'm dropped with equal lack of finesse next to one of the Xians.

''Onyx?'' I say tentatively, remembering what Ben Franklin had said about cats in the dark and thinking that the same goes for Xians—only more so.

In answer, I get a brief, reassuring ''Woman with Coffee.''

The air is scented with overripe apples now. All the Xians but Onyx have drawn back slightly and are studying me with perked-ear interest. When they have rested, one by one, they melt into the dark until only Onyx and I are left.

Onyx shapes a cartoon of the *Shadowsweep*'s shuttle. Then she crafts a more complex picture of me going across the meadow to the shuttle while she watches from the tangle's edge.

"You'll take me," I guess, trying to duplicate her picture, "but you don't want to come with me."

No new picture, so I guess I'm right.

"Come back with me, Onyx," I plead, trying to project my request as a picture. "We need to convince the UAN Survey team to reverse their ruling. We can't do it without you to demonstrate."

The pictures that tumble through my mind are so chaotic that I cannot make sense of them. I see a crowd of Xians, what must be the Survey camp, su-ankh, Chirr, and humans.

"Onyx, you're going too fast," I sputter. "I don't understand."

Then sinking down next to her, I touch her silky nose. She sniffs my hand, bumps it softly with her head.

"Shuttle," comes the picture again, "Woman with Coffee."

She walks a few steps, then looks back to see if I'll follow. I stay hunkered near to ground so that my eyes are level with hers.

"Onyx, are you just guiding me back or are you going to stay?"

The same two pictures: "Shuttle. Woman with Coffee."

"Onyx," I repeat as if the name I've given her actually means something, "please come and stay with me. We need you."

She looks away. I sigh, feeling the muggy air packing its way into my head like damp cotton.

"Will you come back tomorrow?" I ask, picturing a rising sun and wondering even as I do so if sunrises look the same here.

"Tomorrow, Onyx, will you come to the shuttle?" I ask, when she doesn't answer, simplifying my words and hoping she can follow my thoughts. "Please, girl?"

She takes another step and is almost lost to my light's beam. Then the picture of the shuttle in daylight and Onyx emerging from the tree line comes clearly.

"That's 'yes'! You will come."

She repeats the pictures and I haul myself to my feet, thinking, despite myself, of getting out of my waterproofs and having a cup of coffee and light enough to see by.

Onyx must catch something of this, for she sends a picture of her bowl filled with coffee. I laugh and, playing my light before me, let her guide me back.

I hear our encampment before I see it. Raised voices call my name and occasionally Onyx's. Soon broad beams of white light are visible, making a crazy quilt of the tree line. Several are too high to be handheld, so I guess that Tsi Violet has done something with the shuttle. When I can see the meadow's edge and a silhouetted figure nearby, Onyx sends me a picture: Anton.

"Anton!" I call gladly.

The figure casts the beam from his handlight wildly about. "Kari! Where are you?"

I step out into the open, resisting an impulse to shout, "Boo!"

"Over here," I offer, noticing that Onyx is no longer with me.

"Kari?" he shines his light over me as if to be certain, "What happened? Where have you been?"

I walk toward the shuttle. "I went to find Onyx."

"Out there?" he sounds incredulous. "In the jungle, at night, on an alien world when you've never been off-planet before?"

"Yep."

He gets on his pocket comm and tells the others that I'm found. I don't bother to correct that I was never lost.

I don't say anything else until I've gotten back to the camp, a welcoming fairy circle promising a techie wonderland. The others are there before us, and I listen as they bombard me with Anton's questions or ones so close as to be indistinguishable. Against any lack of response, they finally fall silent and then I turn to them.

"If you are finished," I say coldly. "First of all, you

are not my guardians nor am I anyone's idiot child. I find the tone of your queries offensive in the extreme.

"Second," I continue, holding up a finger for silence, "what I did was go look for Onyx. I found her—or she found me—and brought me back here when we were finished talking. She says she'll come back in the morning, but apparently she's tired of alien company."

"Where did you . . ." Toshi begins, but I cut him off.

"I've said all that I care to on the subject, Toshi. What I want to know is what was the UAN Survey team's response to your less than quiet and unobtrusive search for me?"

Quiet. Dead, absolute, quiet. Even the bugs (or whatever) out beyond our golden circle seem to have fallen still.

Tammany shifts. "How very odd. We had no response at all. Tsi Violet, should they have been able to see us?"

Violet hops out from the galley, the scent of fresh coffee swirling after her.

"Yes, we were visible. We wondered at the wisdom of using the shuttle light, but your Toshi said we must, so we did."

"Our Toshi," Tammany says with a smile that's not at all playful. "We sneak down here and then you order the floodlights on, and yet we get no contact from the Survey people. How interesting."

"How lucky?" he suggests, but Tammany is having none of it.

Her chocolate eyes give back nothing of the night as she studies the slender, dark-haired man.

"Drip, drop," she says at last, "drip, drop. Toshi. Toshi."

Eyes widening, Anton looks at her, "Toshi the leak? Tammany, you must be crazy! He was the one who set us looking for it. Why would he do that if he was the leak?"

"Not so crazy," Tammany says. "I think that Karen sees it."

And I had, out there in the Xian forest, dogging Onyx's footsteps towards the bright lights and noise. I nod.

"Yes. I'm not sure why I took so long to figure out that the leak had to be one of us four and most reasonably had to be either Toshi or Tammany—sorry, Tam."

She smiles. "No offense taken. You knew—like I did—that it wasn't you and you couldn't know about me. I had a slight advantage. I presume you ruled out Anton because he was in the field for a long while."

I nod and Anton gives a mock sigh of relief. Freesh is studying us all, his whiskers coiling back and forth as he suppresses questions.

"That's right," I answer, "and my guess is that you eventually ruled me out because I spent all that time in near-isolation with Onyx in the park."

"Pretty much," she agrees, "You could have had your own transmitter, but your other actions didn't support my suspicions. Besides, I couldn't see you blowing the side out of your own home. If you wanted to cast doubt on yourself, you would have picked less theatrical means."

Toshi begins to stand and in Anton's hand a small side arm appears. He levels it at Toshi.

"Sit down, Toshi. You know what we do with leaks."

Toshi pales ivory white and sits quickly.

"What?" Freesh chitters, restraint overwhelmed by the palpable threat.

"We plug them," Anton explains calmly.

"I wanted something to drink," Toshi explains with a poor shadow of his usual poise, "that's all. May I have some oolong?"

Tammany glances over at Tsi Violet, who has been following this from a doorway. The Chirr flicks her ears in agreement.

"So," I say, returning to our discussion, "that left you two, and when Violet said that Toshi had ordered the lights the rest fell into place for me, especially since Tammany was genuinely surprised."

"Yes, I've got it now," Anton says, his words spilling

over each other, but his weapon steady. "Toshi knew where the Xians were at the Complex. He knew the basics of our plans. He could have even arranged for that gang to assault you two on the way to the UAN towers."

"What I want to know, Toshi," Tammany says, "is when you started changing your mind about assisting DuPoy and Chiron."

Toshi's hand jerks, spilling the tea Violet has just given him over the back of his hand. Setting the cup down, he wipes his hand off and looks at Tammany.

"How could you know?" he whispers. "Do you read minds like Onyx?"

Tammany shakes her head. "No, that's Karen's department. I just respect you. You're clever. If you were cooperating a hundred percent with DuPoy and his group we would never have gotten off Terra. You had to be covering for us. Even the shuttle lights were a clumsy choice of signal—one that alerted us as much as anyone."

Toshi bends his head over folded hands. Then he picks up his tea and drains the cup.

"When they killed Qiang and Onyx's kin. That's when."

He buries his face in his hands and Violet hops up to fill his cup, concern in the curling of her ears. She softly whistles something to Freesh that my translator brings back as "Humans are unfathomable."

Toshi continues, "The more I thought about it the worse I felt. DuPoy trusted me, and yet Qiang was one of us. I decided that this was more than I had contracted for."

"Getting out wasn't so easy, was it?" Tammany says with a hint of sympathy.

"No," he whispers, "No."

He continues in a stronger voice, "I couldn't back out completely, but I could misdirect and I could withhold information."

"Not enough," Anton says, "for Vance."

"I know," Toshi says, "believe me. I suspected that

DuPoy had gotten a worm of some sort into our systems, but I'm still not certain if that's how he got through and into our personal files.''

''No matter,'' Tammany says. ''What does matter is what we decide to do next.''

''What's wrong with our earlier plan?'' I ask, deliberately baiting them.

''Have you forgotten, Kari?'' Anton asks. ''No Onyx.''

''She told me she'll be back in the morning,'' I say.

''You believe her?'' Freesh asks, not taunting, genuinely curious.

I nod with more confidence than I feel. ''Yes, she understands how important all of this is. Violet, I was wondering . . .''

''Yes?''

''Has the Survey team formally contacted us?''

She fingers a purple ear tuft. ''No, not through me.''

The rest look at Toshi, who shakes his head vigorously. ''No, neither officially or unofficially.'' He wrinkles his brow. ''That's very strange—they couldn't have missed us. Could they, Freesh?''

The Discoverer whistles qualified agreement. ''No, I agree with what Tsi Violet said earlier, they could not have missed us if their equipment was working and they were looking. Not once we were searching for Karen.''

''Maybe they want to ignore us,'' Tammany suggests, every line in her face disagreeing with her own conjecture. ''We'll take shifts just in case contact is made, but we'd better sleep some if Onyx will be back in the morning expecting our help.''

No one protests, and Tammany rattles off two-member shifts. Anton insists on watching with Toshi. Our erstwhile leader only shrugs, but I don't have to be Onyx to tell that Anton's distrust bites sharply at him. Tammany doesn't miss it either.

''We'll need to watch Toshi,'' she says softly as we make up beds in the shuttle. ''He's going to want to prove himself to us. We need to keep him from doing something dumb.''

I nod agreement, but I'm already drifting off. Sleep has grabbed the insides of my eyelids and slammed them down tight before Tammany finishes undressing. I'm well down the corridors of dream before she shuts off the light.

SIXTEEN

ONYX WAKES ME BY FLOATING A FULL COFFEE MUG UNder my nose and breathing apple spice in my face. Blinking groggily, I vaguely recall spending a couple hours in the middle of the night practicing Chirr verbs with Freesh until Violet bounced out of her hammock and insisting that she would pee on the head of the first one who dared whistle "Run! Run! Run!" again.

I giggle sleepily at the memory and fumble for the mug. Onyx releases it to me and then jumps up and sticks her nose in for a quick swig.

"Hey!" I protest, struggling to sit up, "that's mine!"

She meets my eyes with those brass pyramids and I could swear that she is laughing at me. I do laugh and squeeze her around her skinny shoulders, hoping that she can read my pleasure at her return.

"Who's awake?" I ask after I get some coffee into me.

She flashes quick cameos of each of the others.

"So I'm the lazy one," I decide, "Good. I need to wash before I can consider seeing anyone. By any miracle, has the rain stopped?"

Onyx bends one ear in half, the sign we've agreed on for "Please repeat."

I do, simplifying my language and optimistically picturing clear skies.

Onyx nods. I find myself wondering if her people noticed the human habits she's acquiring.

Once we're all assembled, Tammany initiates a call to the Survey camp. We listen alertly, but there is no answer.

"Freesh," Tammany says, puzzlement evident, "are you certain you've given me the right frequency range?"

He nods, hopping to check the settings. "Yes, but let's try a broader sweep in case they have made considerable changes in procedure since I was last with them."

Silence continues to meet our attempt. Tammany is reaching to switch the machine off when Tsi Violet flips her tail to interpose.

"Turn it up full," she says. "There is something."

Now each of us can hear something beneath the static's spitting. I can't make out words, but Freesh is nodding.

"What is it?" Anton asks impatiently.

Freesh flattens his ears in mute disapproval, but begins to provide commentary. "It is the Survey team, but this is not from a broadcast unit. It is overflow from personal comm dots. Something has apparently interfered with their electronic systems."

The Chirr listen for a while longer while we fidget.

"My impression," Freesh continues when the static levels off, "is that this state of affairs has been in place for some days now. I hear frustration, but not the panic that would be there if this had just occurred. The matters being discussed are fairly routine."

"Are they aware of us?" Toshi asks anxiously.

"I do not know," Freesh replies. "The conversation we temporarily intercepted did not mention us, but that is hardly conclusive."

"I suspect that they are," Tammany says, "or at least we should be prepared to react as if they are. However, if their comm is messed up, we can't expect them to call us first. We'll need to send a group over."

"Do we take the shuttle?" Anton asks.

"No," Tammany says after considering, "We'll keep

a base camp both for security reasons and to give us some diplomatic presence.''

''Tsi Violet cannot be left alone,'' Freesh says firmly.

''I agree,'' Tammany says, ''You and Karen need to go, and Onyx, of course. Anton and I will stay—Toshi should go.''

''Toshi?'' Anton says in surprise.

''Yes,'' Toshi says, ''that will preserve what cover I have and provide Karen and Freesh with protection. Even if I haven't changed my mind—and I have—I would be unlikely to betray the others if you two remain out of reach. Is that how you see it, Tammany?''

She nods, ''Karen and Freesh will be in charge of negotiations, however. You understand?''

He smiles, sees Onyx staring at him with a steady fixation that makes me shudder, and nods quickly.

''I understand.'' He looks at Onyx again. ''You have my word.''

The shuttle's aircar is a utilitarian thing, closer to the redcap from the shuttle port than Vance's Gemster, but it has sides and seats and a place to stow cargo. We decide that our best bet is to have Toshi drive, with Freesh next to him and Onyx and me in the back.

Sweeping up, we follow the twisting course of a brook that is going in our general direction rather than trying to get through the dense growth or exposing ourselves above it. Nevertheless, Freesh directs Toshi to make certain that the Survey camp will get a good look at us before we arrive. Otherwise, certain SOPs from the days when the UAN (humans particularly) feared pirate attacks on bases would come into play.

''And that,'' he comments, ''would be most unpleasant.''

As we circle in, letting them get a good look at us, we get a good look at them. The Survey camp is constructed largely of geodesic domes in a variety of materials. Most are of an opaque pearly blue-grey material that results when a thin fabric shell is coated with a fast-drying lacquer. The end-product is semi-permanent, but can be transported in very little space.

A few domes are of sturdier stuff, constructed, Freesh tells us in the tones of a graduate returning for a college reunion, as defensible centers and places to stash valuable equipment or specimens. These are easy to locate, as they are solid navy blue.

Two shuttles rest to one perimeter of the camp, and a variety of air cars, float disks, and vans are scattered throughout the interior. Perhaps as a concession to Xi-7's frequent rainshowers, most of the domes are connected by covered walkways or breezeways.

The place is mostly utilitarian, but there are touches that show that it has become a home of sorts to some of the occupants. A deep, perfectly round pool—obviously of Chirr construction–provides a focal point at one end. Plantings of bright jewel-like flowers that suddenly make me homesick for my blasted rose garden are clustered near many of the domes.

Yet something mars the tranquility of this otherwise pleasant scene. There is no one there. No one moves purposefully along the gravel pathways. No one loads disks or takes readings with the devices that stand like abstract sculpture around the camp. No one swims in the lake or stops to admire the turquoise and magenta flowers that twine on a rough trellis outside of a cluster of domes.

As we circle lower, it seems that the place has been deserted—abandoned by the people who built it. Then we see a flutter of motion that resolves into three figures: a su-ankh, a Chirr, and a human. Toshi brings us lower, angling to land us by the lake and give us a better look.

''Chiron, Ooohoop, and DuPoy,'' he hisses softly.

I nod, studying the trio. Chiron looks as calm and imperturbable as when he interviewed me in my office. Ooohoop and DuPoy, however, look ragged. Both seem to have lost considerable weight. Ooohoop's snowy white fur is blotched and patchy. DuPoy's eyes are shadowed, and his hair is lank and stringy.

"Su-ankh fast boat," Freesh whistles.

"What?" I ask.

"Su-ankh have a style of ship more swift than any designed by humans or Chirr. Mostly they use it for individual travel for it is not cost effective for any but inert, time-sensitive cargo. Moreover, the ships have a severely debilitating effect on any creature without the su-ankh's unique dual breathing system who travels in one. Special life-support apparatus and drugs are needed even to survive and even then the experience is supposed to be akin to being swallowed and digested alive."

I study our adversaries with new respect. Even though they are bedraggled, Ooohoop and DuPoy stand as arrogantly as ever, watching our car land with a calm that I don't believe I could maintain in a similar situation.

As Toshi switches the car onto standby and motions for us to get out, I realize that my heart is racing and that all of the carefully rehearsed material I've been reviewing since before we even departed Terra has vanished from my memory.

Freesh, however, is undaunted. Bouncing down from his seat, he hops across the soft, vine-covered hillside toward the waiting triad.

Not waiting for them to speak, he begins sputtering indignantly, "Where is Discoverer Hoosh? We are here to speak with UAN scientists, not with politicians."

Ooohoop stiffens, her tail snapping angrily straight behind her. Watching, I realize that Freesh has deliberately insulted her by ignoring that she too is entitled to the title Discoverer.

"They are currently occupied," DuPoy answers smoothly, "There have been some problems with dangerous beasts."

Next to me, Onyx's ears flatten as if she has sensed something unpleasant. Hoping she'll stay in the car with Toshi, I go to join Freesh. Pulling out the datapad to cover my nervousness, I summon up a list of names that Tammany had compiled before we left Terra.

"If Shi Hoosh is not available," I state, "how about Whitman, Sanchez, or Mimir? Any of them have the qualifications we require."

Chiron flicks his tongue out, tasting the air before replying. "We are in charge here, by special UAN charter. You must deal with us first."

"We are," I say, understanding, for once, political posturing and oblique threatening, "and we have. Are you holding these people captive?"

A door opens and a sunbrowned woman emerges. Confidently, she walks to examine us. "No," her voice spiced with a Spanish accent, "we are not captives. Who are you?"

"Dr. Sanchez? Inez Sanchez?" I ask, recognizing the voice from Tammany's records.

"*Sí,*" she replies, "I am Dr. Sanchez? Who are you?"

"I'm Karen Saber," I answer, realizing that my name will mean nothing good to her, "Director at Allain Corp. You must know Discoverer Freesh. In the car is Director Toshi Van Druuik."

An inky spot separates itself from the shadows in the back seat.

"And this is Onyx."

Dr. Sanchez does the last thing I'd expect from a woman who's a renowned interplanetary explorer. She shrinks back as Onyx trots across the hill slope to stand beside me. Beneath her coiled black hair, her tanned face whitens.

"Onyx is originally from here," I say, fumbling for something to say. "You may have met her."

"Met her?" the scientist's laugh has a ragged edge. "I see her in my nightmares, her and those others we took back with us to Terra. I know every hair on their slinky bodies, every glimmer in those cursed brass eyes."

"What nonsense are you speaking?" Freesh chitters.

"No nonsense," Dr. Sanchez replies. "They are driving us mad."

Sometime later, seated around a table in one of the

geodesic domes, a substantially calmer Dr. Sanchez tries to explain. At our request, Sanchez—the authority of record here—has sent away DuPoy and his cronies. Two others have joined us. Discoverer Hoosh, a piebald Chirr marked so like Freesh that I suspect that they're from the same clan, and Mimir, an elegant olive and ivory su-ankh. All agree to Onyx's presence, but are on edge with her near.

''We no longer doubt the intelligence of the creatures of which this Onyx is one,'' Hoosh says. ''Our mistake has burrowed forcibly into our dens. Our problem is they have declared a war upon us and we do not know if we can survive.''

''We can leave,'' Mimir says, ''but as the presence of certain elements makes clear, this would not be a solution. This war would continue, and against the unscrupulous elements who would defy UAN interdict, the Xians would find their tactics less useful.''

''What precisely are their tactics?'' Toshi asks.

''Although there have been some limited physical confrontations, the reality is more terrifying. They've been systematically driving us insane,'' Sanchez says simply. ''Somehow they became aware that the creatures . . .''

''People,'' I say firmly.

''People we took to Terra,'' she corrects wearily, ''had met with less than admirable treatment. We've been having terrible dreams—although that might not be the most accurate word since they come when we're awake as well as asleep. Maybe a better word is visions.''

''The content shifted gradually,'' Mimir adds, ''At first they were inquiring. Images of the Xians boarding our ship and departing with us. After a week or so, they became more centered around scenes of imprisonment and carnage.''

''As if they were learning from you what had really happened,'' Toshi says slowly.

''From some among us,'' Hoosh corrects, ''For many of us these visions were a revelation in themselves—once we began to realize that they were not being generated by someone in our own number who had become insane.''

''You must understand,'' Sanchez says, perhaps in response to the look I give her, ''a Survey team has a great many responsibilities. Those of us who are not life sciences specialists had little contact with any of the creatures brought from Xi-7. We've since learned that the Xians were abused in transit and after and regret this, but we were ignorant, not malicious.''

''Sloppy,'' Freesh says bitterly.

''Discoverer Freesh,'' Mimir says formally, ''No one here will deny that you tried to notify a variety of team members about the abuses. We also admit that we were swayed by Ooohoop's denials. Since then, we have found evidence of substantial records tampering.''

''Damn it!'' I say, slamming my fist on the table. ''We're talking about murder, treason, and a slew of other abuses and you all are talking committees and hierarchies.''

''That's how life is, Director Saber,'' Sanchez says. ''Everything is committees and subcommittees and who knows what.''

''Maybe on Terra,'' I retort, ''and maybe in the UAN, which has learned from Terra, but not here. Whatever decisions the Xians have made have been made. We're not going to resolve anything by seeing how far we can spread the blame.''

''She is naive,'' Hoosh says into the long silence that follows, ''but in this case she is right. We have already had several members of our team disabled from lack of sleep. Two have died, one from sudden cardiac arrest, another from choking. We believe that these deaths were ultimately due to the unremitting strain we have been under. Even those of us who are comparatively healthy are distracted or afraid to leave our compound.''

''Things move,'' Mimir explains with an innocent intensity. ''Small things usually—datapads, sample dishes, food containers. Sometimes machinery turns on for no reason at all or lights flash on and off.''

''The experience is more disorienting than I can explain,'' Sanchez adds. ''We are increasingly short-staffed, which makes matters worse. People don't show up for their shifts; others must be delegated to take their places or care for our invalids. The colony ship is due in sixty standards, and the ground work for its arrival is not in place.''

''There is another element,'' Toshi reminds us. ''The three who met us when we landed represent an entirely different approach to the matter. They also claim UAN support.''

''They are renegades,'' Hoosh says with a dismissive curl of his whiskers. ''We will tell the UAN so, and then no one will listen to them.''

''I wish,'' Toshi says, ''I believed that you were right. However, I think that they will be listened to at least for long enough to achieve their goal.''

''How can they?'' Mimir asks. ''With many of us willing to testify to the Xians' sentience—if not to their benign natures—there is no way that their rights can be denied.''

''I don't believe that's their goal—except in the most peripheral sense,'' Toshi says. ''I believe that their goal is to show the UAN as a flawed agreement by using the Xians as a test case. Then, when no race can be certain that their rights will be protected, they will work to have the UAN dissolved.''

''Why?'' Sanchez says. ''That would be insanity.''

''I never said it wouldn't be,'' Toshi replies. ''Humans, at least, are capable of planning elaborately for what anyone could see is to the long-term detriment. Maybe I'm wrong, but I'm assuming that Chirr and su-ankh aren't that different.''

The aliens pause as if for a brief moment they would deny it, then Hoosh whistles a shrill sigh of acceptance.

''Yes, our ideal is clan, kin, then self, but there are

times when the best way to serve the clan seems to be in promoting the best interests of the self.''

Mimir's eyes are opaqued as a pearly lid slides across their green, ''Yes, Van Druuik is correct. There have even been those who believed that alien claims impede on our natural right to travel into whatever we desire. Chiron may well be one of those and has cleverly disguised antipathy under a skin of xenophilia.''

''If we at least agree that this is a possibility,'' Toshi says, ''Can we agree that they should be restricted in their movement and outside communication?''

''Sanchez and I have authority to order that,'' Mimir says.

Onyx's ears fly up and she stares at Mimir. The su-ankh's spinal fins flare out and his tongue flickers.

''Onyx has suggested a way that we can restrain them,'' Mimir says slowly, ''and I believe that her jurisdiction outranks ours.''

Onyx jumps down from the seat beside mine and walks to the door. She says nothing, but suddenly Toshi starts.

''Yes, that will do it,'' he says. ''It won't be permanent, but the shuttle won't fly until it's plugged back on line.''

Next it is Sanchez's turn to be startled.

''We don't have anything like that,'' she says, ''but we could use one of the smaller geodesics and put a seal on the door so that it can't be opened from inside. If some of your people want to take a turn as guards, we'll try to work with them, but they might be wiser to stay concealed. They've been very effective in making some of our team terrified of them.''

Onyx blows air out through her nose, something I'm certain she's adapted from a human snort. Dr. Sanchez meanwhile has gotten on the intercom.

''Pierre? Would you and Gilgamesh kindly ask the three visitors who arrived yesterday to wait for me in geodesic Five A? Then seal them in until I can get there.''

The man on the other side lapses into French in his surprise, but Sanchez apparently understands him.

"My authority, Pierre. Mimir will countersign if there is any difficulty. Will you do as I say?"

He agrees and she signs off with a wry grin. "We are not a military organization here—in fact, we have no real security force. That would have been excess baggage on a primarily scientific expedition. However, there are times that a clear chain of command would be useful."

"Once your 'visitors' are under wraps," I say, "our next move has to be talking with the Xians."

"Do they speak?" Hoosh asks with genuine curiosity. "We have seen no evidence of this."

"Not in so many words," I answer, eliciting a groan from Toshi at my pun, "but they do communicate. I am hoping that Onyx will act as a translator for us."

"You must accompany her," Mimir says, "to translate for *us*. I only hope that we are not beyond friendly communications. Short of a military cordon, Xi-7 cannot be isolated any more than it can be undiscovered. Can we convince a people who have never left their planet to understand this?"

"I don't know," I say honestly, "but we don't have any choice that I can see—not for us or for the Xians."

"Melodramatic," Toshi sighs, but he winks at me as he does it.

SEVENTEEN

THE NEXT MORNING, AS THE SUNLIGHT IS BREAKING THE mist into a fine haze of rainbows, our small negotiating party leaves the Survey camp. Of the group I departed from Terra with, only Freesh and Onyx remain. Toshi, Tammany, Anton, and Violet are helping the besieged scientists and keeping an eye on the three captives. From the Survey camp, Sanchez, Hoosh, and Mimir all have elected to come along.

Onyx has not commented on the company except to assign them hieroglyphics in her mental shorthand. Even as we shared coffee after her predawn arrival—she'd spent the night with her own people—she had been unusually uncommunicative. I don't have the words to ask her if she's nervous, and so I suppress my own apprehension.

The narrow track through the tangle that we walk along is barely wide enough for one. Mimir moves effortlessly, but I hear the Chirr whistling from a type of exertion for which their planet's veldts and plains had never equipped them.

For me, when I can stop concentrating on the mush squashing beneath my boots and the thin vines and twigs that spring back and swat my face even when I'm careful, I realize that this place is beautiful. My knowledge of plants doesn't go much beyond the backyard garden that

I had on Terra, but I can see that the growth here is different, more succulent, as if even with all the water, they still need to store against dry times.

The creatures I see are strangely pretty—winged skinks, tree climbers like smoky blue squirrels with enormous eyes, jointed millipedes with gemstone-bright segments.

I cannot sightsee as much as I would like. All too soon, Onyx leads us out of the tangle and into a cleared hollow beneath a webwork canopy of trees. There is no evidence of habitation here, at least to my city-bred eyes, but the Chirr whistle softly to each other. From what my translator catches, I realize that they have located what they believe are dwellings.

Then, between one breath and the next, the Xians have surrounded us. Although she tries to suppress it, I hear a low moan of terror from Sanchez. Mimir stiffens, his crests arching outward, but otherwise my teammates hold their ground.

At first, the cluster of Xians around us seem perfect duplicates of Onyx. Closer inspection shows individual differences, and I find myself wondering if we seem as indistinguishable to them. No matter, one—inky black but for a jagged stripe like white lightning across its brow—has stepped from the ranks to touch noses with Onyx.

They stand nose to nose for long enough that the mist that penetrates the canopy has time enough to pool on my waterproof. Of course, I'm stretching in an undignified fashion to scratch when Onyx signals that she wants me to join her.

"Woman with Coffee?" The image is lopsided and disproportioned. With a thrill I realize that the source is the other Xian. As I do so, I try an image of me pouring coffee for Onyx, this one (who I mentally dub "Lightning"), and myself.

In return, Lightning sends an image of himself vomiting at my feet. Hurt and revolted, I look at Onyx as if she can somehow explain what I have done to make Lightning so angry.

Rapidly, the first image is overlaid by a batch of Xian pups—children would be more accurate—but they're so cute that my mind tags them as I see them. The pups happily race over to the regurgitated mess at Lightning's feet and begin to eat.

My revulsion melts before a mixture of pleasure and embarrassment. Lightning hadn't been rejecting my invitation; he had been making a similar offer. Smiling, I try to imagine myself among the puppies, scooping up my share. Briefly, I seem to see my own image join the others. Then the mosaic fades.

Lightning has evidently decided that I can be reasoned with, because his next image is so very complex that I realize that it is to the Xian's form of communication what a formal oration is to verbal communication.

Morning, mist rising from a meadow. Among the ground cover, a group of Xians is busy. Most are dark-coated like Onyx or Lightning, lithe shadows enjoying the sun. They differ, though, not just in markings, but in mannerisms. Some are involved with a group of puppies; others root among the ground cover for shining lizards that vanish down their throats with a snap of fangs and a toss of the head. Snatches of their muted conversations dart like globular butterflies overhead.

Wed to words, my mind struggles to translate. I push the impulse back and strive to listen as the picture changes.

Something, first small and dark, then increasingly larger and bright appears above. A few puppies dart about wildly—whether for cover or from excitement I cannot tell. The adults watch more calmly, speculating on this anomaly. Only when the bright thing is so close that the Xians' fold their ears against its noisy approach do they draw back into the jungle.

When it lands, tearing up the glossy-leafed ground cover and plowing ridges of dirt into near-instantly dried, baked, and cracked furrows, I recognize that thing as a UAN Survey shuttle. It remains there, the rain steaming up off its surface, clicking and buzzing and extending what the Xians interpretation sees as appendages, although the part of my mind that is not attending knows them for distorted representations of a variety of scanning equipment.

Day becomes night and then day again before the shuttle opens and disgorges some still wriggling food. A few of the watchers, seeing this as a friendly and generous gesture, want to move and sample the food. Others, their noses wrinkling against the strange metallic scent of the creature and the even stranger scents of the slowly moving food, counsel waiting.

Lightning continues in a fashion that I would consider long-winded, if wind were at all involved in his oration, to show me how the Xians had gradually realized that the shuttle and its occupants might be some complex creature.

With a blush, I realize that they had almost instantly dismissed any thought that this "creature" might be intelligent because of the amount of noise it made and the considerable attention it gave to picking up and putting down things. I learn that both verbal communication and physical manipulation are considered traits of less intelligent creatures and of puppies too young to focus their mental abilities.

The conclusion that the Xians reach after careful study is that the shuttle and its occupants are a far-flung member of some insectlike hive race. I have trouble catching much of how this reasoning was arrived at—Lightning's images become complex, superimposing pictures of a variety of strange creatures that I have never seen atop each other, but Onyx confirms for me that I do have the gist.

Having decided on the nature of the hive creature, the Xians then set out to find its source. Naively, I've classified the Xians as pastoral innocents; it's somewhat jolting to learn that they have a global communications network. Once queries through this rule out the possibility that the creature is a native to the planet, they shift their emphasis outward.

Stargazing is not an easy task in regions gifted with almost perpetual rain, but in the polar regions of Xi-7 precipitation is much reduced and astronomy is possible. White-furred Xians send messages that the creature could have come from beyond the atmosphere.

When the hive creatures are observed to be loosening the baked earth about their first hive and carrying a variety of items within, several of the younger Xians decide to risk all and make contact with the hive creature. They are not impressed with the creature's intelligence, but decide to leave Xi-7 with it.

Lightning would have continued, but I motion that I need a rest. Behind me, the UAN contingent is shifting restlessly now that they see I am no longer in conference. Despite my aching head, they deserve to be briefed.

Sinking onto the damp ground, I give them what I have gleaned from Lightning's oration. The spate of questions begins immediately and I answer as I can, groping the while for the coffee I'd packed before our departure.

Sitting there with my hands wrapped around my mug and Onyx lapping from her bowl beside me, I let the debate wash over me, thinking that the hubbub wouldn't seem terribly intelligent from a Xian's point of view.

"They think we're a hive entity?" Mimir says. "Chirr, su-ankh, and humans all part of one creature?"

"That's what I gathered."

"There is some sense to it," Sanchez says. "Many Terran insects have evolved different body forms for different purposes. Placed side by side, they differ so that appearance alone is not enough to show that they are all sisters."

"Why would a hive entity travel across space?" Freesh asks. "If they are assuming it is unintelligent, certainly motivations such as curiosity would not apply."

"Many plants," Mimir answers, saving me the effort, "although stationary themselves, have remarkable means for spreading their seeds. From what little I have found time to study here, Xian plants are equally versatile. The Xians could readily deduce such a seeding mechanism.''

''I just hope that they've decided that we're intelligent now,'' I say, ''and that they don't think that I'm some sort of speaker bug.''

''Surely Onyx does not think that!'' Freesh protests.

''No,'' I reply, ''She's granted us sentience—if not sanity—but whether she's convinced the others is still questionable. From Lightning's preamble, I gathered that those who decided to hitchhike on the hive creature—as they saw it—were younger or at least more impulsive.''

''One thing about that story seems flawed,'' Hoosh says hesitantly. ''If they went away on the shuttle believing it to be a creature of limited intelligence, what guarantee did they have that they would be returned home?''

I look at Onyx, trying to picture Hoosh's question. Her answer comes in a graceful picture.

The shuttle is prepared for departure, the baked dirt loosened from its sides, all the crew aboard. However, in all the careful preparations, the geodesic domes have not been moved, nor have the several girder formed towers that support lighting and various other pieces of elevated apparatus.

The picture fades and there is only Onyx studying us with her bright brass eyes. Her ears are arched, however, in a fashion I have begun to believe may indicate a conditional.

''The structures,'' Sanchez says, confirming my belief that Onyx had sent this image to us all. ''I don't understand.''

The Chirr have been rapidly chattering between themselves. Now, Hoosh bounces to get our attention.

''We believe we understand,'' he says. ''Our early orbital surveys of the planet showed no cities, no permanent structures. This led us to rule out the majority of civilizations, since altering the environment to suit oneself is characteristic of those races we have met. However, both Freesh and I have noticed evidence of very sophisticated—the best term I have for it outside of our language is 'landscape architecture.' The Xians apparently do make changes to their environment, but for some reason use a great deal of art to conceal them."

"So when they saw all the junk the shuttle was leaving behind," I continue, "they assumed that the creature had to be coming back, since the job was only partially done!"

"We believe so," Freesh says. "They must have been terribly shocked to see Terra and realize how wrong they had been."

"The other Xian has returned to the center of the glade," Mimir notes softly. "I believe that you are wanted, Karen."

I nod, feeling Onyx's gaze on me. Scooping up what's left of the coffee, I trot off to where Lightning stands. After he agrees to sample the coffee, which he seems to like as much as Onyx does, I am invited to sit on a stack of comparatively dry leaves with a texture like velvet—Onyx's doing I suspect—and to listen.

Lightning begins his oration with material we had already deduced from the Survey team and Onyx, about how the shuttle returned, but without the young Xians, and how gradually they siphoned off enough information to realize that this creature was not peaceful, but was, in fact, quite dangerous. Having discovered there were minds that could be touched, they began to systematically bombard the area with sendings, hoping that—if the young explorers could not be returned—at least the creature would feel their displeasure and leave.

Fear and pain underlie these images, and something else: wrath and the desire for revenge.

Having built to this point, Lightning pauses. The tone of his pictures changes from ornate and decorative to simple, blunt lines. In these, he frames the Xians' ultimatum. The shuttles and their contents are to leave Xi-7. Forever.

Breathing a prayer to pity, I place my hand on Onyx's

shoulder and try to explain what I wonder if my audience can comprehend.

I build an image that starts with where we stand and then moves up and away from it. I know from Lightning's own images that the Xians have gathered the concept of a solar system and that other suns may harbor other systems. Now, with no real attempt at accuracy, I place other stars and other solar systems out in the dark regions beyond Xi-7.

As I struggle to craft this astronomical map, Onyx takes my raw material, sharpening and focusing it before sending it on to our listener. Listeners. With some sense I cannot name, I realize that more than Lightning are watching the images that we are crafting. I fight back something very like stage fright and fall deaf to whispers that this is not my place—I am no diplomat or astronomer. Then I press on; right or wrong, I am getting through.

We select a star and draw a solar system around it like a child's drawing. Yellow sun with planets strung around it like bright beads on avant garde necklace. Now we highlight the third planet, Terra. The moon and the space stations and shuttle hubs orbiting it as the planet does the sun. Then we dive through the atmosphere, Onyx and I harvesting the memories of our journey up so that we color in the mists that become cloud banks, blue and green that become sea and land, brown ripples that only gradually resolve themselves into mountains topped with snow.

We pour down into the cities that girdle the coastlines, showing humans at work and humans at play. Will the Xians know the difference?

Then, before we can show too much, we are up and out back into the black. Coasting through the stars, we find one that will host the Chirr homeworld. My knowledge here is all secondhand, but Onyx coaxes me on. Together we show the Chirr in their rainbow shades of fur. Some crew the ship we ride down the surface. Others perfect the vast maze of subterranean tunnels that are their cities. Others farm the vast, rich plains that make their world's bounty legendary.

My head is beginning to pound, but again we go up and out. More quickly we come upon the su-ankhs' home world. Holding more surface water even than Terra, although gathered in myriad smaller bodies, ringed by three moons and a host of bright asteroids, this world is aswirl with conflicting tides and related stresses. The people who evolved here breathe both air and water and have a high tolerance for variations in both.

Onyx and I show them in their shimmer scales, drawing our portraits with affectionate memory of Kwan Yin, Mimir, and poor Sango. We show them swimming in turbulent seas, meditating beneath a night sky crazed with light, floating on air cars above the water, and so adding dominance of air to that of earth and water.

The images I have to work with are fragmented, taken from documentaries, books, and films. I hope, as I sink back on my heels and breathe to Onyx that I need to rest, that this will be enough. This however, is only our prologue. The real message can only come when the Xians grasp the complexity beyond their world.

Letting Onyx explain the intermission to the rest of the Xians, I stand and stretch. The coffee bottle is empty and wistfully I decide that I can't really ask anyone to run back and get me a refill.

The rest of the crew who accompanied me here gesture for me to join them. Reluctantly, I do so—what I'd really like is a couple of hours sleep.

"What have they been telling you?" Sanchez asks eagerly.

"Not much," I answer. "I've been telling them about us."

"Ah," Sanchez looks disappointed, then brightens. "We've counted over two dozen observers along the glade edge."

"Great. I wonder if they've got their news service here too, and if this is being recorded." I blush suddenly. "I'm not a scientist and I've cut corners to try and get the basics across. Any of you would be better at this than me and yet you're just standing here getting wet and bored.''

''Better?'' Hoosh's ears widen into soft petals. ''Maybe. Maybe more informed, but better here is not a word to use. You have the trust of Onyx. We do not. We may stand, but we also serve who stand and get wet.''

''Boredom is the least of our concerns,'' Sanchez soothes. ''Relax, Karen. Put politics on hold for now. Right now Onyx is barely acknowledging the rest of us. You need to prove to them that all of us are people so that we can start straightening things out.''

With an awkward nod to all of them, I take a deep breath and head for the center of the glade. Onyx is off at the fringes with some Xians. I see small motions in the air that might be the float stone game.

When she sees me, she comes trotting out. Meeting me at the center, she lowers her head and retches. Kneeling to aid her, I realize that the action is deliberate. Controlling myself, I watch her bring up a small heap of something rather like hazel nuts in the shell except that they are a rich purple and covered with a soft quilting of fuzz. Seeing that she expects me to pick one up, I do so, and discover that it is neither wet nor slimy—only warm and vaguely moist.

Onyx raises one in front of her nose and bites it out of the air. Then she takes her head and perks her ears at me.

''You want me to eat one?'' I say.

She looks so eager I expect her to whine, though of course she doesn't, and lifts another.

''I'm not sure they're safe for me, girl.''

The image of the two of us eating dog food nuggets and coffee springs to my mind so rapidly that I'm not certain which one of us put it there.

''All right,'' I say, raising the thing to my mouth, ''but if it poisons me that leaves you to straighten this mess out.''

Trying not to think about where this has been, I pop

the nut into my mouth. "Nut" seems like the wrong word, because the texture is spongy like a mushroom cap. The taste, moreover is wonderful, like the lime syrup used to make gimlets. Without hesitation, I munch into another.

"Karen?" Mimir calls. "Is that wise?"

"I don't think she'd harm me," I call back, "and I know she can eat most of our food."

"Can you give us one?" Hoosh whistles. "I have a small analyzer here and we could test it."

That seems like a good idea. Relaying the request to Onyx, I got her permission and reluctantly relinquish two of my treats. Promising to stop if they find anything dangerous or the moment that I feel ill, I return to where Lightning now waits with Onyx. They have a small heap of stones between them and as I take my seat, one after another spins up into the air.

At first I think they're demonstrating a game for me. Then I realize that a complex pattern is being formed. When I factor out the space that should be there to indicate the void between the systems, I catch on.

"You're doing the solar systems!" I say aloud, forgetting that the words won't mean anything, "The ones I showed you earlier and your own. That's fantastic!"

Now, in addition to the pattern of stones, Lightning sends me a picture that draws glowing rings around each of the inhabited planets. Xi-7 is hooped in pale yellow, the rest in their own pastel shades, pink, blue, and green. Then each of the UAN planets is haloed in a multicolored ring. Only Xi-7 remains in its solitary yellow.

The stones fall to the vines and the colors from my mind.

Lightning stares at me expectantly, but I'm missing something. I look at Onyx, hoping for clarification. She studies me and then a complex image forms.

First, each of the four home worlds with a caricature of the native race standing over it is shown. Then, each of the UAN worlds with the other UAN races represented as smaller pictographs—Xians are conspicuously absent from the mixture.

"I get it," I say slowly, thinking my words. "Each of the UAN races has its own world. If they choose to interpopulate—fine. But Xi-7 is for your people alone."

Onyx lets the image fade.

"That's it, isn't it?" I say, "Well, at least they don't think we're one hive race anymore. Now the tough job. How do we tell them that it's not so simple?"

Onyx stares at me, one ear up, the other down. Idly, I play with the remaining purple fruit as I make and discard increasingly complex plans for showing the Xians that they can't go back to being alone. How do I explain territory and trespass on an interstellar scale? Every time I try to put the ideas into pictures, my brain fragments.

"I'm not cut out for this, Onyx," I'm saying, when an idea so simple that it can't possibly work comes to me.

"Look, Onyx, get them to do that thing with the rocks up in the air again, please. And I need a stick."

I find a length of something that smells rather like white pine but feels like willow. Onyx manages to explain what I want to the others. Biting down on my lower lip, I move to where the spinning pebbles shape solar systems.

"Onyx, please help me—I'll try and show them, but I can't . . ." I stop myself. "I have to, don't I?"

Somehow without my noticing, some twenty Xians have come out of the jungle. I can feel that each one is part of the effort that suspends the swirling stones. They're with me, this far.

Taking a pose I realize a moment later that I'm borrowing from my second-grade teacher, I point to the stone that's Xi-7.

"This is here," I say, feeling inane, "and as Lightning said, Chirr, humans, and su-ankh each have their own worlds and travel between them with some freedom. Lightning says that you wish us to do as we wish with our worlds but to leave yours to you."

I take a deep breath, "But we can't. Even if the UAN

agreed to leave you alone, it can't make certain that everyone else does.''

Using the pointer to help me focus, I picture all of our shuttles leaving Xi-7 and the solar system. The planet spins alone in my mind while I think on the passing of time. Then a ship comes—one far larger than a Survey vessel. I draw its approach with a sweeping wave of my willow wand and a tiny pebble leaps up to follow my trace.

The ship disgorges one shuttle, then a second, then a third. They continue to fall, a strand of steel beads that tear up the ground and vomit forth raffish exploiters.

I pause, my head beginning to ache. Onyx blinks at me. I take this to mean that my point is being received, even if not well.

''Now,'' I continue, trying to believe myself, ''if you allow the UAN to befriend you, the UAN will send observers and scientists who will leave a ship in orbit.''

Concentrating on picturing this, I can feel Onyx somehow amplifying my picture. I add the same rogue ship as before, but this time instead of it disgorging destructive ships they see the resident ship and retreats.

Point made, I stop concentrating, discovering that the Xians are retreating into the jungle again. Our pebble universe remains as a spinning afterthought that patters to a heap of stones as they vanish.

''Do they understand, Onyx?''

She whuffles at me, ears forward, and tosses me a purple berry. I snag it and, still chewing, wander over to the UAN contingent.

''Rest break,'' I announce, ''I'm worried that I did get that across.''

''Worried that you *did*?'' Freesh asks.

''Yes,'' I say. ''I had them reconstruct what Lightning showed me because I wanted the business of the universe beyond their planet to come home. It also made it easier for me to talk. It's hard picturing everything in your head. I hope it also helped you to follow what we were saying.''

"Somewhat," Mimir says. "You are trying to show them that Xi-7 cannot remain alone, otherwise it is difficult to follow."

"Sorry," I say, not really feeling it.

The Xians stay away for a long time and we huddle there in the damp. The scientists have analyzed the purple fruit and come to the conclusion that it is a superlative source of fructose with a liberal dose of vitamins—an organic energy pill. After sampling the plants around them, they have begun a heated debate over whether the fruit is naturally this way or whether the Xians might have hybridized it.

I'm leaning back against a tree with satiny brown bark and leaves that remind me of a French print bedspread my grandmother once had. I'm thinking how nice a cup of coffee would be when Onyx emerges from the shrubs with my hot bottle hung St. Bernard-like about her neck. She is inordinately pleased at my reaction, and as I am fumbling for words, projects a picture of Tammany.

Chuckling, I unfasten the coffee bottle from its sling. While I am unfolding the note tucked into the canvas strap, Onyx floats a satchel from the tangle. It proves to contain a heating flask, some purifying tabs, and a selection of powdered beverages to suit the tastes of the scientists.

Tammany's note reads, "Karen, Onyx arrived here and made clear that you needed coffee. She agreed to take back some things for the others, but you have her charmed. We are fine but apprehensive here. Tsi Captain has made contact with the UAN Survey ship *Blue Jay*, and on the groundside team's recommendation, we have been granted favored-observer status. Chiron's presence has been reevaluated, and they are scanning for his interstellar vehicle with the authority to impound. Tammany."

I pass the note to Freesh. Mimir is assisting Hoosh in mixing hot drinks and Sanchez is eyeing with fastidious concern the pile of purple fruit that Onyx has disgorged at her feet. I decide I could learn to like her as she shrugs and picks one up, popping it into her mouth without even rinsing it first.

Then Lightning and several other Xians return to the center of the glade. Onyx and I take our places. Lightning wastes no time, but in a series of bright mental fireworks reminds me of our previous discourse.

When the new series begins, I somehow know that I am seeing a hypothetical situation. It begins with a shuttle landing much as I had striven to show them. A raffish crew that owes something to my fictional rogues begins ripping down trees, dredging lakes, and throwing up fantastic structures of pearl and shell.

From the fringes of the jungle, the Xians watch, their pyramidal eyes preternaturally wise and thoughtful. By some limit at which I can only guess, the shuttle's crew transgresses the Xian's patience. Then silently war is declared, but this war is fought like no other I know. No weapons are crafted; the enemy is neither bitten nor clawed. They are never even touched. In fact, what is done is more subtle and more terrible.

Lightning and his cohorts embrace me within a nightmare. Tendrils and vines become serpents. Trees sprout pendant tiger faces, fanglike ivory scimitars dripping venom and honey to burn my eyes and sear my merest thought into discordant chaos. The darkness glitters with angular four-pointed stars that resolve into the Xians' watching omnipresence.

I can feel myself rocking forwards as if covering my eyes and forehead with tightening hands will release me from the visions. Beside me Onyx is dropping her mind between mine and the increasingly malevolent demonstration being produced by her kin. She is cotton, padding me from the worst of the force that still oppresses me, from the lambent yellow acid gnawing my skin from my hands and leaving only the bones as a frail lacework tracery to defend me from the ocher and lime bassoon notes that threaten to leave me senseless.

Shrill and keening, a sound slices the images into paper-thin wraiths that shred and fade, leaving my mind my own again, and my respect raised for both the Xians and the UAN team who had withstood their onslaughts.

Footsteps come racing across the ground cover. Human footfalls, Chirr hops and bounds, and the odd hissing slither of the su-ankh's tail following the pit-pat of the feet.

"Karen? Karen?" Freesh says. "What has happened?"

I sit up, pulling my breath in between my teeth.

"I just had a very convincing argument put to me as to why the Xians can take care of themselves, thank you."

"Coffee?" Hoosh asks anxiously, extending my mug.

I glance at the tepid stuff. "No, I'd throw up, and I don't have nearly as fine control over the output as Onyx."

Onyx, I now have the attention to notice, has left my side and advanced on Lightning. Again, I hear that nerve rattling keen and realize with a chill that Onyx is making it—the first vocalization that I have ever heard from her.

The Xians are equally taken aback, and with ears wrapped tight against their heads and tails low are all but groveling.

"I don't need to be a telepath," Sanchez says dryly, "to translate that—they went too far, didn't they?"

"Well, I think so," I answer, managing a grin, "and as long as Onyx thinks so, too, I don't think that we even need to argue the point. Do you think that they could repel invaders with those—hallucinations?"

"Yes," Mimir says, "until it is discovered what chemicals or physical element will reduce the effectiveness. Even then, I suspect that it would rapidly lead to some avoiding the planet and only the bravest, cleverest, most callous deciding to risk both insanity and UAN sanction to plunder it."

"Further," Hoosh adds thoughtfully, "it would not prevent the ecological damage that repeated attempts to establish and exploit would cause. The sensations are terrible, especially when it is combined with the Xian's talent for shifting objects, which can make the entire experience unbearably real—we all know this.''

''They must have really forgotten themselves,'' Sanchez says, kneeling by me and checking my still-racing pulse. ''You were as hard hit as anyone in our camp who didn't actually crack.''

''They must,'' I agree doubtfully. ''Well, Onyx seems to have made them see the error of their ways, so we can get back to trying to show them that spaceships bring more than just people.''

''Rest for the day,'' Mimir urges. ''There is no great hurry now that a dialogue has been opened. Perhaps with some reflection they will even include some of us.''

''Maybe that would be a good idea. Let me ask Onyx.''

I turn only to find Onyx, Lightning, and the rest poised, ears perked forward, intent on some point beyond my shoulder. Turning, I see nothing, but both Chirr have also risen onto their hind legs and are stretched to their full height.

''Ever feel positively deaf?'' Sanchez asks ruefully. ''Hoosh, what is wrong?''

''Something is moving rapidly in this direction,'' Hoosh replies without coming off point, ''and judging from our hosts' reaction it is either something they recognize as dangerous or something completely unfamiliar.''

''Neither's really good,'' Sanchez mutters. ''Let me call camp and see what they know.''

The little comm unit hanging from her belt lights even before she can touch it.

''I don't believe in coincidence,'' she says.

I nod and fumble for my own. The channel opens on a message already in process; Anton's voice is tight and ragged.

''. . . your direction, probably using some look down tracking. Again, Chiron, DuPoy, and Ooohoop have escaped. Ooohoop has been recaptured but the others are believed to be heading your direction, probably . . .''

I cut in.

"Anton, we hear you. How long ago did this happen? How the hell did they get out?"

"Kari!" he sounds so pleased and relieved that my face gets hot. "We don't know except that it was after Onyx came by to get drinks for you. We think they're heading for you, but they have the jump on us. Ooohoop was found getting in their shuttle, so we wasted time looking for the others here. One of the Chirr here caught a scent trail on the other two entering the jungle. Tammany scanned and picked up an odd signal, and with Tsi Captain's help narrowed it to a relay up topside. We're trailing them now."

"Great—I think," I answer. "I hate to say it but you may be right. On our side the people with better ears seem to have something. I'll leave this channel open, but I think I may be needed as a liaison here. Tell the rest?"

"You have it, Kari," he says, "and keep your head low."

Sanchez and Mimir are busy on a channel to their own people and, seeing that I'm available, motion me over.

"Pierre has volunteered to bring a skimmer and pull us out," Sanchez says. "Should I tell him to come on?"

"No," I say, "the Xians are just beginning to see us as people. They won't be able to tell us from them. I'm not certain that they can't crash a skimmer, but I don't want to gamble on it."

"Wise," Mimir replies.

All the Xians but Lightning and Onyx have vanished from the glade. The sounds from the jungle are now audible even to my ears. Whatever is coming must believe there is no need for stealth.

I tense myself against the impact of fire from a long-range weapon. The thought kites across the surface of my conscience that such a death would indeed be ironic justice. Fighting an urge to go and hide, instead I walk over and hunker next to Onyx. I try to get her attention, to warn her of rifles that bite across distance. She does not acknowledge me and I rest my hand on her back in a bid for attention.

Her ears melt down in what I recognize as an angry stance. Hastily, I jerk my hand back, but that momentary proximity taps me into an image I was not meant to see, a glittering trace the yellow white of an old skull that snakes its way through the trackless jungle—the perfect guide for Chiron and DuPoy.

Unmindful of the wet, I sink to my knees. The two Xians are luring these two to us—to them. The line I had seen had not just been a visual trace, but more, a siren's song luring with promise of brutal satisfaction.

Why Ooohoop had not heard it, I cannot hazard—perhaps her motives were not the same as those of her allies. I dismiss that puzzle as unimportant. What is important is my realization that Onyx has an agenda of her own. As vital as breathing is discovering whether this agenda is counter to my own desire to make the Xians understand their own danger.

At that moment, Chiron and DuPoy stride into the glade, no less puppets for all that they are unaware of their strings. I am not certain what proves a greater relief—seeing that they bear no weapons with greater range than a knife or discovering that Hoosh has pulled a side arm from one of his vest's copious pockets and that Mimir is balancing a rifle in the steady support of his upper two arms.

At my round-eyed look of surprise, his tongue flickers out. "I had it in parts."

But my relief and amusement cannot last. Seemingly indifferent to the UAN presence, Chiron and DuPoy are striding rapidly toward the two Xians. The human's face is contorted with a bestial fury; the su-ankh's four arms grope out as if too eager for the moment that they will seize and rend the calm creatures before them.

"Stop them!" Sanchez yells, starting to run forward.

Hoosh whistles for her to get out of the line of fire. Mimir seems to be searching for a clear shot at Chiron, who towers over the rest. From the jungle's edge, torn and soaking wet, burst Anton, Toshi, and Tammany.

In the midst of all this chaos, I do the thing I must. Pulling my arm back, I thrust with a hard bone-breaking strike that my martial arts instructor had taught me could be deadly in close quarters. My hand impacts Onyx's flank with sufficient force that I feel the bones buckle and she is knocked off her feet to thud into Lightning.

My head explodes in a kaleidoscope of clashing colors and competing pains so intense that my muscles turn to jelly and I collapse along the line of my own momentum. There are noises around me—none of which make sense.

I grasp the wetness of the groundcover beneath me, my head rupturing anew as a Chirr hops up beside me and slaps my arm. Then I feel nothing at all.

EIGHTEEN

AWAKENING, I WANT TO FAINT AGAIN. THERE IS NOT A muscle in my body that does not scream for mercy. Even as I try to open my eyes, tears roll forth, burning acid trails across skin that feels swollen to bursting. I am not on a bed but floating in something that is either too warm or too cold—my system cannot agree—but at least it doesn't add to the pain, except where my neck rests in a vise that is steadily sawing through my increasingly fragile neck.

I give up opening my eyes because the light scorches them into brittle soap bubbles that my tears shatter. Someone has seen my motion, it seems, for a voice now adds its cacophonous pounding to the maelstrom in my head.

"Kari? Kari? Can you hear me?"

I want to respond, just to tell him to shut up, but my jaw aches as if every tooth is infected, and my tongue is a furry mass that clogs my mouth. All I can do is weep more steadily, but this seems enough.

The voice, Anton's, yells mercilessly, "Tam! Toshi! I think she's coming around!"

There is more noise then, agreement that brain-wave readings do concur, that I am conscious despite my nearly complete lack of response. Stupidly, they decide that I must want to know what has happened since my collapse, when all I want to do is go back to sleep or—better yet—to die.

Captive to my pain, I must listen and hope that when they are done that they will leave.

"Kari, you're in the medical bay of the UAN Scout ship *Blue Jay*. You've been unconscious for six days."

"Chiron and DuPoy are dead." Tammany's voice is softer but no less unpleasant—timpani thuds rather than the brass insistence of Anton's. "They died just after you attacked Onyx. Autopsy didn't show what killed them, but it did show how they died. DuPoy had a latent circulatory condition that could not handle it when his blood pressure suddenly rose. His arteries simultaneously ruptured. Chiron's secondary brain quit and so did all the autonomous systems that ran through it."

Sounds wonderful, I think, but they're not ready to leave me alone.

"You simply collapsed in some sort of pain," Toshi says, "until Freesh knocked you out. We all then received an image indicating that we had better pack up and get out, all of us. We've cleared off the planet. Look-down shows that the structures left behind have been taken apart and concerted effort is being made to wipe any sign of us off the planet."

"Mimir has taken Chiron's fast boat back to Terra and the *Shadowsweep* has been delegated to stand out-system here and scan for incoming vessels. Gerbil, Violet, and Pearl have been given a smaller craft and are doing the same thing." Anton pauses. "We've tried to shuttle negotiating teams to the surface, but they were hit both times with hallucinations before they could even unbutton."

I don't even want to respond.

"Let her rest," Toshi interrupts almost tenderly. "Get that doctor in here to give her something. We may need to keep her out until she gets over this."

"Over what?" Tammany says with a sharpness that doesn't hide worry. "Nothing is wrong with her!"

"Hell!" I want to protest, "A lot you know," but then

a doctor comes and whatever I'm given smothers my consciousness.

I'm certain I haven't come around, but someone is talking to me. Although I try to ignore the voice and burrow back into slumber, it persists.

"Karen? Karen?" The voice is velvety and female. "Don't ignore me. I have come to tell you how to make the pain end."

This interests me, and I focus and recognize Aino Rand. She isn't there, and if I try and look at her, disconcertingly her presence melts and blurs. My stomach feels queasy and I consider ignoring her.

"No, don't try to look at me, Karen. Simply accept I am here."

"Naw, too hard. Go 'way."

"You want the pain?"

"No, I forget. I hurt."

"Very well, imagine closing your eyes and then listen to my voice. You'll find this easier."

"Okay," I agree, "you're right. Can you make the pain go away?"

"I can tell you how to make it go away."

"I don't hurt so much now," I say. "Being sedated makes the pain less."

"Do you know why you hurt?" she repeats patiently.

"No," I start to answer, then I remember, "Onyx did it. I hit her."

"Why did you hit her, Karen?"

"She was luring Chiron and DuPoy. I think they were let loose by her in the first place. She meant to destroy them, and I wanted to stop her."

"You wanted to stop her, Karen. Why?"

"Why? We need them so that they can be publicly tried for their crimes. They're dead and all we have is Ooohoop."

"That's all?"

I pause. "I didn't like the anger in Onyx—I didn't want to see her do that. It would warp her."

"It didn't work," Aino says, "Onyx and the other one . . ."

"Lightning."

"Lightning. Killed Chiron and DuPoy. Why do you hurt, Karen?"

"I hit Onyx."

"Did she do this to you?"

"She did?"

"No, Karen, did she?"

"Yes?"

"Karen, why are you in pain?"

"I hit Onyx."

"Did Onyx do this to you?"

"Did she?"

"Karen, the answer is yes and no."

"I don't like this game—my head hurts enough already."

"I'm not playing, Karen. Can you accept that you're a telepath?"

"Yes. Maybe."

"Stay with 'yes,' Karen. You are a telepath, maybe a strong one. That's why you could understand Onyx so much more easily than the rest of us."

"I could?"

"Yes, you could. Now, when you hit Onyx, she lashed out at you with all the rage she was holding to attack her enemies."

"Lots of rage," I agree. "She was very angry."

"At whom?"

"At me."

"No, Karen, not at you, at DuPoy and Chiron."

"No, at me. I felt it. She trusted me and I hurt her—I tried to stop her."

"Yes, Karen, she was angry at you, but for a moment only. Karen, where are you?"

I think and remember, "A UAN ship—the *Blue Jay*."

"In orbit, Karen. Onyx is not here. She could not still be influencing your thoughts."

I struggle to comprehend this. "Then who? Then how?"

"You, Karen. You are doing this to yourself. I suspect that you are angry with yourself for hurting someone who trusted you. Self-torture won't repair the trust."

"I'm always hurting people who trust me," I mutter, hoping she cannot see the long trace of betrayals that is my past. "This isn't new."

"This is new, Karen. Reach into yourself and accept that you are inflicting pain on yourself. Then go and apologize to Onyx. If you haven't been wrong, explain your feelings. I'd like to leave you to your latest version of drugs and booze and self-pity, Karen, but I don't have that luxury. We have a volatile situation here and you might—just might—be able to salvage it."

"I can't. I was trying to help the Xians but Onyx wanted other things more."

"So your feelings are hurt. Haven't you ever wanted to get even? Those people tortured her, killed her friends, and left her on an alien planet—finally they tried to sell her for parts. Doesn't that deserve a little revenge?"

"No." My head is clearing, but my heart hurts with a different kind of pain. "Not when your revenge opens the way for innocent people to suffer."

"That's it then," Aino Rand says. "Are you going to pull yourself off the cross and try and tell Onyx this, or are you going to open her and her world and the UAN to the beginnings of a long cycle of destruction?"

"I'm scared."

"You should be. Even with best intentions, we may be too late."

"Is the sedative still in my body?"

"Yes, but I can have an antidote given to you. Do you want me to?"

"Will the pain be gone?"

"It should be, although you may be sore from tensing against the pains you have been feeling."

"I'll take the antidote."

Aino Rand's presence vanishes and I sink back into something like rest. Slowly, I sort out what must be done, who I will take with me. I may be too late, and I am not so naive that I believe that I will make everything right by talking with Onyx. Still, we can try. She might love me a little still.

Awakening, I am hustled from the flotation tank where I had resided for the past several days. The pain is in the main gone, but I have a hangover of abused muscles. When the bemused med techs dismiss me, I decide to satisfy my craving for coffee and companionship.

Departing sick bay, I am accosted by Toshi, Tammany, and Anton. Crowing with pleasure at my recovery, they sweep me aft to the suite of rooms we've been assigned.

The accommodations are not as cramped as they might be, since members of the *Blue Jay*'s crew are taking outguard shifts or have been transferred to the *Shadowsweep.* Tammany in particular is delighted that the Chirr ruffians have been designated as an official UAN vessel.

"I suspect that Gerbil and Pooh Bear want to turn privateer, but Tsi Captain is wonderful. Freesh has been informally made a member of the clan—somewhat to his chagrin. Hoosh has hinted that the Shi clan will be rescinding their previous sanctions in light of the new evidence that Ooohoop was not as honest as she claimed."

"I'm glad," I say, sitting and accepting the mug of coffee Anton presses into my hands. "Now, Aino has said that I may be the only one who can get through to Onyx. Honestly, this scares me. I'd like to take you three with me and leave these UAN folks up here."

Two nods, but Tammany says, "Why?"

I take a deep breath. "I trust you and I trust your motives for getting involved in this. Maybe it started as a job and maybe it continued with coercion, but somewhere I think things changed for you, just like they did for me. Or maybe I'm a fool."

"No," Anton says. "Never, Kari."

Toshi cocks an eyebrow at this declaration, but his blue eyes are friendly and his smile unforced.

"You're right, Karen," he says. "I like the challenge; the pay-off if we pull this one off is more than money—it's the goodwill of an entire people and of some powerful UAN members."

"And you like Onyx," Tammany says dryly, "as do I. Ben Allain was right after all, it seems."

"Hmm?" I ask, afraid to word the question directly.

"Before he died," Toshi says, "Ben Allain argued that we needed to consider more than the money we could make when accepting jobs. Some of us argued that intangibles didn't pay for gear or labs or salaries or anything else."

His face has paled, and I choose not to press the point.

"You'll come with me, then?" I ask. "All three of you? Even though they don't want us there and have some really unpleasant ways of letting us know?"

Three nods answer me, then Tammany pulls out her datapad.

"It's evening down where we last saw Onyx," she says, "We have time to plan and to all get a good night's rest. The Xians don't seem restricted by night or day, but we'll do better after dawn."

Lying in bed after an exhaustive planning session, I discover that my brain won't slow down. We've dealt with so much—landing site, shuttle type, weapons, other gear. Some of the problems were less physical, like a long argument with the UAN representatives over the all human makeup of our team. They would have preferred a representative mix drawn largely from their own numbers. After extensive debate, I solve that one by simply refusing to go unless I can pick my teammates. This doesn't make me any friends, but it does end the argument.

My brain still spinning with advice and nervousness, I'm considering getting a light sedative when there is a ring at my door. I sit up and smooth my hair, expecting a medic.

"Come."

The door slides to one side and Anton enters.

"Kari"—in the dim lights he looks shy and maybe sheepish—"I sort of figured you weren't sleeping and I came to see if I could do anything—get you something or give you a back-rub."

"Anton, I . . ." I realize I'm blushing and feel furiously stupid. "I'll doze off. Probably it's nerves, or too much coffee after abstaining for that week I was ill."

He steps closer and looks down at me.

"We . . . I was really worried," he says. "I'm glad that u're better. What caused it?"

"Something like delayed reaction to the stress," I fib. "Aino helped me to relax."

"You sure I can't get you anything," he says, brushing my shoulder with his fingertips. "I really do give a good back-rub—I took a six-month course in Swedish massage and another in shiatsu for a job."

"No, Anton, really. Now run along and let me sleep."

He backs to the door. "All right. Sleep well, Kari."

"Good night, Anton."

He leaves, and I order the computer to lock the door. Then I smile a bit ruefully and yawn, suddenly tired. The pillow is soft and the blankets warm as I pull Sleep's mantle over my head.

The next morning, I leave the others to shake the shuttle into shape and hurry to the commissary to pick up a special order I'd placed the night before. Violet, recently in from a guard shift, hops over to meet me, a large satchel balanced in front of her.

"Here, enough coffee for a corps of Marines, and those strange nuggets you asked if we could make. They taste terrible."

I grin. "I know. I know."

Anton and Tammany are running through pilot and copilot routines when I arrive. Within minutes we have launched and are burning our way through the atmosphere. My memories afire with the sting of loss, I watch, afraid to even hope, concentrating on finding Onyx, not on what will happen after we do.

Despite the Xians' determined attempt to eradicate all traces of the UAN occupation, Anton easily locates first our original landing spot and then the UAN camp. Remembering how disturbed they had been by the destruction caused by a landing shuttle, Anton hovers us over the lake the Chirr had dug at the campsite.

We get a bit splashed, but manage to land without marring the terrain further. After that, we slog the rest of the way on foot. It isn't easy, especially since we have decided that we won't do any more damage than we have to.

''Damn this stuff!'' Tammany explodes after a supple vine whips back across her face, leaving a brick red welt against the brown. ''When we get out of here see if I ever look at a vegetable again!''

''Funny,'' Toshi says, ''I'd have thought you'd go on a binge in revenge—War against the Greenery.''

''Careful, Toshi,'' Anton says, looking from side to side. ''Remember that they can read thoughts. Are you doing okay, Kari?''

I nod, but my skin is prickling in anticipation of the first mental onslaught. We've been left alone so far, but anticipation is coursing like a snake between my shoulder blades.

The glade is wide, wet, and empty. Aware that we must be being watched, we erect a strange pavilion. The design is modeled on a setup used for arctic exploration, where imbedding support directly into the ice and snow may be neither possible nor prudent. Instead, the supports are based upon an interlocking frame of poles. Over this, we stretch a lemon yellow roof, leaving the sides open.

For our own use, we've brought backless camp stools. A slightly larger and sturdier stool serves as a table, on which I begin to brew fresh coffee.

''When I was seven,'' Toshi says softly, ''my parents sent me to camp for the summer. One of the first activities was a camping trip, and on the very first night the counselors and some of the older kids delighted in competing for who could tell the most frightening story. By the time I unrolled my bedroll that night, every tree concealed a creature, and the wind itself had angry eyes. I never thought I'd feel that way again.''

Tammany wraps long fingers around her empty mug. ''I was the survivor of twins, and for my mother's people this was a very bad thing, for it is believed that the ghost infant will seek to lure its twin to join it in the spirit world. Sometimes when I was very small, I would believe that I heard the dead baby chirping to me, and even the pillow I clutched to me felt as if it was wisping into nothing.''

I listen to them without comment, not answering the unasked question: ''Are these fears our own or are they being planted in our minds by enemies in the darkness?''

The coffee is hot and ready when I arrange a heap of the nuggets in a shallow slate blue bowl with scalloped edges. A stack of empty bowls in the same style sits beside the coffee pot. Anton reaches out and squeezes my hand as I walk to the edge of the pavilion.

''Onyx!'' I call, not attempting to project any image. ''Coffee's ready!''

The hammering of my heart belies the calmness of my manner as I scan the green and silver of the tangle bordering the glade. I cannot bear that she will not come, and yet I am so certain that she will not that I fail to see her approach until she is nearly to me.

Her ears are cupped and she approaches as hesitantly as she had the first time I opened the door of her cage.

''Woman with Coffee?'' the picture comes softly, blurred as if she is whispering.

''Yes,'' I nod. ''Please, come and join us.''

Still hesitant, she steps under our roof. Her nostrils flare as she scents the nuggets in their bowl and I feel the edge of a memory. She greets each of the others with grave courtesy and then takes an open spot by the coffee table, accepting the soft rug that Anton unrolls for her to recline upon.

Toshi pours the coffee with the measured grace and formality of a tea ceremony. When Tammany reaches for the cream and sugar, the tray floats to her hands.

"Why, thank you, Onyx," she says. "Would you care for a cookie?"

Onyx gently lifts a few down to her mat beside the coffee bowl. The small conversation of serving over, Anton draws a deep breath.

"Onyx," he says slowly, "I need to ask a favor of you."

Whether the words penetrate matters less than the novelty that this is clearly meant to be a group discussion. Onyx's ears perk and she focuses her disconcerting gaze on Anton.

He sips his coffee and then continues, "Would you talk with Karen about what happened here a few days ago? She has been ill and we need her to have the full picture."

Onyx blinks, then nods. Her attention shifts to me, but I can feel that the other three are included in her response. She gives me a mercilessly accurate description of the deaths of Chrion and DuPoy. Su-ankh blood, I notice with absent fascination, is so dark red that it is almost black. Compared to it, DuPoy's is scarlet, almost orange as it ruptures from his nose and leaks from his mouth. My hand flutters to my own mouth, but I manage the one word that I am scripted to say.

"Why?"

Like the hanging bulge of a thunderhead, Onyx's fury shapes the images she sends—of being strapped in cages, kept alive by tubes while hunger washes acid in your belly, of helplessness before the deaths of those bound to you not by mere kinship but by a dream, of having your ability to speak—even to your own—taken from you, and yet knowing that those who have gagged you are condemning you for having nothing to say.

Now comes the hardest question. "Did killing them make it right?"

And in answer she sends me and me alone one picture—the face of Ben Allain.

Angry at myself for finally admitting the truth aloud, I say, "I was wrong, Onyx. What I did didn't help him and probably hurt you. If you're going to justify yourself, don't try and do it by showing me how little right I have to question. The issue still remains: Did killing DuPoy and Chiron make anything better for the dead ones?"

She shows me blackness that collapses in on itself, folding origami-like into an angular self-portrait.

"For you," I whisper, "that's the one thing revenge like this does—it makes the pain go away for a while. Can you understand that it must stop with those two or we will never see an end? You're the only one who can convince your people that some of us might be worth getting to know."

Her answer is stillness, then five of the hard nuggets erupt from the bowl to stop one before each of us. I take mine and bite a chunk from it, chewing determinedly.

Tammany imitates me and nearly spits hers out. "These taste terrible!"

"Yeah," I grin at Onyx, who eats hers in two snaps. "I know. UAN synthesized kibbles—the bread of captivity or misunderstanding or something."

"A symbol?" Toshi asks, nibbling on his.

"A memory," I answer.

NINETEEN

THE XIANS EVENTUALLY AGREE TO ALLOW A RETURN OF a UAN team under the condition that protocols are established so that the damage to the terrain is as limited and as restricted as is feasible. As the next several weeks go by, studies and negotiations continue. The work is slow and prone to misunderstanding because the electronic translators that work on a verbal speech cannot handle the Xian's images. Some clever tech may solve this in time, but for now the bulk of the liaison work falls to Onyx and me.

Aino Rand, Kwan Yin, and others take the responsibility of explaining to the UAN that despite apparent differences the Xians share many goals and ambitions with the known races. Already, there's talk of Xians traveling to the other inhabited worlds.

Stepping from my geodesic into a drizzling morning that is beginning to seem normal, I am intercepted by Anton.

"Kari, a ship arrived last night with news. The guidelines we drafted for the UAN/Xian incorporation have been accepted. The holdouts were largely parties that had been planning on profiting from colonial ventures. There will probably be some lawsuits, but they won't affect the main picture."

"Great," I answer, feeling odd now that the job I've

been doing is effectively completed. I'd expected to feel happy, but there's a sense of loss.

"Great? That's it?" Anton studies me. "Well, Kwan Yin and Aino are here along with a mess of UAN stuffed shirts. There'll be some formal ceremony later for the record. Kwan Yin asked if you would see her some time this morning."

"Sure." I shake myself. "I'll go over now if you think she'll be free."

"She seemed to be. The reporters and recorders are still upside until this afternoon."

Leaving him, I amble across the restored complex, my boots thumping softly on the wooden walkway that now helps keep muddy pathways from forming. Kwan Yin will be in the largest geodesic, the increasingly cramped Administration and Research Center. The Xians have agreed to let the UAN expansion go down, Chirr-style, rather than sprawling out or up. There always will be topside buildings, though, because humans and su-ankh tend to like open areas.

Sanchez and Hoosh wave as they hurry by, sketch pads in hand, on their way to some meeting with the Xians. Inside the dome, the light is warm and yellow. Shedding my coveralls and hanging them on a drip hook, I consider that seeing the sun for more than a hour or so a day will be nice. I realize, though, that I can't remember what month it is back home.

Kwan Yin and Aino Rand are working over some documents when I am admitted to the office. A few other people I've met, tagged as bureaucrats, and promptly dismissed from memory, murmur greetings as I enter.

"Karen." The su-ankh rises and gestures for all but Aino to leave. There is an expectancy in the air that I cannot read as they file out.

"Yes," I answer as the room empties, "I was told that you needed to see me, Honorable. Anton also told me that the agreement is finished and accepted."

"Yes, all but a few details. I will be returning to my

neglected post on Terra, but Aino will remain some time longer as an advisor to the new UAN ambassador.''

''Good idea,'' I reply, ''Who's taking the post—Hoosh or Mimir?''

''Neither, actually,'' Kwan Yin says, ''although both were considered and even interviewed. They both felt that there was a stronger candidate for the post—someone with more general experience. They are both scientists, you see.''

''Ah.'' I'm disappointed. I'd hoped that someone who has been through the worst would take the job.

''That rules Freesh and Sanchez out, too,'' I say. ''Is someone being imported?''

''No, Karen,'' Kwan Yin says. ''Hoosh has agreed to be interim ambassador if our first choice refuses. We all agree that we need someone who knows the Xians first-hand.''

''And that they don't have hands,'' I quip, covering the odd feeling that had been with me since I realized I'd be shipping home soon. ''Who do you have in mind?''

''You, Karen,'' Kwan Yin says softly. ''Surely you had expected.''

''Me?'' My shock is genuine. ''I'm not a diplomat. I'm just a translator.''

''You are far more than that, and it is false modesty to deny it,'' Aino says sternly. ''The Xians we've spoken to universally respect you, and your lack of ambition for the position they find rather endearing.''

''Oh.'' I sit back suddenly. ''Me? I can't be an ambassador. Look, it's been hidden, but you need to know. I have a criminal record.''

''Yes,'' Kwan Yin reaches for a datapad with her small hands, ''DuPoy and Chiron had collected some interesting files on all of you Allain Corp directors. This Mr. Allain was a wizard at creating false identities; our initial checks on you had found none of this. However, only Aino and I have seen the contents of DuPoy's blackmail packet.

Although we suspect that Ooohoop may have been told something, she is disgraced and cannot harm you."

"Still," I protest, "you must see that a criminal cannot be an ambassador."

"No," Kwan Yin says, "I do not. That was long ago and you have gone beyond that; the air is different now. Will you accept the post?"

My thoughts are merry chaos, but my feelings are constant.

"Sure, I guess so, especially if Aino will be here to train me."

"Only for a time," she reminds me. "I am tired and retired. An advisor, yes, de facto ambassador, no. You need to consider who you want for your staff. The UAN will be happiest if it is a mixed-race group, but, given that you have never left Terra before this trip, it has agreed to accept a human-heavy beginning."

"This is too much," I say, wishing for coffee. "I'll need Onyx, of course, and I'd like Tammany, Toshi, and Anton, but it's a bit much to expect them to give up the business and move to a soggy planet. The Tsi clan is low-ranking, but if Pooh Bear or someone could be spared, they'd balance all these scientists."

"Talk to people," Aino advises. "The announcement won't officially be made until nightfall. You have time to assemble a beginning staff."

"Thanks," I say, still dazed. "I'll be back."

I walk for several minutes until I come to the pond—lake, really, now. One of the first things the Xians insisted on was no landing field, but they did agree to a larger body of water so that more than one shuttle can port.

The silvery grey water is dimpled by gentle rainfall, so that the reflections are less representations than suggestions. Still, I have no trouble telling who is walking up beside me.

"Hello, Anton."

"Hi, Kari. Quick meeting."

"They want me to be ambassador, Anton."

"Of course. Who else could do the job?"

"Really?" I turn and grin. "Want to be on my staff?"

He smiles. "Of course. What's the job?"

"What it has always been," I say. "Troubleshooting."

"Fine. Let me guess. The announcement is tonight and I should keep quiet until then."

"Right. Do you know where Toshi or Tammany is?"

"Tosh is doing something with media arrangements. Tam is in the commissary."

I find Toshi on my way to the commissary.

"Can I speak with you?" I ask, snagging his sleeve and pulling him to a sheltered bench. "They want me to be ambassador."

"Congratulations." His smile is warm. "It had to be you—something everyone but you seemed to know."

"Will you be on my staff?"

He pauses, looks uncomfortable. "I want to say 'yes,' but in honesty I can't. It's not you Karen, or the Xians or—no matter what you may think—my plans for the Allain Corp. It's something so stupid that I hate to mention it. I'm embarrassed."

"Go on."

"It's the rain. It never stops here except for a few hours some days. I know a drier season is supposed to be coming, but I think sometimes that I'll go crazy if I don't wake up some morning under a hot full sun." He stares at his hands. "I'm sorry."

"No, Toshi, I understand." I touch his arm. "Just a few hours ago I was thinking that one of the nicest things about going home would be having a chance to be warm and dry. Will you work with me from Terra, give me a break if I need something done and channels are too slow?"

"You bet. Think what it'll mean to the Corp to have an ambassador as a Director Emeritus!" Although his words are flippant, his eyes thank me for not embarrassing him.

We both laugh. I excuse myself to go and find Tammany.

She's in a quiet corner of the commissary. I get a cup of coffee and a Chirr breakfast roll with the taste of spinach and eggs. She moves her rice and pickled fish to the side to make room for me and looks sleepily up from her datapad.

"Morning, Tammany."

"Morning, Karen. How goes?"

"They want me to be ambassador."

She looks at me, eyes no longer sleepy. "Do you want to be?"

Slightly taken aback by the lack of congratulations, I consider. "Yes, I think so. I feel better about the work I've done since I met Onyx than about anything else."

"Good then." She smiles now, toasting me with a clump of rice in her chopsticks. "I am very pleased."

"I was wondering," I begin, Toshi's rejection still fresh, "if you would consider being one of my advisors."

She studies me, a thread of a smile playing about her lips. "Before I say 'yes,' will you answer a question for me?"

"If I can," I reply solemnly.

"Did you kill Rhys?"

For a moment I consider denying it, then I nod. "Yes, I did."

"I thought so," she says, rolling a piece of rice with her finger, then picking it up and studying it as if it is the most fascinating thing on earth. "He mentioned that you might be stopping by, and I know that his wood should have been untainted—I'd been his supplier. There was no proof, though."

"No," I agree. "What do you plan to do?"

She looks surprised, "Do? Advise you or whatever this job you're offering takes. Rhys deserved it. We all did for what we let happen to Ben. He'd scared us, you see, reminded us that our pasts were still there and that maybe we owed something, if not to him, to the world—the universe—for what he'd done for us. None of us really liked that. The past was finally gone, and here he was reminding us. We forgot that he had been our benefactor and started thinking of him only as a blackmailer.''

We sit silently for a moment, then she grins at me.

''What happened was that when we lost the threat Ben offered, we also lost his protection. We also gained the tension of knowing that too many of us knew what we had done.'' She snorts humorless laughter. ''Ben had his revenge, and the strangest thing is that he was right from the start.''

''I'm not saying anything about it,'' I answer. ''DuPoy's files have been found and will be destroyed. I am no threat to you. I've lost my belief that Mr. Allain should be avenged. Now all I want to do is move on. Everything is over.''

''Sweet, naive Karen,'' Tammany says, ''The past is never over. Count me in on your new venture, though. The Corp is haunted by ghosts past. Time for seeing what the present and future offer.''

''Thanks, Tammany. Keep it quiet until this evening, okay?''

She smiles. ''What next?''

''I need to find Onyx,'' I answer, ''and tell her everything.''

I am grateful that Tammany refrains from telling me that Onyx most certainly knows already. She's thinking it though. I can tell.

The rain and mist make sky and horizon a paper box melting at the edges. Onyx meets me before I am ten paces from the commissary. Tammany is right, she does know everything, and her pleasure is warmer than any sun.

In a splash of bright, angular pictures, she suggests that we go for a ramble so that I can get better acquainted with this world I will help her to represent. I agree, happy as a kid on holiday from school.

Nightfall and all it will bring is many hours away. The rain patters on my umbrella as I walk beside the Xian, and the bustle of the preparations for our inauguration fades to nothing. The jungle we lose ourselves in is noisy in its own way, and dark and deep.